MAY BE FATAL ©

A Thriller

TAYLOR MARSH

Cover image background by Lane Jackman, upsplash; photo of woman, Deposit Photos

ISBN 978-0-9982125-6-2

The Evil Men Do – F.B.I. Profiler Roy Hazelwood's Journey into the Minds of Sexual Predators, Steve G. Michaud with Roy Hazelwood

The Mary-el Tarot, by Marie White

"The History of Slave Trade" by Scott Shane, BaltimoreSun.com (1999)

ABC 20/20: "What Really Killed Prince" (9.28.18)

First draft editor Effrosyni Moschoudi

Cover by Angie @procovers

Technical: Amy Gibbs

Always, for Mark

"The experience of the feminine is the psychological key to both the sickness of our time and its healing."

Marion Woodman

CHAPTERS

September 2009: Thursday

No one saw him.

He made certain.

It had been two months since Raymond Drake's last indulgence. He'd disciplined himself. Waited. But his fantasies weren't enough. Tried to survive on the thrills inside his mind. Couldn't anymore.

Had eyes on the front of her office building before anyone came in. Watched people enter. Delighted in their ignorance of what would come. Felt their surprise deep in his gut, as the pure pleasure of the fantasy played in his mind.

Held his excitement at bay.

She arrived in a sunflower yellow pantsuit. Virgin white blouse made him snicker. Four-inch cobalt blue strappy sandals. Her chestnut brown hair bounced at her shoulders. Long sterling silver wavy drop earrings dangled from each ear and peaked in and out of strands of her long locks. Streaks of red highlights flashed in the morning sunlight.

Oh, to grab her hair. Bend her to my will.

Dressed in black. Workout clothes formed to his physique. The leather jacket bulked up his frame to a formidable presence.

No one would glean a hint of viciousness.

It was good to be handsome. Unattached. A man with straight white teeth. His manicure flawless. Lace-up leather boots. No detail too small.

No one would suspect him.

Cunning was the initial wound. Delivered with a smile.

Before she blinked twice.

Strike.

Thoughts of it aroused him. It began.

A gurgle of euphoria.

Visualization of her face. How it would be when he had her. In his grasp, to watch her lose her will.

Sublime surrender.

He would set her free.

Deliver peace to her.

Unlike previous Thursdays, she'd exited the building alone at 7:11 p.m. Raymond had seen her colleagues leave earlier. They'd scheduled drinks at an upscale bar. The same time each of the last three weeks.

But today she walked off alone to the employee parking lot next door.

A sign.

He followed unnoticed. The lateness of the hour buoyed him.

On her phone, oblivious, she hadn't seen the tall, handsome man enter the garage. Had missed the quickened pace of his steps.

She laughed. In her own world.

Raymond Drake smiled. Followed his prey.

Better for him if he took her happy. But he must not catch her in the middle of the conversation. "Goodbye" was the signal.

He would purchase the look he craved through force. Terror to replace her uplifted mood.

The instant she realized her mistake. The look in her eyes.

What he craved.

Thoughts of it increased his breathing. Quickened his pace. A whiff of her. Wanted to stop and savor. Fierce need propelled him.

They were alone.

Behind her.

Closer.

3...2...

It happened in slow motion in his mind. Raymond's hand over her mouth. She seized up. His strength lifted her off the earth. Midair, he beheld the moment.

Eyes wide, her mouth agape, shock, no power to protest.

Slammed down on the hood of her car, their eyes locked. She scooted backward. He grabbed her legs, pulled. Straddled the beauty below him. Towered over her. She lay still. Silent terror spread across her face.

The blade in his hand. Fingers to his lips. "Shh. I want to play with you."

Her face scrunched together. Defenseless. She'd allowed herself to get distracted. Tears dropped down her cheeks.

Savor each second. This delicious fight. The moment of collapse. She would be his.

A pitiful whimper.

"Shh." His teeth gleamed. Bright eyes. A smile from ear to ear.

Grunts, groans, she shook her head no.

"Oh, yes." The roundhouse right hook landed with a crack. Raymond watched her slide off the car to the concrete.

Head tilted. Pursed lips. His victim lay at his feet. "Beautiful girl."

Checked his surroundings. Nothing moved. All quiet.

Leaned down. Turned the woman's head. Whipped out a knife from his belt. Slashed at a section of hair near her scalp. A flick of his wrist caught flesh. The wound began to drip. Drip, drip.

A swipe of his index finger over the red droplets. The taste of her. Not her sex, but the flow of life itself. Eyes closed. The ritual he savored. Euphoric moments when he proved to be invincible.

The tune in Raymond's head came across his lips in a shallow whisper. The thrill simmered inside him. His rigid member strangled against his pants.

In the moment of triumph, Raymond Drake believed no one caught him because his mission was divine.

Didn't stop to secure his own safety. Over his shoulder, a fireman's carry. He must be quick. His car nearby.

Opened the trunk. Extracted the needle from his bag. Plunged it into her thigh. Enough ketamine to knock her out for the drive. She'd not awaken until he reached the far edge of Maryland's Eastern Shore.

No one worries about a stranger who looks like a Hollywood star and drives a classic sports car.

But experts agree white males commit most deviant sexual crimes.

It starts with a fantasy.

It ends in actualized terror.

Present Day: Friday Night

"Where is she?" Jack Stone looked at Trevor.

Lily saw him enter. She got up and moved closer to the back door. The look on Stoney's face from across the room warned her what would come next.

Revelers packed the room. Music was loud. Small groups gathered in different parts of the living room. On a table was a punch bowl. Large empty liquor bottles rolled around on top. A cooler on the floor filled with ice and beer was half-full. There were other party treats available in the kitchen.

His voice. Amanda heard her dad from the room she was in. She perked up. A smile. The plan was in motion. He'd see her in the room with three men.

It's what he deserves.

A tall Asian with jet black hair, perfect physique, thin and lithe, glided across the room. "Amanda's in the last room down the hall," Trevor said. He nodded in the direction. Jack Stone moved toward the room, but Trevor stopped him. "Stoney, be cool. You won't like this, but she wanted to party with them."

"Party?"

"Yeah. Amanda's a grown up. Not much you can do."

"She's my daughter. *She* called me."

"Yeah, well, we both know why, don't we?" The words hit low. The tone of his voice, the look on Trevor's face worked as an epithet.

Stoney tensed up. Stepped closer to him. "Just say it."

"Do I need to, *boss*?"

The shorthand language between them revealed their history. Trevor provided the deference required to discharge the tension between them. He worked for Stoney, but he didn't intend to coddle him. The strained relationship between Stoney and his daughter Amanda was well known.

Respect required straight talk.

Stoney exhaled, looked up at Trevor. He saw Lily out of the corner of his eye.

She froze when her gaze caught his. Lily sped past people by the back door. No need to look behind her.

The second Stoney saw her he took off in the same direction.

Trevor saw Lily leave. He watched his boss tear across the room after her but wasn't interested in why.

"Wait. Lily." Stoney yelled as he ran.

She stopped in the middle of the backyard. Wicked, late summer rains had left the ground soggy. He walked toward her.

"Talk."

"What happened? Everything was good."

"I told you. It's over," Lily said.

"Tell me how I can make it work."

Lily shook her head. Looked to the trees, which bent in the breeze. Deep breath. "We were supposed to have fun, remember, no strings?"

"We did. There aren't any."

Laughter was her response. "You are too intense. There is never any let-up. It's always about you, your company, your problems. I'm too young for this shit."

His jaw dropped a little. The stare from him made her uncomfortable. Stoney cracked his neck. Opened and closed his mouth, the tightness in his jaw made his face muscles constrict.

"What do you want from me?" Lily looked around for a quick exit. Trees on all sides of the yard and a drop-off to the creek behind her.

"Nothing."

"Then let me go."

Stoney stepped back. His demeanor turned dark.

Lily didn't move.

Amanda watched her father and her best friend from the window. Their relationship public for the first time. No one had seen what she had. The gooey center of her father's infatuation on display. The scene outside was less obscene than what she'd witnessed before.

He thought his secret was safe. Didn't bother to call out, but assumed I wasn't home. I saw them.

Not a word from Lily to her best friend about her sloppy heart, or how she'd wandered into treacherous territory.

The daughter now watched her father proclaim himself to a woman who treated men similar to the way her father treated women. Disregard bellowed from the body language of her dad's lover.

Amanda was numb.

Even after I call him for help. He can't stop himself.

It would have been simple to hide their affair.

She wanted to humiliate him.

Her thoughts were a conglomeration of disrespect and loathing.

Therapy made it worse. Amanda had ditched it many times. Hard to keep track of all the doctors, therapists, and quacks her mother dragged her to see.

Daddy thought I'd grow out of it.

Instead, Amanda had grown from hard to handle adolescent to out of control teenager. Both of her parents prayed high school would change her. No such luck. During a date with a young man, she'd gotten aggressive. The high school senior said they were making out when she attacked him. Tried to get his pants off. It terrified the young man because Amanda had a pocket knife in her hand. He told police, when he fought back she said, "Shut up. I won't cut it off. But you need a little trim."

The police had been stymied. Amanda's parents said it was absurd to think a young woman would sexually assault someone who was bigger and stronger. They sloughed it off to teenage hormones.

No one could handle the truth about Amanda.

Experts told her parents girls don't commit sexual acts of aggression. Not possible. "Think about it," they had said. When Amanda's therapist at the time said she believed his daughter had assaulted the young man, Stoney fired her. Nothing made Amanda happier. It would take weeks to find another shrink. She would be free of them all until they found another doctor.

One month became two, which turned into six months. Amanda had graduated with honors from high school. "I told you I'm fine," she said. Desperate to believe it was over, her mom and dad relented.

Therapy was in her past.

Nothing to see here.

Adulthood freed her.

Amanda stewed in her mania until she had seen Lily with her dad. What had her best friend done to him? She waited. Watched. Made sure no one challenged her sanity again.

A stable job as a research assistant to a Washington, D.C. think tank convinced them all. Years of diligence. She was normal to the outside world.

Amanda watched her father with Lily. He was desperate.

She doesn't give a shit. It made her hate her friend a little less.

A young man came up behind Amanda. "Hey, come on. Let's party." He kissed the nape of her neck. She didn't respond. Her eyes were glued to the scene in the backyard.

Another guy in the room took off his shirt. "Let's go, baby. I'm ready." He jumped on the bed.

The third guy turned the lock on the door. "No one but us. We won't tell."

Her father reached for her friend, but Lily backed away.

Amanda smiled. Her hand came up behind her. She put it on his head. "Mm, I like it."

The scene outside shifted.

Lily's hands came up in front of her. Amanda didn't need to listen to what was being said. Lily was pissed. She let her dad have it.

I call him for help and look where he goes.

Amanda smiled. "Come on." She took the guy's hand. They started to join the other young man on the bed.

Clothes hit the floor.

"I'll watch for a while," one guy said.

"I don't care," she said.

The knock was loud, followed by more bangs on the door. "Amanda, I know you're in there." Trevor kept it up. "Your dad's here. You got what you wanted. Don't make it worse."

Peals of laughter from the other side of the door.

"Okay, I'm out." Trevor walked away and into the kitchen.

"What's up?" The man had a swastika tattoo on his forearm. Dirty brown teeth.

"You're sure this is cool?" Trevor looked at the tattooed man who had offered the house for the party. "No one will get jammed up for being here, right?"

"Relax. The boss owns the house. We're good."

Trevor was unaware the drugs the man had brought were laced and lethal. The man's boss was a habitual criminal. Part of a syndicate who imported counterfeit narcotics laced with fentanyl out of China, via the web.

Trevor shrugged. "Okay. So, you guys set?"

"Yeah. Happy customers."

The drug dealer's partner walked into the room. A rugged, lean African American male, with a shaved head. "Hey, I'm Tack." A nod. "You leaving? We just started."

"You've got my cell," Trevor said. "Work fast and don't get comfortable. I have a hunch you won't be here long."

The tattooed man moved closer to Trevor. "Good man." He patted his shoulder. "Is there something you need to tell us?"

"One of the women called her father. He's got juice."

Tack nodded.

Trevor walked out of the kitchen, across the living room. He saw a woman he recognized on the couch. She appeared to be asleep. He walked over. "Hey, you okay?" He touched her. She didn't move. "Hey. Janet, hey." Trevor slapped her face, but she didn't respond. "Shit."

He dialed 911 on the way out the door. "Party at Riverbend Road. Some chick overdosed." Trevor hung up. They would trace his cell phone, but he didn't care. He was protected.

Ducked his head back into the kitchen. "What did you guys do? Ambulance on the way. Police will be..."

The men were out the back door before Trevor finished speaking.

Present Day: Friday Night

"Don't do this," Stoney said.

"Oh, you've got to be kidding." Regret hit Lily. *What have I done?*

"I love you."

She froze, shook her head. "This is…No, you don't. You want what you can't have."

"Don't tell me how I feel."

"You sound like a girl."

"I told you, I'd do it. I'm divorced now…you and I can be together."

The air drained out of Lily. She stared at the man she'd had fun with for two years. She no longer recognized him. "Your divorce has nothing to do with me."

"I…" Words wouldn't form. "You're right. Doesn't change the facts."

"No, it doesn't. Fact one, your daughter is my best friend. Fact two, you were a distraction. Fact three, this is your midlife crisis."

Stoney shook his head. Looked away.

"Remember what I said when we started? Do you?"

He ignored her.

"Jesus. Talk about denial."

When he looked at her again, Lily saw it. Fury and frustration. He didn't like being told no.

"You're scared."

"What did I say or do to give you that impression?" Her voice trailed off. She turned, started toward the trees at the end of the yard.

He grabbed her arm.

"Let go." Lily stopped, looked down at his hand. He hadn't released her. "Stoney, don't start this again."

"You came into my marriage and..."

"Whoa." Stared at him. "Don't you dare. Don't try it."

"You're right. Sorry."

The tension dipped.

"It doesn't have to end like this. We had fun. Let's part as friends, okay?" The look on his face was her answer. *Was he going to cry?*

"But I want you."

"Get over it."

"I can't. I won't."

"That's unfortunate. We had fun, but I'm done."

"Nice rhyme."

"You're, what, fifteen years older than me? Not going to happen. I told you."

"Things change."

"We want different things."

"I want you. You want me. Simple."

"Wanted you, past tense."

"So, you used me."

"What? What are you talking about?"

"I didn't need to hire you, but I did."

"I'm the best researcher you've got."

"You got what you wanted and now you're not interested. Callous bitch." Stoney's voice was loud. The veins in his neck stood out. His cheeks flushed.

"Guys do it all the time. I'm so done."

"I won't take no…"

Lily turned to bolt, but Stoney grabbed her again. She pushed back at him. He pulled her close. She brought her knee up and her foot down on the arch of his right foot. He yelped. Strained not to buckle while the pain shot up his leg. She broke away for an instant. He leaped for her. She slipped on the slick grass. His hands on her shoulders, Lily's effort to escape escalated. One last push, she would be free. Stoney grabbed at her again but as he did, Lily gained traction on the grass and fled.

Stoney tore after her. Chased her to the end of the yard. Lily was over the crest of the hill where the ground turned to a slick mudslide. He grabbed for her backpack purse hiked high on her shoulder. Felt something and pulled, but the purse stayed in place. Her feet slipped. The lack of traction propelled her down the hill.

He was left alone.

Lily was gone.

Present Day: Saturday, 2:00 a.m.

Closed eyes cleared her mind.

Why won't it work?

A walk through the living room didn't soothe her dread.

Dr. Kate Winter watched as the police tramped through the vacant house. The Stratford Police Department's forensics squad accumulated the evidence and exited.

It must have been one hell of a party.

Summer's last gasp, the humidity made everything cling. Reactions slowed, crime scenes turned to goo.

An involuntary twitch of her nostrils didn't squelch an aroma that reminded her of an unburied corpse stewing on a sweltering day.

Smells attached to ugly pictures fired up her synapses. But the stench came from Kate's own thoughts. Powerful sense memory transported her to cases best forgotten.

Darkness shrouded the backyard.

Shadows can unnerve the soul and cause a mind to spin out. The questions came in a contagion.

Why here? Seventh or eighth party broken up since summer began. Keep coming back.

The uniform police who remained to guard the crime scene didn't speak to Kate when they passed. She trained her eyes on the marred landscape beyond the gigantic picture window with a view of the forest behind the expansive ranch home on 1154 Riverbend Road, White Hills, Maryland. Twenty miles south of Washington, D.C.

Kate set her case down, then walked closer to the picture window.

A large burnish-red spot on the aged wood floor stopped her. Images whipped through her consciousness.

Floodlights kicked on in the backyard.

Snapped her out of a dark memory.

The stars were out. The night air cooled things off even if the humidity strangled the breezes. Hottest September on record.

Dr. Kate Winter worked best by herself.

It made it easier to sense what lay beyond what could be seen after everyone had left. Yet, her consciousness offered no clues.

Too much interference.

A walk. The manicured backyard carved a simple path which plunged toward a swollen creek beyond the trees at the edge of the grass. The bright floodlights lit the way.

Vacant for over a year, a "For Sale" sign replaced by a "For Rent" sign had not worked. She made a note of no yard sign at all.

Headed to foreclosure? Wouldn't surprise me.

Nobody wanted to live in the home of the deranged. Psychopathy is not contagious, but fear is. It crept into minds to make victims of those who should have better sense. A house can't absorb the evil of those who lived inside.

Can it?

Everyone who watched cable television had seen the news about this house, the horror stories. A daughter had bludgeoned her parents to death. In and out of mental health facilities until she became an adult. The courts couldn't keep her away from her prey.

An unexplainable tragedy to everyone but Kate.

No imagination.

The girl's parents had missed the signs. The way they saw their daughter defied reality. Perhaps she got sick of it and ended her own misery. The thought terrified people.

The incomprehensible act of parricide defied decency. A child who had killed both parents? During Kate's "Today" show appearance, the NBC network's switchboard had lit up.

Children don't kill their mothers.

Women aren't psychopaths.

No clues or any answers to what had happened at the Riverbend Road party. Two 20-something women in the emergency room for toxicity had imbibed strong alcoholic drinks laced with MDMA, also called ecstasy. It got worse. They had found toxic black-market drugs at the party.

The paramedics were pros. Overdoses from OxyContin laced with fentanyl, a powerful opioid, were on the rise. News reports of it daily. They had revived a young man at Riverbend Road after paramedics had administered Narcan nasal spray.

Counterfeit drugs from China were notorious for surprises and deaths.

Enter Dr. Kate Winter, who discovered what others missed. Brought in to explain to the uninitiated the unexplainable. Who was responsible for a person in the throes of death's grasp? Bad choices?

As the world became more connected and more dysfunctional, behavioral scientists got busier.

People called when desperate.

Professionals who discovered bodies at crime scenes, which baffled forensic experts who deciphered them, wanted deeper answers.

People who had lost the battle with their own mind, which left them ravaged. Beyond their rampages, they hid their disconnection with life.

Comments on newspaper pages, websites, and social media squealed connection amid a frenzy of alienation.

Loneliness, the incurable disease of modernity, detonated.

The birth of an epidemic.

The new interconnected world had inspired Kate Winter to get a Ph.D. in psychology. Her doctoral thesis was on the homicidal urge, which she believed was recognizable through intuitive tools. Research into the psychotic to the psychopathic, emphasis on behavioral and physical flashpoints. A second major in gender studies because the scientific community ignored women.

As for intuition, a reminder wouldn't have been necessary if humans listened to themselves and recognized their own voice.

Reconnection with the emotional self was the initial salve to soothe a wretched mind tortured by psychosis. No elixir existed for psychopathy embedded in a sick brain.

The backyard turned into a steep incline and ended in a fast-moving creek. A row of medium-sized boulders, slick from the rain, at the end of the manicured lawn made her walk precarious. One careful step onto the boulders for a peek at the terrain below.

Kate felt herself lose traction but too late to do anything about it. The hill sucked her down. She yelped an expletive and tried to stop her glide, then grabbed the ground. A low branch from a small tree worked for a second. The move changed her trajectory down the hill.

A shiny object appeared.

The floodlights caught the charm's brilliance. It lit up. She spit something inaudible, reached for it, and got lucky. Her fingers clutched the object connected to a chain.

Lily was spelled out in sterling silver. Kate assumed this referred to the woman named in one of the anonymous phone calls to the police that had brought authorities down on this address. Several people interviewed at the scene said Stoney had a fight with some woman outside, in the backyard. Someone identified her as Lily.

What was Stoney doing at this party?

It wasn't a good sign.

Trouble can be a magnet for women between the ages of 16 and 28-years-old. The invincible cloak of youth protects them, they assume. Social media unlocked a world parents once kept away from their child's life. Sexual revolution in perpetuity. Stupidity replaced adventure with men of a certain age. A young woman's sexual persona became a tool for some, a weapon for others.

For the uninitiated, the power of youth became a trap.

Back up the hill. The Lily charm in her pocket. Kate stopped and stared inside the house wondering if someone had watched the partiers from here. So easy. It meant they could see outside, too.

People watched Stoney and Lily. Why make a scene at a big party? So many witnesses.

The full story buried deep. Not for Kate.

Stoney's back at it.

Womanizing as sport.

No way to clean off all the mud that clung to her clothes after her slide down the hill. A small wire brush in a basket inside the porch helped scrape the caked mud off her boots, but some debris remained stuck in the tread. Her clothes clung to her like a second skin. Mud seeped between the fabric and her flesh.

The rest of the Stratford County Police interviews would take time. People bolted when Trevor called 911. Roundup was a nightmare.

One woman didn't make it.

Kate drove away with the Lily necklace tucked deep in her bag. It nagged at her and stirred memories from dark uncomfortable spaces. What this meant wasn't lost on her.

It was an omen.

Present Day: Saturday, 3:30 a.m.

The peace of quiet wrapped her in comfort. Lily didn't want it to end.

Minutes passed before she assessed the situation.

She'd broken away. No going back to where it all waited for her. It would start all over again.

"Ouch." Her shoulder ached. Tight neck, a head roll-around to loosen it didn't work. She'd passed out in the driver's seat of her truck. Aggravated a high school shoulder injury. "Oh, man. What a headache."

Shook off the last hours.

A night turned into craziness.

People would search for her.

The cabin was over an hour from Washington, D.C. Parked her truck where it wouldn't be seen.

Was this the moment to split?

The plan concocted on her drive could still work. Her small bank account and savings combined would be enough for a new start. She needed a job. Being a competent researcher and a writer helped.

Her things on the front seat. Opened her satchel, checked for her Mac. No connection. Offline notes would be enough. Time to write it down.

She brought her notebook and satchel, purse, phone and Mac inside the cabin.

I'm out. The party last night got wild. I didn't expect Amanda would get ripped. Stoney would show up.

Things got out of control.

It starts when I get rattled. Overwhelmed.

Stoney said he loves me.

It triggered me.

"So, I ran." Lily's words came out in a whisper. "She talked to me. Again. Afterward. Amid my visions."

She ran back to her truck. Behind the driver's seat, she pulled out a small suitcase. Back inside, Lily tried to open it. Locked. Dug around in her purse, got her keys. The tiniest one worked. She'd packed a change of clothes.

Lily used the small kitchen sink to clean herself. Wiped off the grit from her night flight. "Maybe go to Mechanicsville tonight."

Wait until darkness.

She had slipped. No control over her thoughts.

The visions were back.

There is no way to evade the mind. The machinations of a person's thoughts. There are necessary triggers sent to manipulate the reality preferred. A place where crushing moments of betrayal revisit our psyche. When people force themselves to face the divots knocked into their own sanity. A confrontation with their primal self, the part they try to ignore. Authenticity escapes us when we're robbed of manifesting who we are at our core.

More thoughts to put down.

"Oh, Lily."

I hear her when the Cardinal's song dies at sunset.

Needn't be afraid. It's I who calls.

Won't get away. Yet, not afraid.

I'm invisible, hidden behind what they see.

When the day bursts through, run like the mad mind has a reason. It doesn't matter why.

Called.

Something better awaits.

I'm gone.

No desire to return.

All day to find a spot.

No one follows. They are lost.

By myself, I am found.

April 2011: Late Friday Night

Spring on the wind.

A whiff of rotted flesh.

Time to move her.

The far Eastern Shore of Maryland had been Raymond's home for years. Near the waterside town of Oxford, a short ten-minute drive to work. A remote spot on the map. They had designated the town as one of two original ports of entry. The other was Annapolis, first named Anne Arundel's Towne. After the American Revolution, the town changed, and the ritzy tobacco plantations and a way of life vanished.

An on-call security officer at a large medical facility outside Easton was the perfect job. It surprised Raymond how kindness manipulated people. Became a path and a way to exploit and experience his darkest fantasies.

He lived off a generator in a single-wide mobile home. Dug his own septic. He was safe. Had a stable job. Lots of time off for his passion. His purpose.

The proximity of where he lived meant more to him than his job. No one must ever find out the reasons. Secrets buried deep inside he'd carry to his grave.

No one bothered Raymond.

After sunset, he claimed what he stalked.

A small boat on a speck of property near the Blackwater National Forest. Many waterways offered an exit. No one thought a thing about a man tootling around in the Chesapeake Bay by himself.

Dr. Kate Winter was on the news again. Yack, yack, yack. Pissed Raymond off. Made him restless. So smart, she thought. He had to meet her.

Raymond's obsession filled his dining room. On one wall, photos of his women. Locks of hair taped to each face. Trophies in every color. The opposite wall was about her. Dr. Kate Winter's face, every article he had found. Photos blown up to cover the wall.

Her voice in his head.

Two mother-daughter pairs dead in Prince George County. The networks coveted her expertise. Colleagues in law enforcement and government revered her. A woman behavioral scientist was the draw in a year where women had stepped up to lead after the failed attempts of men.

"I'm here with behavioral scientist, Dr. Kate Winter. When you compare the homicides, two pairs of mother-daughter deaths, do you agree with federal law enforcement? It's the work of two separate killers?"

"I disagree with the F.B.I. assessment. It's too soon to state the crimes are unrelated. The killer has sent us clues but confused the details. Wants us to get bogged down. We lose nothing by waiting. He will strike again, maybe has already. I need more information."

Raymond muted the television. He had work to do.

Whistled as he walked to the car. The tune calmed him when he worked. An old Ford coupe hid his secrets.

Flies buzzed around him. The closer he walked to the car the stronger the stench. The closest neighbor was a farmer's field away. It had started days before, but he had been called into work. The delay couldn't be helped.

Death gasses wafted from the trunk as he drove away.

On Alms House Road, he merged onto US-50 East Ocean Gateway. The showers began half-way through the drive. The familiar road seemed to float atop the marshland it cut across.

An innocent trek with an ominous shadow.

A road with no shoulder.

Darkness hypnotized.

A sudden downpour.

A treacherous trek.

May be fatal.

The only car around, Raymond straddled the narrow two-lane road. It calmed him to see the ground on both sides of his car. Over the Choptank River, he moved at a faster clip. Continued on Church Creek Road. Past the Harriet Tubman Underground Railroad National Historical Park and multiple markers honoring the brave abolitionist.

In Blackwater National Forest, a dramatic slow-down. The path invisible in a night with no moon.

Drivers in daylight saw the reality beyond the road.

At night, drivers beware.

Where the side of the road ends, the water begins. Tall grass and reeds sprout from a shallow bottom near the road that deepens before awareness.

Where the Great Egret finds solace to stalk their supper in the shallows.

When the rain hardened, Raymond slowed to a crawl. The road difficult to see as the storm kicked up. The forecast was accurate, but he had no choice.

A rotted body.

It was an error.

His error.

The road disappeared in the black. One visible sign of the world around him was above him. Brilliant stars danced between storm clouds. Shadows thrown on the ground. His eyes darted from side to side. Attention paid to where the water lapped up and the road disappeared.

Firm ground found beneath the splashes.

A Ford 150 appeared around a curve.

Raymond steered as far right as was safe. But the truck drove down the center of the road and when it passed him, he felt his tires on the edge. His car so near water, fear ratcheted up.

A drop-off splash into the marsh.

A jerk of the wheel.

The threat of his own demise.

Held on tight to the steering wheel. Jerked the car back left. Skidded into the oncoming lane. "Shit." Little control.

The longer Raymond drove, the darker it got. He no longer saw the water at the edge of the road. Focused trained ahead. Road, water and atmosphere, all was black.

The tension in his shoulders traveled to his extremities. Shook one hand, then the other. A dull ache rose from his neck.

Light rain turned into yet another downpour. Nature's special gift. The torrent of rain forced him to stop in the middle of the road. Waited.

Pop. Pop. Bang. Tat-tat-tat.

Water on his vehicle. The torrent blinded him. Raymond started to count. Numbers calmed him. 1...2...3... He got to 11 before it started.

Car idling, it moved on its own. Sideways.

The marsh eclipsed the road. His car carried by the current of the downpour.

"No. No. No." His guttural screams filled the car. Turned to look behind him. "Stop it. Quit laughing."

Who had Raymond addressed?

"Shut up. Don't talk."

Panicked.

Desperate words to the dead. The cadaver locked in the trunk.

Turned off the car, started it again. Floored it. The car swerved to one side of the road. Skid to the other side before he regained control.

The water lapping up taunted him.

Kept driving. Car on water fighting him. Low land danger. Raymond had to get to the higher ground ahead. Focused until he arrived. Pulled over. The car sunk inches into the waterlogged ground.

Rain kept up.

Lightning flashes across the wet sky over the wide Chesapeake Bay.

Raymond drove until he arrived on Hoopers Island Road, which led to Old House Point Road in Fishing Creek. Past ramshackle houses, modern remodels, and the lone restaurant within miles.

To the spot where he kept a boat. Paid a local for the privilege. Delivered payment via PayPal, so they never spoke after they first met.

No one saw Raymond take her out of the trunk.

Reached into the back seat to get the drill and his flashlight. He needed to be quick. The spotlight a beacon.

Touched her chest to find the spot. Two holes would do it. He pierced both sides of her lungs.

A body bobbing up in the Chesapeake Bay would not be good.

She didn't weigh much, so the transfer from car to his boat was a cinch. The motor would make more noise than he wanted, but no one would peek out or be interested.

People lived on the far edges of society for a reason. Nature's beauty, tranquility, the birds, and a middle finger to the masses. Residents had to brave the mayflies, the massive influx of mosquitos in summer, and the wrath of mother nature in all seasons.

No one cared about a man out for a late-night boat ride.

No one witnessed the splash.

No one saw the body float for seconds and then disappear into the water where it would become a future crab hangout. Claws gripping the flesh off a human carcass as the body decayed to become a host for a community below the surface of the Bay.

Calm had returned.

Motored the boat back to the modest dock. Drove 50 miles per hour until he was home. The water spilled across the road was a mere nuisance now.

Raymond's fear disappeared with the dead.

The rain subsided as he drove. His clothes clung to him. Soaked. The air chilled his wet skin.

Another girl gone.

Nothing would lead back to him. People sailing on the Chesapeake Bay would never discover death so deep below the surface.

Invincible.

But it wasn't enough. He couldn't wait six months for the next one. Raymond's appetite had escalated.

Power lust drove him.

The thirst was back.

His thoughts fixated on her.

The first time he had seen Dr. Kate Winter was on television over a year ago. She was a looker, 5'10" tall, he'd bet. Her cocksureness made Raymond twitch. Her eyes on him felt dangerous. Had experienced it before.

An obsession reborn.

Raymond convinced himself she could read his mind. His thoughts became transparent when she was near. She stalked him, he thought. In his dreams, during the day and at night. The conversations in his head about her escalated.

It wouldn't stop until he ended it.

May 2011: Monday

A security guard at her colleague's office building flirted with her each time Kate arrived to see her.

He's intense.

But it was the way Raymond Drake's eyes darted toward other women as they walked through the lobby to the elevators.

Kate asked him for help she didn't need.

"Dr. Carlisle is on the 11th floor," he said.

His smile is too wide. Too much effort. "Elevators?"

"To your right and straight ahead." A plastered smile.

"May I borrow your pen?" Kate reached over to take the pen on the security desk. Brushed his hand on purpose. Eyes glued to see his reaction.

The instant their flesh touched, Raymond Drake recoiled.

There you are.

It takes an instant for walls to crumble when the mind behind them is petrified of being seen.

Tried to recover. Too late.

"Sorry. Wanted to make a note," she said.

Eyes locked. Kate caught a glimpse. She kept Raymond's gaze until he broke from hers. He turned and walked across the marble lobby. She watched him.

The other guard at the security desk hadn't noticed their interaction. "Hello, Dr. Winter. How are you?"

"I'm well." She pointed toward Raymond Drake. "Is he new?"

"Transferred." He stared back at her.

Nothing came to mind to say. "He's... attentive."

The guard waited. "Can I help you with something?"

"No. Thanks very much."

Inside her colleague's office, two coffees sat on a low table between two floral-design armchairs.

"How was your spring break, Dr. Carlisle?" Kate had a wise-ass grin on her face.

"Who told you?"

Surprise on Kate's face. "It's not a secret, Bridgette. Your grin says it all. Has your family adjusted?"

"Depends on their age."

"They'll get there." Her lips tightened. She had something else on her mind. "What's with the security guard? Tall, athletic build, but I get a vibe from him." Kate shook her head.

"Who?"

A tilt of Kate's head. Eyebrows raised. "You didn't notice him? Those eyes."

"What don't you like?"

She shook off the question. "Can't explain it. Nothing."

"We all missed the signs, Kate. It's not your fault. You tried to tell the bureau."

"I didn't convince them."

"You cannot spend your life weighing a stranger's intent when you meet someone new. You are not a cynic. And you are not clairvoyant."

"But I sensed something was wrong with the nurse. It came from..."

"Your gut? Tsk...tsk...tsk. It's a signal, not proof."

"But it was foreshadowing. Sad for the families. It was sick."

"Tragic," Dr. Carlisle said. "So far, you've been immune to most of the side effects of your work. But looking for psychological abnormalities in every weird person who gets your attention will drive you mad. Have you kept up with your journal?"

Kate rolled her eyes. "What do you think?"

Dr. Carlisle closed her tablet. "My work is done here."

Kate sighed.

"I'm not here to push. You asked for these sessions. But we are done... for now."

"Worry when I'm not haunted by a nurse who whacked 15 of her older patients."

"Point taken. You're as healthy as anyone who combs the minds of serial murderers."

"I need to get laid."

"Can't help you there."

Kate grabbed her purse to leave. "But I'd like to keep my appointment time."

Dr. Carlisle shook her head and smiled. "The guard?"

When Kate got out of the elevator, the security guards were different. She walked outside.

The intense security guard she'd noticed was in a chat with a woman. A column nearby provided cover. Kate eased forward so she could spy on the two. She was flirtatious. He leaned closer. She laughed. He backed away and waved. She turned.

Kate watched him.

The smile of the guard contorted as he watched the blonde leave.

It was a split second.

He caught Kate's gaze.

She retreated behind the column. Prayed he wouldn't come close or engage her. Cursed her recklessness and her impatience. So curious, she let an UnSub catch her. In an instant. She had revealed her curiosity to him.

Raymond would never forget it.

Present Day: Early Saturday Night

Picked up on the first ring.

"Hey, Kate. What's going on in Stratford County? Rumor about a missing woman. Disappeared after a wild party?"

"If you're trolling me for stories it must be a slow night, Micky."

"No sense in being modest. The cops don't call you in unless something big happened."

"Jesus, you still think this shit works?"

"Flattery? You bet. Women find me irresistible."

"Oh, dear god."

"Can you confirm the part about a missing woman?"

"I cannot confirm or deny."

"This story will blow up. So, you'd better remember who called you first."

"What does that even mean?"

"Give me the story, *your* story."

"I'm boring."

"Yeah, right. You've heard of the Netflix series called 'Mindhunter.' Who isn't interested in psycho killers? Women have gotten into the game."

Kate grunted. The flippancy by which people labeled psychopaths. "You're a sensationalist."

"And you pick psychopathic murderers out of comfy communities. My sources inside Stratford PD remember what you did on the Drake case."

She had stopped listening. No way another case would be about her.

The press and reporters from up and down the mid-Atlantic had descended on her home during the Raymond Drake case. They plastered her face across social media. "Psychic Solves Serial Killer Crime Spree" had brought crazies to her inbox. Fictional reportage, an outlandish fantasy, or a penchant for click bait? They called her psychic. Kate Winter? No way.

"Hello, you there?"

"Yes, but we're done here." She hung up.

Her mind took off.

"Stop. Not enough information."

Another lost argument with her mind.

They partied. No drama. Until strangers with lethal party favors walked in.

Kate replayed the scene. Trees surrounded her. She saw lights from houses on 2-3-acre properties in the distance. The police would finish the initial interrogations, which would give her the landscape of the case and identify each person who attended.

Too many questions at this point. The Center's motto: stay skeptical. Social media hadn't provided definitive answers to what happened at the party.

Who brought the drugs? Who is Lily? Maybe she came out for a smoke? To light up a number? Someone she didn't like got friendly with her, so she split?

Patience gave Kate the edge.

The long view made for fewer blunders.

AMANDA STONE

June 1999: Saturday

Amanda tiptoed around the back of the house. Saw the boy from next door go inside. He'd come home from a baseball game muddy, with a big smile across his face.

The girl with him was a cheerleader at his high school. She glommed onto him, all giggles. It was pathetic. Fawned over him.

He disgusted Amanda. Other girls had been to his house before this one. She was clueless.

At the window to his room, Amanda was careful not to make noise. Branches from a recent tree-trim scattered the ground. An errant crack or snap of a twig might alert them. Closer to the window, she looked to see if he was in his room yet.

"Get in here," he said.

More giggles.

The door shut behind them.

She watched them. No curtains, the window cracked, Amanda saw them both. Watched him scooch up her ultra-mini cheerleader skirt, pull her panties down. The girl grabbed his neck, kissed him hard.

They grunted.

Her lip curled upward, a scowl on Amanda's face.

When the boy pushed the girl on the bed, she grabbed for his pants.

Amanda ducked down so they didn't see her. The grunts continued. She slid back up to watch.

His hands grabbed for her breasts. She pushed back.

"I didn't say we'd do it." Her hands on her miniskirt. The girl bit her lip. Her eyes wide.

It was a signal to Amanda. Scared little girl. She picked up a discarded piece of wood, splintered at the end. Slammed it into the muddy earth. Kept jabbing the ground as she watched.

A car door slammed shut, then another. She bent down and slithered away from the window to see his parents had arrived. They'd catch them in the act.

Amanda laughed as she crossed into her backyard. Walked to a tiny shed in the back of her dad's property. Above the door was a sign, "Amanda's Hideaway." She locked the door behind her. A ramshackle structure, it provided enough privacy for her to indulge her whims and darker impulses.

The naked Ken doll was on a small table inside. Two small stools nearby. Movie posters of *Jumanji* and *Jurassic Park* covered the wall. A stack of old women's magazines on the floor. Her mother's discards.

The November 1988 *Vogue* was on top. Eleven-year-old Amanda didn't care it was an iconic cover. A Christian Lacroix jacket paired with jeans. Anna Wintour's first cover, which had been defaced.

The model had a big smile, but her head was no longer attached to her body. Amanda had cut off the model's head and pasted it to the cover page next to her torso. A jagged line across the model's belly made in red ink. Blood droplets drawn below her tanned skin.

Scissors, colored paper, pencils and other art equipment on the floor nearby. There was a bag with Amanda's initials stitched into the front flap. Rummaged through it. Grabbed one of her favorite tools.

Amanda picked up the Ken doll. Put it on the floor. Stabbed him with the ice pick over and over again.

Loud giggles and euphoria erupted as she bludgeoned the plastic totem. Amanda's delighted fury drove her until she stopped and pulled his head off.

Threw it in the corner.

A beheaded man doll.

Sat for a moment.

"I'm hungry." Walked out of her hideaway, shut the door tight, and skipped toward the house.

Present Day: Sunday, 5:15 a.m.

Eyes opened, the murderous headache pinned Lily to the floor.

Legs didn't want to move. Pain pulsed through her upper torso. Limbs heavy, grogginess drenched her.

She peeked out. Nothing was familiar.

Where am I? No memories. The last few hours didn't register. Jumbled mind.

Tightness in her chest.

Unfamiliar surroundings allowed fear to seep in.

Breathe, exhale.

Anxiety rose.

Lily removed the tarp. Found discarded in the corner of the shack, it made a perfect blanket, a shield. Her protection, she thought, like a cape. Last hours proved it. No one had found her.

A shawl draped over the chair.

Why she'd driven here came back into her mind. Her friend's cabin hideaway. No one would find her here.

She'd fallen back asleep.

A temporary respite.

Now, a full-blown migraine.

Moments later Lily's stomach turned, a foul taste crept into her mouth. She retched. On all fours. Head pounded. Too many cocktails, but something more. Lame to blame the booze. Spun up, on the way to a freak-out.

Take a breath, get control.

Party night with friends. A guy hung around, more than one. She couldn't remember all the names. Brain blank, no answer to her question. Bad idea to stay here long. The sun would be up soon.

What was that? It sounded like it came from beyond the front door. Nothing in the room. The surroundings gave no clues.

Eyes closed. Willed the pain to end.

"Oh, Lily."

Whose voice? Sounded like a smoker, gravelly. No reply. She stayed silent.

"Oh, Lily."

Nothing visible, but the voice sounded closer. Up on her knees, she whipped around to see behind her. This simple move made her head spin. Tried to stand. Dizzy, she couldn't find her center. It came out of nowhere. Back she fell. Her head hit hard against the wood planks of the floor.

"Oh, Lily."

A hiss from inside her head.

The sound shrouded her thoughts, occupied her brain. A presence.

Torment from the center of her mind.

She stretched one leg, then the other. Another deep breath.

A flash of Stoney's red face.

Bound to the moment. Memory unfolded with pictures of Friday night.

People do things to themselves.

The air moved when the tarp came around her body again.

Blackness descended.

Would anyone hear her deepest scream?

The dilemma made her giddy.

The calm came to confirm the choices of her own existence.

Strength came from rational knowledge she possessed but couldn't unravel.

Alone she was safe.

Dialed the number. It rang and rang. Tried again.

"Hello?"

"Sorry to wake you."

"What time is it?"

"Not long before sunrise," Lily said.

"Give me a second to wake up." A restless sleeper. Duchess had fallen asleep outside on her large veranda. "Where are you?"

"Your cabin."

"Good, you're safe. What happened?"

"You don't mind I came here?"

"If I did, I wouldn't have given you the key. But what drove you there?"

"Why don't you live here? You never told me."

Duchess smiled, shook her head. "You can ask, but it's not your concern."

"You're so guarded. I don't understand."

"When you've got more life under you. It will make sense. For a woman, mystery is a weapon, a tool, and a safety net."

"I want to survive. It would be enough."

She felt sad for Lily. So much talent, a first-rate mind, but the unstable nature of her thoughts was crippling her natural strength. "Don't settle. You will regret it."

"I had it out with my ex-boyfriend Friday night. Bad scene. Lost my necklace."

"Aw. I'll buy you another one."

"Maybe a crystal this time? I'm ready for it."

"Hmm. Good idea. Would you like to pick it?"

"I would."

"Good. We'll choose a time. Have a little ceremony. I'll prepare the crystals, so things are ready whenever you want."

Lily got quiet.

"You didn't answer my question." Duchess waited.

"Sorry, my mind's a jumble."

"What made you drive to my cabin?"

"The public fight with my ex-boyfriend. I wanted to hide."

"Good reason. Is it over?"

"Yes. I'm done. Why did I start up with him in the first place?"

"A question worthy of an answer. Got one?"

"Boredom makes me take risks I shouldn't. I hate it here."

A chuckle. "If you hate it here it will be the same if you go somewhere else. The issue is inside you. A new city is a band-aid. Until you go deep within yourself, every place you move will not be enough."

"The voice came again last night."

Duchess perked up. "No apparition, a voice alone?"

"Yep."

"What type of energy?"

"Hard to tell. I was a mess. But it didn't scare me. I'm free alone."

"Good."

"Do you ever sense you don't belong? Like everyone has a life but you?"

Duchess changed the subject. "Are the events still happening?"

"One late last night, like I said. A couple of hours ago. Why?"

"Want to make certain you haven't given up on your meditations. They're critical to the changes you said you want to make. When you get comfortable with your wisdom you won't take lethal risks anymore."

"Nice way to say I'm self-destructive."

"Don't be so hard on yourself. We have come out of a rough season. All the summer energies and eclipses. The retrogrades. Mars, the planet of action, was hobbled. Nothing moves unless the energies align."

"When summer ended, I had to do something. Change things." *Duchess has the most lovable laugh.*

"Patience, it will come."

"But I've fucked up. Amanda found out."

"Are you scared of her?"

Lily hesitated.

Duchess didn't speak. *Bad sign she can't respond with a quick answer. There is more to this drama than she will admit.*

"Be honest with yourself. Why did you choose him?"

"He was there when I wanted," Lily said.

"Let Amanda vent. Your punishment won't hurt for long."

"I'll be by later."

"You are welcome anytime. Let's plan to have supper on one of your visits."

"Okay. Thanks so much for the cabin. After the fight, I would have been lost without it. You're a lifesaver."

"Sometimes. Meditate. Center yourself. I'll see later."

The call ended.

She always changes my mood for the better. Maybe the crystal Duchess gives me will ward off the dread I sense. It gets stronger every day. I hate it. Didn't ask for this... gift, Duchess calls it. Gift? Ha.

Present Day: Late Monday Afternoon

Long afternoon of calls. One after another. Chaotic Monday after an event. Kate dialed a number. "Can I buy you a drink tonight?"

Micky chuckled. "I think it's my turn."

"Yeah, but I need something from you."

"I'm a man. Of course, you do."

"You will never change."

"I'm divorced, 55, drink too much and eat at the sink. What's to change?"

"I see your point." Micky had money. If he had his shit together, there might have been a connection. He didn't.

"Are you anywhere near The Tavern?"

"Meet you there in twenty."

A glass of red wine waited for Kate on the bar opposite an empty stool next to a man dressed in shades of beige, expensive shoes. He dripped money.

"You remembered."

"I'm a pushover for redheads."

"You're not that picky."

"Health to us both."

"You need to lose weight, Micky."

"What? I'm all muscle."

Kate laughed. "Right."

"So, why am I here?"

"Remember the vacant house close to the bluff? Daughter killed both parents."

"Riverbend Road. Can never forget it."

"Well, it's being used for a party house. An overdose. Two women in the hospital. A young woman is missing."

"Yes. And?"

"My client doesn't think the police leveled with them," Kate said.

"Your client?"

"Humor me."

"Okay. Why not? Explain."

"Nothing from the missing woman's friends who came to the party. No one saw her leave. No one gave her a ride. There is also no information on who brought the drugs. I need what the Stratford PD won't share. You're a reporter, so I figured your police sources might have answers. You can call without raising the temperature."

"Riverbend Road proves true to its nicknames," Micky said.

"Murder house?"

"Something evil inside lives."

"Oh, brother. I hope everyone doesn't react as you did." *Smooth wine*, another sip. "This one is worrisome. The missing young woman's name is Lily Cates. She didn't vanish. She's hiding, and I bet she knows a lot."

"Not the first time, watch 'Dateline'."

"Someone is lying."

"Good one, Sherlock, people lie."

"Police interviewed the people at the party. More names to call. Talk to your sources. See what you can find out."

"If the police aren't talking to you about this Cates woman, who's gone missing, it's a bad sign, babe."

Kate tossed a baggie across the bar top. The evidence should seal his involvement. Micky did a double take. Took the baggie into his hands and stared at the contents.

"A necklace named Lily. Sweet."

"The missing woman's."

"Where'd you find it?"

"After the team swept the crime scene, I needed to see for myself. Took a door to the backyard, ended down a hill near the creek. Found this as I climbed back up."

"It's evidence? What the fuck?"

"Interested, aren't you?"

"Now, I am. Someone ripped it off the abducted woman? Someone named Lily," Micky said.

"See, you're spinning a story. There is no evidence of an abduction."

"What other answer is there?"

"Do your job. Inspire the police to answer your questions."

"What are you going to do with it, the necklace?"

The last sips in a wine glass are tragic. "I'm going to deliver it to someone with the power to do something about it."

"I'll cite an unnamed source."

"Appreciate it, but if it will get you more detailed information, use my name. Don't lie on my account."

"Who, me?"

Time to meet up with her partner, Jack Stone.

Soon the headlines would take over.

Resurrected horrors on social media.

Riverbend Road made into a predictable scene for the next local drama. The current case dragged down into the rumor machine, where the truth disappeared amid fake news.

May 2010: Thursday, 7:30 p.m.

"Ain't No Sunshine" by Bill Withers played over the speakers.

The hostess was super chipper.

"Hey, Clay. Want your regular table?"

She fluffed regulars and F.B.I. agents got special treatment in this well-traveled tavern near Capitol Hill.

"I'm meeting a woman. Redhead, 5'10" …"

Contorted face, her reaction was swift. "Oh, sorry for you. Be careful. We've poured her two glasses of wine from different bottles and she still says it's rancid."

Terrific. "Sorry."

The hostess waved him off. "This way, sir."

The smile on Clay Zach's face disappeared when he saw her. He'd seen her filet law enforcement on CNN when they objected to her theories. Plastered on his charmer smile as he approached the table.

"Is the wine any better?" The hostess waited.

A smile. No comment. Kate looked up at the man in front of her. They hadn't met before.

The hostess looked at Clay. "What's your pleasure?"

"Dirty vodka martini, please."

"You got it." She walked off.

"Clay Zach, from the bureau." He stretched out his hand, she took it.

"Dr. Kate Winter. Have a seat."

She was better-looking than he'd first assessed. Expensive threads, she made over twice as much money as he did as an F.B.I. profiler. It made him happier about his change.

"What do you need?"

Clay chuckled. "You get down to it."

Kate waited.

"We suspect a serial murderer is active in the D.C. area."

"What do you need from me?"

"I need a woman to go undercover. We've tracked the UnSub across five states. Current whereabouts is down to Maryland. We think."

"What about the BAU?"

They fell into a shorthand conversation. The Behavioral Analysis Unit (BAU) of the F.B.I. referenced a department of the National Center for the Analysis of Violent Crimes. An "unknown subject" was shortened to UnSub.

"The available undercover agents have little psych training, which I think is essential on this. They've told me you've been effective with..."

"Serial killers love me."

"Works for me." Clay put a single sheet of paper on the table, which he had stashed inside his jacket pocket. "There is an access code to the website and a secure password. If you accept the contract, all the info you need is on the site."

She perused the paper.

"Is it true you worked with interrogators in Iraq?"

Kate looked up. Stared at him. *He's worn out. What happens when you have a non-stop diet of death, with no personal life.* "My work in the Middle East is classified."

"No problem. We can't let him... He's slipped through before. We've tracked him for the last six months, but we think he's been active longer. Long enough for the media to dub him the Chesapeake Slasher."

"Nice nickname. What's his trophy?"

"Hair. Different colors."

"So, you're desperate."

"Officially, no. Between you and me, you bet."

"I'm the right age." Kate held up the paper he'd handed her. "What's your plan? Hit the area he's been trolling until we find him. He hits on me, offers a ride home, and then knocks me out in the car?"

An accurate guess. She's seen what these maniacs do to women. "Last Friday, a man tried to pull a woman into his car in the St. Charles area. She'd had self-defense training. Caused a ruckus."

"Sounds disorganized."

"Yeah."

"Not your guy," Kate said.

"Agreed. He's organized, plans things out. As sadistic as we've seen."

Kate eyed him. "Your name sounds familiar."

"I've worked inside BAU for the last nine years."

"Oh, right. You're one of the protégés. You trained with the first manhunters, the serial killer gurus."

"Guilty."

Kate laughed. "Do you agree with them?"

"They were prescient. Serial killers have to experience it. No fantasy will satisfy these bloodthirsty savages."

"Like sugar. Once you start, you feed off the high and want more."

"They need to top their last experience."

"Desensitization and escalation?"

A single nod. "And you're the lucky woman I want to put in the middle."

"The cheese."

"Jesus, no."

Silence.

Clay took a drink of his dirty vodka martini. Kate sipped her glass of white wine.

She leveled a gaze at him. "You need to trust I can get in his head. Use whatever I can to seduce him. Make him comfortable. You sweep in at the end. When he's on his knees."

Frozen by her description, he didn't respond for a moment. Tried to digest it. "You think you can seduce him?"

Deadpan stare. Kate shook her head. A smile cracked through. Her right eyebrow lifted. "I flip the script. Serial killers like to charm their victims. The Chesapeake Slasher won't be immune to the tactic. Is he impotent?"

Former colleagues had read Clay in on Dr. Kate Winter. A brilliant woman who chased men who kidnapped, tortured, and mutilated women. She worked outside traditional lines and produced results others didn't. Took risks in procedures she'd developed. The definition of fearless leader.

"No," Clay said.

"How do we set it up if he's a ghost?"

"Evidence leads us to believe he's in Maryland." Reached into his jacket. Set a small photo in front of her.

"Is this?" Kate pointed downward at the table. "It didn't register when I walked in. Two months ago…"

"A woman and her girlfriend walked out of this bar. We found one woman. Parts of her. Still haven't located the second. We can start there."

"What if he doesn't come on to me?"

"Yeah, it's... Since you have walked inside their minds. We thought you might have a suggestion."

"He has to think I'll sleep with him. It has to be real all the way down the line. We'll get naked together, so he'll trust me."

Clay leaned back in his chair. Speechless.

"What?"

"Nothing."

"Oh, this is precious. You don't approve?"

Clay held up his hand. "No. I mean, yes. If you can handle it. We can keep you alive."

Kate reached for her purse.

This woman is tough. Didn't flinch. "So, you have sex with these animals?"

Kate stopped. Shot him a look. "Who said that? Undercover, I seduce them. I don't fuck them." Shook her head.

Nodded. "Good to know."

She said something under her breath, but he couldn't make it out. "Sorry?"

"He doesn't crave consummation. It's about power. A woman can take a psychopath all the way to arousal. But he'll turn on her. Surrender is anathema to his need to conquer. The thirst to obliterate his obsession is the root of his fury."

Clay stared at her.

"I'll be ready," she said.

Kate walked out of the restaurant. No goodbye.

Present Day: Monday Night

A loose atmosphere ruled inside the Ransom Center, which was located along the Potomac River in National Harbor, Maryland, south of Washington, D.C., near the Woodrow Wilson Bridge.

The open floor plan encouraged camaraderie and chaos. The noise level represented collaborative jostling in a rapid response environment. Brutal hours and possible 24/7 workweeks required specialized orchestration. A roomful of hackers, tech geeks, and social media nerds brought an atmosphere of frenetic energy, brainstorms, and outbursts, due to copious amounts of caffeine and other legal stimulants required to do the job and focus their genius minds.

Kate walked across the cavernous workspace, up the stairs, and knocked on the door to Jack Stone's office. Peeked in. "Hey, Stoney, you busy?"

"Depends. Do you bring good news or bad?"

She walked over to the full-sized stainless-steel fridge. Took out a Corona Light. "Want a Guinness?"

"Sure."

They clinked bottles. Kate stared at the workspace below on the other side of the glass. Stoney's second-floor view to an ocean of laptops, desktops, phones, and large screens trained on Twitter, Facebook, Snapchat, Tinder, TMZ, cable news channels, and whatever other newfangled social media platform was trending these days. Experts divided into regions, broken down into cities, and focused on data breaking in active cases, or potential new business, which often came in the form of breaking news.

The Ransom Center catered to the rich, the infamous, and the nosey.

A local private school board got the idea to track their students on social media platforms. It came after a brutal set of sexual assaults. A wife in a vicious divorce whose husband owned half her business wanted his online footprint investigated.

To make up for the appearance of corporate greed, the Center performed pro-bono work for rural communities around the country whose law enforcement and political leaders found themselves in the middle of cases they couldn't handle. After a mass shooting in a church in a small Missouri town. City officials hired the Ransom Center to dissect digital footprints of witnesses to identify potential suspects. Government agencies also sought their help on specialized cases, multiple murders and assaults.

The Ransom Center was free of boundaries, the annoyance of oversight committees and the scrutiny of shareholders.

Trevor Kim, Callie Diaz, and their colleagues tracked people and their connections. Team leaders were managers in a collaborative environment. Meetings kept to a minimum, otherwise, burnout set in.

Their data center amassed enough information to make the company worth tens of millions of dollars.

"A connected world is a safer world," was Jack Stone's motto. He'd courted Kate to partner with him. A businessman, he needed her expertise. She'd driven a hard bargain because she was content as a contractor. Demanded every full-time employee also be an owner of the Center, which brought strict guidelines. Transparency in all cases. The kicker was an ethics clause which brought a penalty of partnership loss if either one of them betrayed the foundational purpose of the Center.

The enemy, according to the Ransom Center, was public fear stoked by bad actors who spread misinformation, however it manifested.

But no one could stop fear from spreading.

The Center looked to expand into homeland security entrepreneurship, which in the era of hyper-vigilance would triple the company's value.

Most of Stoney's pals thought he ran a global call center for government, corporations, and foundations. The cover stuck. Few had a handle on the scope of the Center's reach.

"Okay, so what's going on? Did you find anything at the scene?" Silence. "Kate?"

No answer, so Stoney waited. He'd fought for her with the Tripp Foundation, who endowed the Ransom Center. A hard sell with the money men. Emphasis on men's club. Her psychological techniques and intuitive talents weren't quantifiable to board members, accountants, human resource models, and "endowment weenies," as everyone at Ransom called them.

Dr. Kate Winter operated beyond the elite superstructure of law enforcement created in Washington, D.C. and she had talents the men who ran this world didn't understand or respect.

"Riverbend Road, what a location for a party. People obsess over it. Want to be where it happened," Kate said. "It titillates. Explains why scary movies make great date nights."

"An unimaginable act, both parents killed by their daughter. People don't want to think about it because it scares them. The fear makes it visceral and, it excites people."

"As if the power to obliterate lingers in the air. It also scares the hell out of men to think a beautiful teenage blonde would lose her shit and murder the people closest to her."

"True."

"Anyway, we got lucky." Kate fished the plastic bag out of her satchel. "I found this in the backyard."

Stoney took the bag from her. "Police missed this?"

"I guess. The house was a disaster zone by the time I got there. No way to tell the state of the interior before the party started."

"Hmm." He swiveled his chair around, his back to her. "Lily means nothing to me." He lied.

"Because that would be too easy."

He wouldn't make eye contact. His laugh was forced.

She watched him. *Uh-oh, what's he not saying?* Kate pushed. "Last name is Cates. Have you talked to the police? Do they have anything else?"

Stoney held up the bag with the Lily necklace in it. "This will cause a problem. They'll want to talk to you."

He looked at the necklace too long. Rubbed his thumb across the letters. Kate made a mental note.

"At least they're used to me now."

He forced a smile. "Well, tolerate is closer."

"I'll take it."

"A Stratford PD liaison officer is in place, so we can funnel information her way."

"I told Micky, the reporter at the Baltimore Post."

"Is he going to help or be a problem?"

"Both. I showed him the Lily charm, so he understands what's involved." Kate picked up her phone, which had vibrated. "A text from him. Says he talked to one of his police sources. Neighbor saw a black Porsche tear down the street at around 1:30 a.m. Plates on the Porsche registered to..."

Kate stared at him. "What were you doing at Riverbend Road?"

"Personal reasons."

"Stoney. Come on. It looks bad. Tell the police. If Micky's in the loop, it won't be long before everyone else will be too."

"Amanda was at the party. The guy she's dating got drunk and passed out. She told me people came they didn't invite. It got out of control afterward. People buying drugs from two guys."

"How many people?"

"I called when I got there. Amanda came out. We left."

Another lie.

"What did she have to say?"

"We didn't talk. Came in here to prepare action items for the team. Called our liaison with the police. I need to call her again. Your little addition will make them crazy."

"Has Amanda mentioned anyone named Lily?"

"What? No."

"I'll go check in with Callie. Hang around a while to see what the gossip is."

"I'll update the police on the necklace."

"You'll need something stronger than a beer. They will be pissed I found an item at the crime scene their guys missed, and because I brought it back here. Tell them two uniforms guarded the house. Not their job. No way to log it, so chain of custody would be in doubt either way."

"We've been through this before. Won't be like the first time. We've got history now, some trust."

Stoney watched her leave his office. His face changed the instant the door closed. His jaw tightened, and a wave of tension washed over his face.

Kate sensed eyes on her, stopped walking. Turned around. Peered up into Stoney's office. The glass wall overlooked the work area below. The look on his face. His intense stare. From where she stood his fury was palpable.

A sense of dread kicked up in Kate's consciousness. Stoney had done more than pick up his daughter. He had gotten numb to Amanda's antics. His reaction to the events at the party was personal. He didn't want to share. So, he lied.

What 30-something woman calls her dad to pick her up from a party?

Something else to figure out, and one difficult task to mete out.

Callie and her team had eyes on Amanda's social media accounts. Tracked all of her friends.

Kate would need to stay in Stoney's face to make sure he did nothing stupid. His reaction to his daughter's situation warned her.

The old anger had resurfaced. The roadmap to what came next had shown in the tension in Stoney's body.

When Kate's instincts yelled, she never ignored them.

July 2015: Friday Night

The man she'd seen inside the bar got her attention when he exited. Tall, handsome, but he couldn't hide his shyness from her. The type of man Amanda loved. Easy, arrogant, and weak.

Perfect.

She flipped the visor down. Checked the mirror. A touch of lipstick helped her pout pop. "He won't be able to resist." Got out of her car. Leaned over, tussled her hair. Whipped it back when she stood. Walked across the street.

No one around paid attention. Restaurants and bars lined both sides of the street. Georgetown was abuzz on the weekend.

A stunned look when he saw her. His smile turned quizzical.

"I saw you in the bar."

Her flirtiest smile beamed at him. Amanda had used it many times. Few men resisted.

"I waited until you came out," she said. *He's loaded.* "Haven't seen you since the party."

A good bet he'd play along.

"Been busy."

"Me, too."

"Need a ride? My car's around the corner," he said.

"How did you find a parking space? It's crazy here tonight."

The man chuckled and kept walking.

Amanda dug inside her purse. Turned around. No one was near. Opened a zipper compartment. Touched the instrument she would need.

He opened the passenger door for her. "Milady."

"The back seat is more comfortable."

She got in. Looked out at him. Patted the seat cushion next to her. "Promise, I won't bite unless you ask me to."

Roaring laughter. "Good one." He slipped into the back seat.

A large yawn. "Whew, I'm tired." Laughed.

"Let me loosen your tie. You'll be more relaxed." Amanda leaned in to kiss him.

Hunger fueled his response.

It's always the shy ones.

Amanda moved to straddle him. Kissed his neck. He moaned. Unbuckled his belt and unzipped his pants. He tugged on them but couldn't get them down. He was too inebriated. She grabbed his pants by the pockets and pulled. He lifted up. Got his pants off and pushed them onto the floor.

"Beautiful man."

"Hot woman." His eyes fluttered. Shut tight. His breath deepened. He'd fallen asleep.

Swift movements. She took the syringe out of her purse. Quick look out the windows. No one around.

Lifted herself off him. Untied his right shoe. Pulled off his sock. Grabbed the syringe and injected him between his toes.

Waited. It was the longest five minutes of Amanda's life.

Convulsions came in waves.

She held him. "It's okay. You can't help it. It's why I'm here." When the convulsions stopped, Amanda watched his eyes. Saw them flutter. Spittle and saliva foamed from his mouth. His breathing was shallow. The effort was obvious.

The street remained filled with people. She wouldn't get caught. Disgrace would ruin her dad, which would be fine with her. But she wasn't done.

Opened the car door and exited. Turned back to look in. "Maybe you'll make it through the night."

Watched another convulsion and then he was quiet.

The drugs she'd gotten from a new source, although her dealer wouldn't say who. It was a heroin-laced concoction circulating in the area since the spring.

Walked in the opposite direction from where she came. Amanda's head on a swivel and on the lookout for police. Certain no one had seen her. The street was one of quiet suburban safety.

She dialed. He picked up on the second ring.

"Talk to me."

"What a way to greet a lady."

"Who's this?"

"The woman of your dreams."

Quiet. "Give me another clue."

"Party at your place?"

"Hey, Amanda. Why not?"

"See you soon." *When I get finished with him, he'll get 'why not.'*

The night ended as she'd planned.

They'd had cocktails, chatted and she'd taken him into his bedroom.

"If you're my dream woman, assume the position." Shoved her on the bed. She'd remembered him, so was prepared for his aggression. His condominium was the perfect setting.

Amanda took a deep breath, screamed and screamed again.

"Shut up." His left hand came across the side of her face in a thwack. The pain seared into her mind what she had orchestrated, what the man deserved.

Laughter exploded from her mouth. "That's all you've got?"

Another blow, same place, the pain coursed through her body. A deep breath, a louder squeal. His neighbors needed to hear her.

Faint sirens.

He jumped up to look outside. Stared back at her. Amanda kept her eyes closed. It would all be worth it.

A misogynistic monster would be locked up.

And she'd never be suspected of the murder in Georgetown.

July 2015: Saturday Morning

A knock.

Lily opened the door. Amanda's self-satisfied smile alarmed her. Then she saw the bruises on the right side of her face. "Oh, no. What happened?"

"Victory for women everywhere."

"Get in here." Lily went into the kitchen. "Want anything?"

"Nah, I'm good. I am *so* good."

Came back out with a package of frozen peas. Handed it to her friend.

"Are you high?"

Amanda placed the frozen pack on her face. A small gesture with her right hand, index finger, and thumb. "A bit. Enough to appreciate genius."

"I'm scared to ask."

One shoulder shrug. "Then don't." Amanda plopped down in a chair. Saw Lily's tea. "Got anything stronger than tea?"

"You've been here before. Help yourself."

Lily watched her walk into the kitchen. Amanda's purse was open on the floor. A glance down, a syringe was visible. She didn't have to look any further. Her best friend had been on a downward spiral since her mom and dad split. It was clear she hadn't hit bottom yet.

Picked up her phone on the table. Scrolled through her Twitter feed. Stopped on a news item. "Oh, man."

Amanda walked out of the kitchen. "What's up?"

Held up her phone. "Your usual on Twitter. A guy got sent to the emergency room last night. Wonder if it's the same woman?"

A shrug. "I haven't read anything, what?"

"They think it's a hooker trying to get even. This is the third man."

Amanda smiled. "At least they're alive."

"Well, not this guy. He didn't make it."

"Tough luck."

Lily eyed her.

"What?"

"How'd you get the bruises?"

"It's nothing."

"Swiped the wrong way for the wrong guy?"

Amanda shrugged. "Maybe." Sipped her drink.

"Bullshit. You don't use dating apps."

"It's a good story, isn't it?"

Lily had been friends with her for a long time. Amanda had anger issues, and she was a liar. Had been caught in plenty of whoppers over the years. She'd covered for her more than once. Had been present during several public outbursts. Saw Amanda throw things, break precious items of her mother's, and be cruel to her dad.

She's clueless her dad came on to me. Wouldn't be able to handle it. "You're up to something. You lie when you're guilty. What did you do?"

Amanda looked at her. They'd been besties since eighth grade. Lily had listened to her problems for years. Watched her struggle with therapy. Saw her spiral from one emotional event to another. The drugs started earlier this year.

She was on her way from troubled to institutionalized. Her parents had fought over it. Her mother had been adamant. Amanda had talked her dad out of it.

"Righted a wrong," Amanda said.

"You aren't going to tell me?"

"I'll show you." Her iPhone open, Amanda scrolled through news items. Clicked on a link. Handed the phone to Lily. A news story about a man's arrest.

"This is the guy who hit you?"

"Sad." Her face beamed.

"What?" Looked down at the phone again. "I don't understand."

"Sheesh. If you can't figure it out." Walked back into the kitchen.

"Wait a minute." Lily followed her. "What are you... Don't tell me... Amanda, what did you do?"

"Don't get hysterical. It needed to happen. The worthless creep."

"The man assaulted you?"

"What?"

"How did you get the bruises on your face?"

Amanda laughed. Grabbed Lily to hug her. "You are so gullible. You think the world is..."

"Let go of me." Backed away. Lily sensed her darkness. Looked at Amanda.

They stared at one another.

I can't be around her anymore. "You better go."

"So soon? But we have so much to talk about." A maniacal laugh. Amanda turned and walked to the door. Opened it. Slammed it after she walked through.

Lily flipped the deadbolt the second the door shut. Hurried to her laptop, logged in and began a search. Tried different words, locales too, including Washington, D.C. "This will take too long."

Put in a call to Trevor at the Center. Explained what had happened when Amanda came over. He listened.

"Something is wrong. Look for any assaults. She had been banged up."

"I'll do the research myself."

"Don't tell Stoney. He'll freak if he sees Amanda with bruises on her face. The man is witless when it comes to her."

"He won't do anything," Trevor said. "Stoney's scared of her. Told me stories about Amanda when she was younger. Hot chick, but I wouldn't go near her with my roommate's dick."

"Ew. Stop. Call me back if you find something useful."

She decided to take a run. Got dressed and was out the door in ten minutes. Lily took her phone, which was turned off because it distracted from time needed to clear her head. Half-way through, she stopped to take a drink of water. Powered her phone back up. Three text messages, all from Trevor.

The first said nothing had gotten his attention, so he had expanded his search. The second mentioned "a man taken into custody at his home. Name not released. Neighbors called when they heard squeals for help." About an hour later, the third text, but she focused on the last three words. "...description fits Amanda."

It came as confirmation, not a surprise.

Amanda's specialty was outrageous risks. Games meant to punish an adversary. She saw enemies everywhere. Punished them for thrills, she had told Lily one day in high school. A teacher everyone at their school loved had rejected Amanda's advances. Because he'd spurned her, he was now a registered sex offender without a job.

Life was a cage match to Amanda Stone.

Weaklings, beware.

Present Day: Thursday Morning

"Thanks for yesterday," Callie said. "It was too much after I found out Lily was missing."

Kate smiled at her. "Hey, we're flexible here. Events shift our focus. If we don't react in the moment, what are we doing, right?"

"So, we put eyes on Amanda's social media accounts, Facebook, everything, friends included. They informed Stoney, so don't worry."

"Got it. I'm still worried."

"The team is on the social media accounts of the people we have proof came to the party. The crew who came in uninvited wasn't random. They got there through Trevor. The drugs were unexpected."

Drugs are never a surprise at a party. But Trevor? No way. What had Callie left out? Kate needed all of it.

Callie stood. "I'm going for coffee. Want anything?"

"Double espresso, please. Find a table in the quadrangle."

She nodded and took off across the office.

The quadrangle was an enormous outdoor space attached to the Center. Trees, flowers, tables to eat meals, and stations where people plugged in and worked when weather permitted.

Kate walked outside to where Callie had settled.

"Freakish warm weather. Perfect spot, right?" She handed Kate the double espresso.

"This will do the trick."

Kate waited before she launched into a conversation fraught with conflicts of interest for her. Stoney was her business partner. They'd become friends. His daughter and ex-wife complicated his life because they hated each other. It mattered less now that Amanda was on her own. Stoney's ex continued to blame him for her relationship with Amanda. Typical stuff. Their daughter's mental state wasn't.

None of it explained Stoney's presence at the Riverbend Road party.

Amanda was not a victim.

Callie opened her phone, whipped through her messages. Took another drink of her coffee. Played with her hair. Opened her computer, typed, clicked on a link. Cracked her knuckles. Looked up at her boss. "What?"

"I've never seen you fidget like this. What's up?"

She shrugged. "Nothing, I'm like this when I'm stressed."

"I can see. You don't have to talk about it."

"I'd like to, can't."

"You can't? Who's stopping you?"

Callie smirked, shook her head. "Come on."

"What's with the attitude?"

"Whatever we tell you goes straight back to Stoney. So, I can't talk about it." Callie stared at her. "Don't ask."

"Give me a second." Kate got up and walked across the stone path connected to the field beyond the quadrangle. Furious, she had no one to blame but herself.

The partnership was a dream. It fit what she did best. Map out actions for private citizens, authorities, and outcomes for people who take a wrong turn, and are a danger to society and themselves. Make the Ransom Center famous for behavioral science techniques turned into practical applications for institutions, corporations, schools, and private citizens. The partnership also gave her institutional power she'd never had before. As money poured into the Center, she benefited.

Kate's specialty remained the immersion in tormented minds, crime scenes, and the malevolent acts of unhinged humans. It was her foundation, but she had bigger ideas. If the Drake case taught her anything it was to trust intuition as part of the process. Coupling facts and proven profiling theories with instinctual perceptions would break new ground for the Center.

Stoney remained resistant to her idea. He'd insisted and pushed to expand nationally. She'd relented, although she wasn't sure how they would pull it off. The fast growth concerned her, but so far, they'd been able to invest, pay their bills, and make a profit.

She had worked with him for years, but he'd changed. His drinking made him volatile, and he'd closed himself off.

Our secrets make us sick. It was more than a paraphrase from Alcoholics Anonymous. *It's not my job to save him. But would he risk the Ransom Center? It would explain a lot.*

Kate sat back down across from Callie. "Let's change our focus. Detail the situation between Amanda and Stoney. I give you my word it will not go beyond this table. Understand?"

"Yes. You can't tell anyone I told you."

"Anonymous tipster, got it."

Callie laughed, a loud yelp. "My new sideline."

"I want all of it."

"There's not much to it. Her habit caught up with her. Amanda got busted for heroin last January. Her dad pulled strings to keep her out of jail. They've been at it since. After he found out she had gone to the party at Riverbend Road, he blew up. Amanda got ahold of Oxy and got rowdy. It was laced with another narcotic, I was told. A guy from Ransom saw her. Three guys were all over her. She encouraged them. Amanda also called her dad. Talk about clusterfuck. The guys here are protective, have seen a lot. Trevor found out. Headed Stoney off when he arrived."

"Heroin? You're sure?" Callie shook her head. "I expect to find this in our work. This is too close."

"Come on. You've been around. Amanda in the middle of both her parents."

"It's desperation."

"Amanda was in the bedroom with three guys when her dad arrived. Trevor warned him. I'm shocked there aren't pictures all over social media today. I hacked into Amanda's FB account, where a 'friend' posted a gross picture she wouldn't have let anyone see if sober. She was wasted. In bad shape when Stoney picked her up."

It was easy to visualize how things had escalated.

"Amanda's got issues, a lot of them," Kate said.

"You're tight with Stoney, but he and her mother did a number on her. Like you say. Some people shouldn't have kids."

"Yeah. All the conflict between Stoney and his ex-wife. Terrible for them and Amanda. Where was her boyfriend last night?"

"Boyfriend?" Callie shook her head. "Amanda doesn't have one."

"Stoney said her boyfriend had gotten drunk. Amanda called him to pick her up."

"Weird. She can't stand either of her parents. No way Amanda would choose her mom. Nothing is ever enough. Amanda was a straight-A student, except for one B. One. Her mom grounded her. The bitch is cra-cra."

"Yeah, but…" Kate's voice trailed off. "Stoney's ex is a handful." The thought of Amanda's new trouble cut into Kate's heart. "Nothing else?"

Callie shrugged. "Wait five minutes."

"Huh?"

"Amanda's on self-destruct."

"Oh. Stoney never talks about it with me. The divorce ended the conversation although not the drama."

"I like this job, so I keep quiet. Prefer ignorance over the alternative."

"Stay focused on the party at Riverbend Road."

"We have eyes on one guy from last night, his social accounts. Shady dude, white supremacist type, we got his social media handles from Trevor."

"Mmhmm." Trevor had more than the Center in his life. *He's wound too tight. What's he up to?*

"Takes a lot of risks. Trevor loves it. This job is his universe," Callie said. "I asked him about the drugs at the party. He refused to talk about it." She shrugged.

Kate had seen Trevor take chances. What she wasn't sure of is how far he'd go. Risk also meant mistakes.

How did an Asian super geek get tight with a white supremacist? Was it about the money?

It didn't fit.

"One last question for you. Who is Lily?"

"Um... What about her?"

"You know her?"

"Nobody *knows* Lily. We used to be friends. Now, she's a wild one."

"It could mean a lot of things."

"Off the charts smart. Hates it here. Not the same girl she was in high school. Lily isn't part of our crowd."

It wasn't what Callie had said about Lily that set off Kate's mental alarm. Callie's mood had changed when she talked about her. Her demeanor made a statement.

"What's so different about her?"

"I can't say because I don't understand what happened. We drifted apart, I guess. Why do you ask?"

"We think she's the missing woman."

"Oh, no shit?"

"The search isn't over."

"If Lily doesn't want to be found, she won't be."

"Odd for you to say. You assume she disappeared on her own. Maybe she had help."

"No way. Lily is different, sure, but she won't let anyone fuck with her. She's a loner. Not friendly, keeps to herself."

"What about her parents?"

"Dad split before her mom died. Lily never talked about them. Can't help you."

"Her dad abandoned her? Whoa, rough. She your age?"

"I'm two months older. I turned thirty-two last May."

"I'll quit bugging you now. If Stoney asks what we talked about, tell him I asked you about a young woman named Lily. Note his reaction. We need a lot more on the two guys at the party peddling Oxy, MDMA, and counterfeit pills laced with fentanyl."

"Got it."

"Take another crack at Trevor. He needs to explain the guys who brought the drugs."

"Will do."

"Keep your work quiet."

"Don't expect much from Trevor. He didn't want to talk about it the first time I asked."

"He can explain it to you or me, his choice."

Present Day: Thursday Afternoon

Trevor sped across the unpaved dirt road. He had a package to pick up from his new best friend. The guy who had turned his life upside down. His situation brought meaning to the term family obligations. He could have said no.

"Door's open."

The two-story metal structure was on property in rural Maryland. From the outside, it appeared as a storage facility. Inside, a massive stainless-steel table was near an industrial kitchen. Steps up to a loft were visible, but no way to see what was upstairs. Two large couches made up the living room, with a hand-crafted, cabriole-leg desk nearby. Beyond the living area at the back of the room was a large wall, with doors at the center. What lay beyond the doors was not for visitors.

Trevor walked in.

Tack Marin eyed him.

Neither man spoke.

Another man entered through two French doors at the center of the back wall. Straker Kent was bald. His tanned flesh stretched across overworked muscles. He wore a skin-tight t-shirt, with black workout leggings. He didn't need a bodyguard.

"Can I get you anything?"

Silence.

"He asked you a question," Tack said.

Trevor looked at him. "I heard him."

Tack grunted, smiled.

Trevor's mood was at a boil. "Something I said was funny?"

"Tack is anti-social," said Straker.

Trevor looked at him. "What's wrong with you?"

Instant recoil from the insult. Straker tensed up.

"I'll be around if you need me." Tack exited through the French doors, his shadow now visible through the frosted glass.

"Why are you here?" Straker stared at Trevor.

"Friends in the hospital. One woman missing. They mobilized the Center. Who laced the stuff your people brought to the party? It's no secret I'm the one connected to you. Fentanyl? The police have questions."

"Was everyone an adult?" Straker waited.

"Who do you think you are? I can crash your world." The instant Trevor said it, he regretted it. *Shit.*

New to this game, he had let emotions strangle him.

"So, pull the trigger. Drop a dime. Call the coppers..." Straker snickered. "You won't. You love your brother."

Trevor's jaw clenched. He took a deep breath. Controlled his fury. "Here's a thought. Play it straight, so no one gets poisoned."

"Tell that to my satisfied customers."

"You're sick. I'm out. I'll find another way to pay you off."

He had Straker's attention.

"There is no other way. You will do as you're told. Honor our deal. Because you can't face what happens if you don't."

"You don't give a shit about anyone."

His head jerked back. Straker grabbed his chest. "Oh. That hurts. What are you going to do about it?" He walked to his desk. Opened a large drawer, took out a package. Tossed it across the dark wood surface. "I'll text you later with an address."

"What's in it?"

"Excuse me? Not your business. Now, be a good man and your brother won't wish he'd died instead of survived." His gaze on Trevor, Straker saw him seethe. The tension in his body was clear from across the room. "Something I said?"

Trevor had many questions but wouldn't dare ask a single one. He walked over to the desk, took the package and turned to walk out.

Tack came back into the room. Stood by the window near his boss's desk.

"Don't make me regret this," Straker said.

Trevor stopped. He turned, shot a glance at Tack. Stared at Straker. Recovered his calm. When he spoke, his voice rumbled in his chest. "My brother and I were never close. He won't expect a rescue. I wouldn't. Don't push me."

A slit of a smile broke across Straker's face. "Your decision." Straker dropped his head back and laughed. His attention diverted for an instant.

Tack straightened. Prepared for what came next.

Straker had hit Trevor's trigger point.

He was back when his mother had called him from San Francisco to say his younger brother was in trouble. His girlfriend saw two men whisk him off the street and throw him in a dark grey van. No identification on the vehicle.

There were places men in vans took young, gorgeous girls and boys who didn't come back.

Straker's threat.

The event had paralyzed Trevor's family.

Blackmail came next.

Trevor had been on the hook to the men involved until he had more to go on. A way to find his brother.

After one month, Trevor threatened to go to Stoney. It's when Straker had shared a revelation. Stoney wasn't who Trevor thought he was. No specific details, except Stoney was broke, and Straker had come to his rescue. Trevor forced himself to accept Stoney had betrayed everyone at the Ransom Center and made his brother's situation worse. The news gutted him. But none of it mattered because he would do anything for his mother.

In fact, his brother's kidnapping was as much to squeeze Stoney as it was to control Trevor.

It's when Trevor turned his skills over to people with more power. A private intelligence firm had contacted him. He met with former F.B.I. profiler, Clay Zach. Took the chance when they made him an offer. He told Clay everything about Straker, including the drugs. Then Trevor trained. Promised back-up and a team on watch, he prepared to go undercover. Dangerous decision for an amateur but he and his family were out of options and time.

Trevor had taken orders for months. Gotten close to the man responsible for his brother's abduction. But Straker had pushed him. Threatened to hurt his brother whenever Trevor refused to help him with a pop-up party at one of his foreclosure properties.

Straker had also asked too many questions about the Ransom Center. No way Trevor would get in the middle of a fight between Straker and Stoney. Yet, he was.

"Fuck it," Straker said. "I'll tell my men to send your brother to Thailand."

Trevor had little to lose.

He lunged, struck Straker and moved him back into the desk. Over him, Trevor punched him in the face. The downward force landed with a crack. Blood spurted from his nose. Straker fought to respond.

Trevor unloaded strangled emotions, and he screamed at Straker. "Tell me where—"

Tack rushed in behind him. His grip came down on Trevor's shoulder like a vice. He lifted his body off of Straker.

Tack's warning was a whisper. "This will hurt."

"Get it over with," Trevor said.

He yelled as Tack lifted him up. The next second, he hurled Trevor through the air. A loud thud. A guttural grunt. Trevor lay still on the floor.

"That gets it done," Straker said. He picked up a small brass pipe in an ashtray on his desk, lit it.

Tack reached down, pretended to take Trevor's pulse. His eyes opened. Trevor looked at Tack.

"Get me out of here." The words mouthed.

Tack nodded at him.

Trevor stayed still.

Tack looked at Straker. "He's dead, boss."

"You broke his fucking neck." Straker laughed. "One loose end gone."

"I didn't plan it. He came at you."

"Get rid of him."

"Are you going to call him?"

Straker side-eyed him.

"Better to get in front of this. Jack Stone will be pissed." Tack hoisted Trevor's body up and over his shoulder.

Straker watched him leave. Hit speed dial on his cell phone.

Changed his mind before the call connected.

This news could wait.

Present Day: Thursday Night

The sound of a bark, then a shriek of a fox carried across the night air.

Kate rolled down the window. Tapped into the pulse of her surroundings. Sat in her car to think through what came next. The hardest element of her work depended on the opposite of effort. She had to relax her mind. Let it come to her.

To traverse a vacated crime scene and bend reality to reveal secrets meant blank space. A canvas to welcome in another world. Intent and motive to fill in holes.

The repetitive sounds of wildlife became a cacophony.

"The crime scene won't analyze itself." She got out of the car, hoisted her bag onto her shoulder and walked toward the house. The code to the police lockbox hadn't changed. Nobody had been inside since the police left early Saturday. The first step onto the porch set her instincts on alert. A normal reaction for anyone who visited Riverbend Road.

"You'd never guess what has happened here." Kate set her bag on a nearby table, opened a flap. Took out her night vision binoculars.

Peered through the binoculars from the front porch. Nothing moved, nothing discovered. The goggles had become a wrench for her subconscious. Tools turned into a security blanket. The result of a tough job done in difficult spaces.

Turned to go inside. A high-powered flashlight guided her way. The picture window across the room appeared like a portal. The script to whatever played out here reached beyond this space.

"Someone ripped the necklace off. Chased her, grabbed her?"

The necklace and the woman who wore it preoccupied Kate.

A walk toward the back room on the main floor where the young men had taken Amanda. It was Stoney's story. He had held back a lot, saying she'd awakened here. In this room.

"Makes little sense." The most powerful tool in her arsenal balked. Her gut didn't buy it. "Stoney's bullshit, again." His interior world was a minefield. Being here, clear of obstacles, the night revealed secrets that hid in plain sight in the light.

A look outside from this room made her calmer until she heard a strange noise. The walls dispersed the sound. Did it come from the yard? Her night vision intensified through the binoculars. Surety regained. Nothing visible, no movement.

So, what had caused the sound?

There was no wind.

Kate closed her eyes. The next sound came from inside. Muffled. Seconds later, nothing. "Now, I'm hearing things."

Work to do.

It didn't begin for Kate until she was alone. Absorption of the crime scene, all aspects, demanded no distractions. Where her imagination encouraged her to dissect the results of a collision of souls. Humans at their worst. Trails of energy left behind to diagnose. A story to unravel.

The crime scene techs left the room as they'd found it. They'd collected enough DNA to keep the lab busy for weeks. Science worked by method, not time.

Force had not been an issue with Amanda. The consensual sex with multiple men happened through choice. Inhibitions were minimal with drugs and alcohol.

She has a score to settle with her father. Heroin arrest, multiple-partner sex, Amanda out of control. Narcissism on steroids.

"A lot more to this." Her subconscious mind plowed through obvious trails of previous drama with Stoney. None fit the current scene.

Dr. Kate Winter was immune to petty frights because of experiences that would have wrecked ordinary mortals.

The picture window provided a lens in the blackness. She stared out while her mind did a deep dive.

Fear spiked at night.

We take risks under the shield of the moon.

It exposes our emotional insecurities and personal fault lines. Opens wounds we don't admit exist to anyone.

Our need to annihilate what haunts us taps on our weaknesses, so we act out. It makes our vices appear as a tonic, an escape. It doesn't have to last long. We don't expect relief. We settle for a respite.

Dull the emotions.

Drown manic impulses.

A moonlit night peeks in at our subconscious and the unclaimed parts of our unconscious. Where our weaknesses wait to betray us.

Light defuses the time bombs we bury while the night infuses our mind's darkest thoughts like a detonation charge.

Our actions repulse us when we react. Driven by inner battles, we cannot help ourselves.

It was the same every time.

When the earth shakes, the seabed roils until the organic reaction fulfills itself in a wave or a tsunami. Same with our subconscious. Our ugliest thoughts are strongest in the deep darkness.

Extreme choices can seduce us.

Our subconscious calls from the depths for us to remember.

When we refuse to comply, our excuse is to self-medicate.

Memory is the first step. It reminds us of our torment. We torture ourselves to find our footing without it.

When we can't, we run.

Present Day: Thursday Night

"It's what happened to Lily. The young woman is alive, no doubt about it. The crowd was chill. She ran. But who chased her?" Recorder on, Kate continued. "He got close enough to Lily to break her necklace chain. A struggle."

To understand terror is to live with it. What it means to cause it. To analyze the aftermath is to be inside the perpetrator's mind. To be where it happened helps to absorb it.

The rancid emissions of a human amid death throes. The noxious expulsion of body waste, the rotting flesh amid clues. The putrid combination comes with Dr. Kate Winter to every scene. The fetid smell of dead bodies.

It doesn't have to make sense.

Variables, however, must fit like a puzzle.

A flashlight-lit walk through the house, room by room, delivered familiarity. "Walk through the past before you excavate the present." Into the kitchen where the double murder had happened, and how the myth of this house began.

Hesitation.

Kate's steps slowed. Jolted by forensic pictures, her steps were heavier. An accumulation of mutilated corpses bathed her brain, red walls of arterial spray, and of victims turned vigilante. She stopped.

Inside the kitchen, a haunted void.

A daughter's vendetta.

The visual carnage resurrected tonight.

The ooze of viscous tissue had dripped off the counters. The blood on the floor from the brutal battle had left a mirage of slick red tile. The bodies of the two people who'd given her life were covered in the patina of red lacquer.

Memories of the double murder scene photos flipped across Kate's brain.

Knife as a weapon, the daughter delivered her verdict in an epic tirade. The choice of weapon forced intimacy in death. Her rage a secret until she exploded.

The deed played out over many minutes, two against one was a death wish. The daughter gained strength through her retribution, enough to overtake both her parents. Minutes passed, the end took time. With every strike she made, another wrong was rectified.

Exhaustion came at exsanguination.

Don't get distracted.

"There it is again."

Quick steps back to the main room. She listened.

The sound came from the other side of the house. The earlier one was different. "There's nothing to absorb noise, no drapes or furniture. It's the house."

Sounds in darkness travel deeper than our best efforts to block them. A thud in an upstairs hallway when no one occupies the space ignites our imagination. But a house with vinyl siding has less to block the noise than a brick or stone structure.

It caught Kate's attention when she walked down the short hallway by the bedrooms.

A brass hook-and-eye positioned on the hallway side of one bedroom door. She looked closer. Revulsion bubbled up. A crude system intended to keep whoever was inside the room secured. A motive of cruel intent? The room across the hall didn't have one, but the bathroom down the hall did.

She turned on the recorder.

"I'm in the hallway on the opposite side of the house from where Amanda was found. One bedroom and the hallway bathroom have brass hook-and-eyes on the *outside* of the doors. The daughter's room? Paltry method to lock her inside. Recheck the crime scene notes."

Across from the hallway bathroom was another room.

A small but impressive built-in library. A contemplative room in contrast to other parts of the house.

The extreme shift in energy made Kate stop.

Book after book on the Civil War. Foreign policy and history books packed one wall of shelves, pages of war stories, fragile peace, and how the world became what it is today. Fiction commandeered another wall. The last wall of shelves held books by mystics and New Age thinkers. Spiritual books, philosophy, and writings meant to challenge people.

"Weird." An aroma different from other parts of the house. A bothersome sign.

It wasn't her imagination.

Humans leave traces of themselves behind.

Chaos screamed from several rooms in this house. Not here. A cozy hideaway. One room safe from the mayhem.

"Wait…" One wall was a wall-papered facade. The closer Kate got to this wall the stronger the energy. She stopped. Far enough for now.

A signal, she explained it to people as her gut.

Then, a chill.

Her reaction answered the questions.

Explained the noises.

She wasn't alone.

Present Day: Friday, 12:30 a.m.

Kate walked out of the library.

The fake book wall opened with ease. He squeezed out of the hidden passage.

Back in the main room, Kate's cell phone rang. She ignored it. Rummaged around in her bag.

The man opened the library door to slip out. Silent footsteps, agile moves put him at the entrance to the main room.

He waited. Watched. An unobstructed view to the woman who'd interrupted his search.

The wind kicked up. Rooftop sounds, a loud clang.

"I know you're there," Kate said. Binoculars back in place. No response. Reached deep inside her bag. The cold metal intensified her alertness. Pulled out her gun. Held it close to her side. Her back to the man in the hallway.

The man saw the front door, thought about a fast split. The woman's voice was serious. There was no hint of nerves from her.

He rejected the idea.

No clean options.

"You can stand there all night, but I won't leave." Speed dial, a quick answer. "I'll hold."

He didn't move.

"This is Dr. Winter. I need a squad car out here on Riverbend Road." She listened. Hung up. "Listen up, pal. I'll have two shots in you before you cross the floor. Maybe more. It's fascinating, but police often don't recall how many times they pull the trigger when they confront a criminal. Time for you to decide."

"No need for the gun."

"Thanks for the advice. Time for introductions. You first." Her flashlight lit the way for him.

He stepped into the room, his hands in front of him. "Easy. I'm unarmed."

"Take a seat on the couch."

"Listen, I—"

"Not interested. Who are you?"

"Clint Grant. My sister came to the party and ended up in the hospital."

"Let me see your identification."

"You, first."

"What's her name?"

"Janet."

"Get comfortable."

She watched him. Dialed a number. "Hey, it's Kate. I need the names of the two young women hospitalized last Friday."

The man moved to the end of the couch. Checked his watch. Scratched his face. Cracked his neck. Changed his position again.

His mannerisms scream withdrawal. Amphetamines? He can't sit still. Guilt? Oh, yeah. "Thanks. I appreciate it." *He's caught and a liar. And he came here unarmed.* Kate tucked her 9mm Glock pistol into the back of her pants.

"I assumed you were police. What kind of doctor are you?"

"The kind that doesn't patch up bodies after a gunshot wound. I'm an analyst with an organization that works with authorities."

"Tells me nothing."

"You're quick. Two kind officers will be here in less than 10 minutes. What were you doing in the library?"

He didn't speak.

"Look, I understand you're upset about your sister, but you will not find answers here. Let authorities handle it."

"Right."

"It just happened. Be patient."

"This is bullshit."

"No, it's a fucking travesty. What are you doing here?"

Nothing.

If he bolts, I can't shoot him. So, why is he still here? He is desperate to find something in this house.

"This is out of character for Janet. She's not a party girl," he said.

"How do you know?"

"What?"

"You're her brother. Does she tell you everything? Intimate details about her life?"

"No, but… It's not like her."

Kate walked closer, still on guard. He'd developed a tick. Kept tilting his head to one side. A permanent kink in his neck.

"Oxy and cocaine is one type of high. Add fentanyl and it's Russian roulette. It happens too often. Your sister was lucky."

He ran his hands through his hair. Exhaled.

If this guy could climb walls, he'd be on the ceiling. "Janet almost died."

He grumbled. Looked down.

She saw him check for exits.

"I didn't know about the fentanyl," he said.

Kate took another step forward.

He stood and walked over to look out the picture window.

"Why did you hide in the library? What were you looking for?" She walked closer to him as she spoke.

He didn't respond.

Kate was less than five feet away.

"They will pay for this. I'm not their fall guy."

"What did you say?"

When he turned around his face was flush, his eyes darted around. She was too close. Alcohol wafted from him. Mixed with the flop sweat she'd smelled in the library. The unmistakable odor of panic.

Her gut sent an alert. Simple message. Back off.

He took a step forward.

"You're not Janet's brother."

"No, I'm not." A slit of a smile crept across his face, but he wasn't happy.

He lunged in Kate's direction. But instead of attacking her, he fled out the front door.

Present Day: Friday, 1:00 a.m.

The headlights of the squad car flashed across the front window. She grabbed her bag, headed out.

An officer walked half-way up the stone walkway. "What's up, Dr. Winter?"

She walked over to him. Another squad car pulled up behind the first one.

"What are you doing here?" The police officer checked his watch.

"She works at night." A tall slender man with sandy blonde hair walked up. He was in civilian clothes.

"Where'd you come from?" Kate looked at the man in disbelief. Her eyes wide at the sight of him.

"Police radio. Wanted to see what happened." He looked at the police officer. "It's okay. I've got this. Told the liaison officer I'd be on scene."

"Sure thing, Clay. Captain authorized 24/7 after Dr. Winter's call. We'll be close." The officer turned to go back to his vehicle. Gave a signal to the policewoman who had pulled up behind him. They'd be on watch until the shift changes at dawn.

"Good to see you, Kate."

"You, too."

"What happened?"

"Are you working this case now? Small time for you."

"Spider's web."

"I got that impression tonight. Needed to go over the crime scene. Had to be here to grasp it." *Why is he here? Keep things on point, doesn't matter.*

"When no civilians are around to disturb the vibes," Clay said.

She saw him roll his eyes. "Are we going to do this again?"

"No. Sorry. I'm an asshole."

Silence.

"Report to write. I'd better head off," Kate said.

"That's it?"

She stopped. "What do you want?"

"Tell me what happened tonight. Why you called in back-up."

"I'm not a policewoman. It wasn't back-up."

"Why did you call it in?"

"I went through the house. It's the way I work."

He chuckled.

"Have you been through the house?"

"Yeah," Clay said.

"Did you go into the library?"

"The fake wall?"

"My instincts were correct. A man hid in the compartment when he heard me. It's the only explanation."

"You still carry?"

"It's part of the job."

"Good. Your work is..."

"Don't say it."

"Wasn't going to."

"He concocted this story. Tied himself to one woman who landed in the hospital. Said he was her brother, Clint something. Wait. Grant, that's it."

"Can you describe him?"

"Stocky. Not tall. Strong body odor."

"You smelled him?"

"The guy stunk. He was twitchy. Nervous type."

"Why do you think he came out?"

She looked at him. "No clue. He had no idea I'd sensed him there. Maybe... Wanted to see if I was after what he came to retrieve?"

"What would you have done if he hadn't shown himself?"

"The same thing. Called it into Stratford PD."

He walked past her toward the house.

"I've got to run, Clay."

"I want a copy of your report." Said over his shoulder.

"Sure. Are you still at the F.B.I.?"

"I'm touched you remember. No. Private outfit. Trevor has the details."

Trevor? Now what?

"I miss you, Kate." Clay said it walking away.

She turned to watch him go into the house. Closed her eyes.

Moments passed.

"No. Don't complicate your life, Kate."

It needed to be said out loud.

She threw her bag in the back seat.

Clay shows up here out of nowhere? And Trevor has details on his new private gig?

The last nugget of news threw her.

The man who called himself Clint watched her drive away. She'd remember him. There would be a sketch. Two police vehicles close to the house meant he couldn't go back in tonight. It might be better to split town than face Straker Kent's wrath.

September 2011: Saturday

Reports had escalated about women abducted across several states from Illinois to the mid-Atlantic region. Another woman had disappeared in Maryland.

The perpetrator had skipped again.

Gone girls, but these women were innocent victims. Clay was stumped. At an impasse. He'd left the F.B.I. but remained involved with the Violent Criminal Apprehension Program (ViCAP) as a private contractor.

Kate had worked for the Department of Defense, so a security clearance was no issue. They had verified her expertise.

But Clay didn't trust her methods. Couldn't navigate through the minefield of the seduction of a serial killer. It was the first experience he'd had with an undercover partner cut loose to investigate alone. Her tactics were too aggressive for him. He'd kept Kate out of the loop on what he was doing to protect himself and his new company.

He dialed. "Dr. Kate Winter, please."

"This is she."

"It's Clay."

Her breath caught. *What does he want? We haven't talked since he asked me if I slept with psychopaths.*

"Hello? You there?" The questions came out in a croak. He cleared his throat. Chest tight. *Jesus, I'm like a teenager with this woman.*

"Yes." *He will have to work for it.* "What can I do for you?"

"Wasn't sure you'd take my call."

"Why wouldn't I?" The answer clear. Wanted him to say it.

"When we met it didn't go well."

"I got the contract."

"Yeah, but..."

"You're not the first male to react as you did."

"Thought you might hold it against me. Didn't plan to piss you off. Didn't realize I had until..."

"I walked out?"

"It was a moment."

A smile spread across her face. "I was annoyed."

He stifled a laugh. "Yeah."

Quiet between them. Awkward.

She didn't intend to cut him any slack. He'd pitched her, then disappeared. Never intended to collaborate.

"Your female colleagues slammed you, didn't they?"

"Yep. It was merciless."

"I'd like details."

"Short version: sexism." He paused. "When you respect someone enough to hire them. You've got to trust their methods. Expect they can take care of themselves."

"Nothing impresses like examples from women who have been through it. Their expertise siloed or ignored."

"Bullshit. That's not fair. You intended to get personal with a serial killer. When I say it out loud it sounds as nuts as it is."

"It's dangerous, yes. My methods work."

"It's why I offered you the spot," Clay said.

"Boy, you must have dreaded this call."

"You have no idea. You are an expert at what makes a serial killer do what he does. The motive. It's your life, your risk."

"I appreciate it."

"Won't happen again."

I made Clay Zach self-conscious. Good. Now, give the guy a break. "Why'd you call? What's up?"

He wanted to tell her more, but next week would come soon enough and then Kate would understand.

She sat back in her chair, listened, as he continued. Swallowed the snarky comments trolling her brain.

"All the women were professionals, mid-twenties to early thirties, single. Several worked in health care facilities. Not all."

"I've followed the news reports. Remember our last conversation."

"The last few weeks, my team has done exhaustive interviews with the healthcare staff members where the women disappeared. We got a break. First suspect is a security guard. Several of the staff we interviewed mentioned him."

She perked up at the mention of a security guard. *No need to tell him until I'm sure. But I'm close.*

"A lot of potential targets in a healthcare facility."

"So, why does this one security guard stick out?"

"This is awkward."

She exhaled. "What don't you want to say?"

"The profile we got back on him. My instincts kicked in. My gut..."

Kate's laughter cut him off. She didn't hide her enjoyment. "Oh, this is priceless." The laughter continued.

"Are you done?"

One last chuckle. "For now. You've got to admit it is hilarious. The man who called me a ... What did you say?"

"You will not let up, will you?"

"No."

"All right. I said if we were all as psychic as you are, we could start our own circus."

"Right. And you said it on the record to a reporter who ignored my years of study in psychiatry, criminology and behavioral science."

"Shit." Said under his breath.

"And now the great F.B.I. profiler does a gut check on a guy with no evidence to back it up. I am so glad you called to share."

"You're welcome."

"I'm not sure how I can help."

"I've got one piece of evidence." He had more but didn't want to share it.

"Shoot."

"The women all disappeared on the new moon."

Her face lit up. "Lunar cycle. Now, that's a connection."

"Not crazy. An organized, sadistic bastard."

"'Crazy' implies psychosis, which is different. You called to talk it out, right?"

He paused. "I also wanted to apologize. Slacked on your role in the task force."

"Thanks." *I still can't tell him.*

"Now for the other reason I called. The security guard on our radar."

"Do you have his birth name?"

"Aliases galore. My gut won't let me sleep."

"Trust your instincts." Kate rolled her eyes. *He doesn't want to share the UnSub's name. These fucking guys.*

Clay laughed.

"What?"

"Nothing. I need to be reminded."

"What about his social life? Girlfriend?"

"We talked to a woman who dated him a couple of times. Said he took her to nice places. But she couldn't get close to him. And then she said something that lit me up. He was fixated on the lunar cycle. Would tell her in advance when he wasn't available. It was the first man, she said, who ran his life around lunar cycles. Creeped her out."

A chill crept up Kate's legs. An involuntary shudder.

"That's it. Wanted to touch base." Clay closed his eyes. *I dread next week.*

They hadn't worked well together. But his voice stirred her. Clay had it all. When they first met, she thought he could be a nice distraction.

"I'm gone most of the holiday season," Kate said.

"Skiing?" *A lot can happen before December.*

"A group of us from grad school meet in Colorado. One of my friends has a condo. Should be fun."

"I'll call when we get a tangible clue."

Last thing I expected today. Kate googled lunar cycles. The new moon was this weekend. It would happen this week or there might not be another victim until next month.

This was the worst thing about the job. The wait for what's coming.

Hours and days and weeks of it.

A psychopath plotted his next move while law enforcement lined up clues to pinpoint where he might strike next.

And not a damn thing Kate or anyone else could do to stop him.

September 2011: Wednesday

A stroke of luck for her.

Bad omen for him.

Raymond Drake watched Dr. Kate Winter walk into the Mid-Atlantic Health Pavilion. The first time he'd seen her here was last December. He took it as a sign. He had recognized her from the news. Her face plastered across his mind for months.

He watched her. The sound of her heels clacked on the marble floor. A smile crept across Raymond's face. Walked back to the main desk in the lobby. Eyes and ears trained on the elevators. Planned to catch her when she came down.

No need for his efforts.

When the elevator door opened, Kate stepped out and headed toward the reception desk where everyone had to sign in and out. When she arrived in front of him, he handed her the clipboard to sign out.

As she signed, she tilted her head up. Their eyes met.

Kate smiled, Raymond chuckled.

"How's your day going?"

"A lot better now," he said.

His reaction the first time he saw her had seemed harmless at first. Flirtatious. He'd smiled at her. Had come over to help.

But with each week, Raymond got more familiar. When he stood next to her, he got a little too close. Touched her arm. And he smelled odd. Not body odor from a gym workout. The kind she remembered from interviews with frightened men. A villain caught doing unspeakable acts.

It was time for a little test. "How was your trip?"

"What?" His eyes darted away from her.

I caught him off guard. "I asked about you last time I was here, in July."

A piercing glance in her direction. Kate held his gaze. Raymond looked down, picked up a pen, then tossed it across the desk.

Mood swing. Hello, bad boy.

Next, he grabbed the clipboard and tossed it back up on the counter.

She watched him.

He's nervous? What did you do, Raymond?

He looked at the guard seated next to where he stood. "I'll be back in fifteen minutes."

The other security guard stared at Kate. "Can I help you?"

"What's his name?" She pointed in the direction of the guard who'd left.

"Anything I can do for you?"

"No, Mike."

"It's Raymond."

"I see you both so often. Nice to put a name with a face."

A simple question had made Raymond skittish. He doesn't want to talk about his life. He could not get away from her fast enough.

He showed himself.

Kate walked out of the building preoccupied. It had been that way since she'd met him. Ruminated about the events as she walked across the sidewalk on her way to the parking garage.

Not paying attention. She didn't notice the man. He came up on her. Grabbed her arm. Walked and pushed her in a direction she hadn't intended to go.

"Don't say a word. Keep moving," he said.

The man wore a large parka. Kate didn't recognize him.

"I will not." She pushed against his force. He gripped her tighter. Made a left at the next corner. The entrance to the Mid-Atlantic Health Pavilion building out of sight.

"I'll take it from here, Diego."

The voice came from behind Kate.

"Yes, sir. I'll be in the van," Diego said.

"What…?" Her mouth agape. *What is Clay doing here?*

"Hello, Kate. Sorry about that, but we had to get you away from the building."

"What's going on?"

"I'll tell you, first answer a question. What were you doing in there?"

"I don't have to tell you."

The conversation they had days before vaporized. It became adversarial in a flash. The tension between them electric.

Stepped closer, stared at her. "Dr. Winter. You have walked into surveillance amid a criminal investigation." When he pulled his jacket back to extract his phone, she saw the strap of his gun harness. He dismissed the incoming call.

"Whose investigation?"

Clay ignored the question. "We've discussed parameters of it. Why were you in this building today? Why have come into this building for the last three months."

He's been watching this building for three months? Maybe longer. Not a word?

He stared at her.

"A meeting with Dr. Bridgette Carlisle, my psychiatrist. But you know that, don't you?" Her words came out in a clipped cadence.

Clay didn't respond.

It all made sense to her now.

"A professional check-in. She keeps me on track. My cases get intense. Bridgette keeps me healthy. Helps me do my work, too."

He nodded. "Did you speak to either of the security guards in the building?"

She smiled. "Yes." Looked around. Saw a van parked nearby. The driver with the standard windbreaker with no alphabet soup on his chest. Wrinkled brow. Her lips pursed.

"Kate, answer me."

"I did."

"Anything else?"

"Yes."

"What?"

"Hey, you've been surveilling the building, so why don't you tell me?"

Clay didn't speak.

She exhaled. "It isn't the first time I've talked with this guard. But you know that too. Smart move, he's got all the signs."

"Explain it."

"Nothing special. The usual."

"Humor me."

"Why should I? You've seen me come in here for months. Said nothing."

"I'm asking now."

They'd been on the same UnSub. On the same team. Two separate efforts converged.

"Call it serendipity. Or is it synchronicity? I get the two mixed up," Clay said.

She stared at him. "Why didn't you tell me?"

"I'm informing you now."

Kate didn't respond. Brutal self-analysis eclipsed her fury. *He was on the same security guard. He didn't tell me when we talked because I'm not by the book. I'm not honest with him, either. But it stings. Being watched, not told.*

"But why didn't you mention this in our conversation this past weekend?"

"You were due back in Dr. Carlisle's office this week."

"So much for professional courtesy. I'm supposed to be on your goddamn team." Kate paused. "Would you treat a male colleague this way?"

"No male I trust has your background and experience. Look, you did what you do, and we ended in the same place. Didn't trust your methods, but I do now. We want the same thing."

Kate looked to the side. Bit her lip. Shook her head.

Clay turned away. Head down. Turned back toward her.

"What do you want me to say?"

She didn't respond.

"First impression of the guy. Give it to me." He paused. "Please."

Deep exhale. "Okay. He didn't mention my name, but he recognized me the first time I walked in the building. Said he'd seen me on television. But the way he looked at me said something else."

"Be more specific."

"You know the look. Then today, when I asked him a simple question, he froze. Like a light switch. Anger flared up. Walked away."

"We've seen it," Clay said.

"He walked off and took a break. His mood shifted. Each time he's approached me it's been personal. Gave me the creeps, so I wanted to talk to him to see more. It's what I've done."

"Wait. What did you ask him?"

"I asked, 'how was your trip?' He was off for several weeks this summer."

Kate watched the tension drain from Clay's face. It hardened to a look she'd seen before. An 'aha' moment.

"You're coming with me."

"I've got a packed day."

"It's now unpacked. Sorry." He escorted her to the nearby van. She looked at him. "I'll explain inside."

"No, you won't. I'm not going anywhere with you until you tell me more. Is this the guard you mentioned in our conversation?"

"Let's talk inside the van."

She didn't move.

"Please."

It was bare bones inside. One side of the van filled with electronics, monitors. There was a driver in the front, Diego and one other person in the back.

"Give us a minute."

The female sitting at the console of monitors smiled. "I thought you'd never ask." His team exited.

No one paid attention to the security guard who walked out the side door of the Mid-Atlantic Health Pavilion building. Lit up a cigarette. Stood on a landing with an unobstructed view of the surveillance van.

Clay took out a picture.

"Who's this?"

"It's a disguise the security guard inside uses. The one who chatted with you."

"Okay, I see the resemblance. What's his name?"

"An alias, Raymond Drake. We suspect him in murders across four states, several in Maryland. He's why I brought you in."

"What's your plan?"

Clay ignored her question. "What did he say to you?"

"Nothing. Pleasantries. Until I asked him about his trip."

"When do you see Dr. Carlisle again?"

"Anytime I want." She stepped out of the van. Turned around to look at him. "What's on your mind?"

"I'll get back to you."

"You do that. I'm all over this. Raymond's got an obsession and it's me. So, expect to see me next week, same time, same place. Unless he asks me out."

"Don't do anything without backup. I'm a phone call away."

"Right, *boss*. I'll be sure to run my every move by you."

Kate's boisterous laugh echoed as she walked away.

The guard dropped his cigarette, squashed the butt. And watched until she disappeared at the next corner.

Present Day: Friday, 2:00 a.m.

Tack pulled over when it was safe. Walked back to the trunk. Opened it.

Clay Zach had rescued Tack Marin from brutal investigative undercover work. Three years in character inside a violent sex trafficking gang had almost wrecked the man. Now a fixer for Clay's small private outfit, Tack had special skills that made other people squeamish.

"What the fuck. I've been in here for hours." Trevor untangled himself. A large bruise on the left side of his face. "Help me out of here. You fucked up my shoulder."

"Princess. It's been 62 minutes. I had to make sure Straker had no one on me. The man's got trust issues."

"I think it worked."

"That was too close."

Trevor stretched his body. He was a black belt in karate, a master at yoga. "I'm out. That's what matters. Have you been to the Riverbend Road house to do a search?"

"I'm on a leash."

"That's where they do their drop-offs for now," Trevor said.

"Seems risky."

"It's temporary. Been using it for months. Parties are part of it. They'll shut it down without me. But not until they get whatever is in the house out. Assume it's drugs."

"Nothing on your brother."

"Yeah."

"So, we keep going."

"I'll call Clay to tell him it worked. I'm dead," Trevor said.

Tack handed him a prepaid phone.

"What about the Center?"

Trevor ignored him.

"You can't hang them out. Call them."

"I can't, but you can."

"Anonymous?"

Trevor nodded. "Call Callie. Tell her I said Aaron Andrews sucks. She'll get the message."

"Okay. Get out of here. Stay invisible."

"I hope it won't be much longer."

"Clay wants you on a flight to San Francisco."

"No argument from me. But I'll have company."

"Not a problem."

The men shook hands, made body contact.

"Don't take chances."

"Too late," Tack said. "I've got to get back."

Tack dropped Trevor two blocks away from his condominium. A back entrance would allow him to enter without notice.

Present Day: Late Friday Night

The Center buzzed.

It was 11:00 p.m. EST.

Peak time for crime on the East Coast. The country's criminals hadn't started to do their worst.

Stoney walked up. "Where's Trevor? Stratford PD has three individuals they want us to track. I need him."

Callie played with her phone. Closed one app, launched another. Quick keystrokes. Hit send.

"Hey." Stoney snapped his fingers in her face. She jumped.

"Oh, sorry. What do you need?"

He exhaled. "Have you talked to Trevor?"

"That's what I was doing. I sent him another text. He's not in."

"Tell him to come see me when he shows up."

She leaned on her desk, hand on her forehead, stumped. "Come on, Trevor. Don't do this to us." Her desk phone rang. Picked it up.

"Callie. Don't talk."

She stopped, listened.

"Trevor is safe. You will hear reports otherwise. Ignore them. Whatever you're told, play along. No one can think he's alive."

"Who are you? Why should I trust you?"

"He said to tell you Aaron Andrews sucks." Tack waited.

She exhaled. Smiled. Aaron Andrews had won one of the network talent shows. Trevor had bet her he'd flame out. "He's full of shit."

"Don't I know it. Now, remember, stay quiet. Don't tell a soul. No one." Tack hung up.

The dial tone hummed.

Callie stared at her phone.

Present Day: Saturday Morning

Twelve hours of sleep. Lily was recharged. She dialed. On the fourth ring, her best friend's voice.

"I almost didn't pick up," Amanda said. "Where the fuck are you?"

"Are you okay?" *She doesn't need info on where I am.*

"No."

Neither spoke.

Lily tried again. "What happened after I left?"

"Hmm... 'left.' You mean ran, don't you?" Amanda's tone was cold.

"When your father showed up, I didn't have a choice."

"That's weak."

"It was a party. Did you want us captured on social media? Father, daughter, and girlfriend, everyone's mouth agape?"

"Don't give a shit."

"Don't lie. You care a lot. What makes it worse is you took it out on yourself. If you're pissed, yell at me."

"If?"

"I didn't intend to hurt you."

"The heart wants what it wants, right?"

Lily wanted more from her. Soberness had become her lifeline. They had to talk about it. She had been there through the worst of Amanda's rehab. "I don't understand why you'd take the risk. And three guys?"

"It was desperate." Amanda exhaled. "I'm embarrassed. All those months clean. So, where are you?"

"Took a drive to the beach." *I can't trust her.*

"Must be nice." *What bullshit. She's not at the freaking beach.*

"It is."

"To get away."

"That was the plan."

"For how long?"

"Haven't decided. It depends," Lily said.

"Ask the question."

Amanda waited.

"Huh?"

"It's okay. Ask it."

"Maybe you should ask me. I never wanted the secret. It was his choice."

"Oh, I'll bet. He didn't want me to find out."

"True."

"How did it start?"

Lily would never share the details of a relationship she regretted. Amanda couldn't cope with the truth. She'd have to first process the pictures in her head of her best friend and her father in bed.

"It's not mysterious. He asked me out."

"Why'd you say yes?"

"It was complicated." Lily stopped. "He's your father. How do I explain the attraction to you? Older man, Stoney's fun. I told him no strings. No attachments."

"But my father? And why didn't you tell me?"

"Stoney didn't want it public. I have friends at the Center *that he runs*. Remember? He didn't want it to become a thing."

"When did it start?"

"It's over."

"Not what I asked."

"It doesn't matter now."

"Matters to me."

Lily had played this moment out in her head. She never got through it before giving up.

"We can talk about it all you want." *I will never tell her the whole story. It's none of her business.* "But you haven't told me anything about what happened. What made you get ripped after so many months sober? What triggered it?"

"Nothing."

"I don't understand."

"Not everyone is like you."

"What does that mean?"

"Loner. Needs no one."

"You have a genius I.Q. And support from friends."

"Yeah, my life is great." Amanda laughed.

Lily ignored her. Asked a question stuck in her mind. "Why would you call your father? It's no surprise how he would react."

"You wouldn't understand."

"Amanda, come on. Be honest."

Silence.

Lily was tired of it. The months she had held Amanda's hand. The long talks in the wee hours. *Her dad can enable her, but I won't. Tough-love time.* "You like the victim role. You got blasted, then called daddy. Face it. Your constant drug binges and drunken stupors are about him. Intelligence means nothing if you can't grow up."

Sniffles. A cough. "Give me a second."

Conversations with Amanda had been hard for months.

Lily contracted with the Center, so the rules were different for her relationship with Stoney. His marriage had failed, he had told her. His wife wasn't happy, either. Lily didn't care. She told Stoney not to talk about his marriage when he was with her.

The marriage had ended before they dated. The relationship between Stoney and Lily had started fast. Instant chemistry had morphed into a torrid sexual affair. Lily had told him it was casual. She wasn't interested in a long-term commitment. Wanted to have fun. Laid it out for him from the start.

Two months before they finalized their divorce, his wife had shown up at Lily's front door. She didn't want to let her in, so she went out on her porch. The conversation enlightened her.

"You broke up our marriage."

Lily would never forget those words. She didn't believe it. *If two people want the relationship, nobody can break them up.*

How to explain it to Stoney's soon-to-be ex-wife? She had unloaded fury that should have been directed at him.

"You don't understand him."

But what she said had gotten Lily's attention.

Stoney had blown through all their money. He was in deep financial trouble. The Ransom Center was insolvent. "That's your problem now," she had said.

No, it wasn't. Lily made sure. "I've moved on."

"Stoney hasn't. You need permission from him, first." It came out as a warning from his soon-to-be ex-wife.

People weren't aware of their affair yet. No one at the Center, Lily was sure. Amanda had used it as an excuse. Blamed her problems on her dad, her friend or anyone but herself.

The personal drama was minor compared to the bombshell about the Center's perilous financial reality. It had made Lily dizzy to consider the ramifications of what Stoney's ex had said.

"You still there?"

"You okay?" Lily knew she wasn't.

"I feel like shit."

"Are *we* okay?"

Quiet.

"I don't understand why you'd do it."

What to say? There was no answer Lily could give to soothe her friend. Amanda was in a battle with herself.

"This is so stupid," Lily said.

"What is? That I don't like you fucking my dad?"

"We're adults. It happened. It's over."

"I can't stop seeing you with him. In bed. It's gross."

"I'm not doing this with you. I called to see if you were okay. The picture on Facebook freaked me out. If you don't want to be friends, I understand. But I will not justify my actions to you. Can we move on from this or not?"

She waited.

"Yeah, *not*." Amanda hung up.

It was over.

Lily had called to clear things up with her friend. Doubted if it would work. She had tried. It left Stoney, who hadn't let go either.

He worried her more. Marriage, daughter, and now the Center was in jeopardy. Stoney's world revolved around it. He'd given everything. His ego was intertwined with it. He would hold on tight. Fight all the way.

Lily wanted to let go of it all. She couldn't yet.

Her phone rang. She didn't recognize the number. Let it go to voicemail. When the notification icon popped up, she tapped into her voicemail to listen.

"Hello. I need to reach Lily Cates. I've got her necklace. This is Dr. Kate Winter. You can reach me at..." The number left on her voicemail was the same as the Ransom Center.

She stared at her phone.

Will I ever get out?

Present Day: Midday Saturday

The intercom buzzed. "Hey, that call is still on hold."

"Okay, I got it." Walked to his desk, hit the speakerphone.

"This is Stoney."

"You fucked me," Straker said.

"You can't call me here. We capture every call."

"Your man? Gone. It's on you."

"What?"

"Trevor."

"What did you do?"

"Me? Nothing. He got aggressive. Paid for it."

"Tell me what happened." Stoney sat down, stared into space.

"Short story. Trevor stepped out of line. Came at me. My man laid him out."

"Where is he now?"

Silence.

"Are you retarded? He's gone," Straker said. "Like in you won't see him again."

News as bad as it gets.

Stoney had tasked Trevor as the go-between with Straker. The situation straddled Trevor on a thin limb. No way out until he found his brother. But why Stoney was involved with Straker was a mystery to him, until he opened one of the duffle bags.

"Bad move," Stoney said.

"What did you say?" Straker's voice rose.

"This is too far. It will come back on us both."

"Who will make good on that threat?" Straker laughed. "I'm not worried."

The line went dead.

Stoney stared into space. Despondent.

A knock on the door.

"Hey, Stoney, got a few minutes?"

He nodded. "What's up?"

"You don't look so hot," Callie said.

"Bad news. Have a seat."

"What happened?"

"How to say this? It's Trevor."

Put your best poker face on. She sat down. Licked her lips. "What about him?"

"I don't have details yet, but I got a call..." His voice trailed off. Stoney stood up, walked to the window with the view of the bullpen below. Screens lit up, small teams in several areas worked over details of an event happening in downtown Baltimore. Police had called it in. The Center's teams culled through social media accounts to follow the tick-tock of the event. He was proud of what he'd created.

"Kate, have to tell her." It was a whisper.

"What?"

"It's Trevor."

Stay cool. Goosebumps on Callie's arms. "What happened?"

Stoney looked at her. "You okay?"

"Um… Yeah." Cracked her knuckles. Pulled the sleeves down on her blouse. She hoped her reaction made sense to her boss because of how close she was to Trevor. The more she talked, the worse it would get. Callie was a bad liar but had to convince him.

"Tell me about Trevor." Her voice steadied.

"I'm sorry. I know you're close." He walked toward her. Sat in the chair next to her. "No details, but he got into a fight down by the docks. Ugly characters. It's bad."

Fucking liar.

It was easy to put emotion into the idea of Trevor's death. Her lips tightened. A hand came up to her mouth.

Stoney put his arm around her.

Callie stiffened.

He stared at her. "He's gone."

She wanted to look into Stoney's eyes, but he'd looked down. He wouldn't meet her eyes. Jaw clenched, she pulled away and stood up.

Stoney looked up.

It was the moment. She thought about the phone call. Forewarned of this news. If it had been true, Callie would have lost it. How to replicate it? She was no actress, but for Trevor, she'd do anything.

Think hard. Come on. You need tears.

She'd seen a video on Twitter from The Dodo about a dog hit by a car. A man tried to help him, but the dog was so terrified he dragged himself away with his two front paws. This video had a happy ending, but the start of it had made her cry. Thoughts of it worked on her.

Callie's face scrunched up. A tear trickled down her cheek. She put her hands over her face.

"Oh, no, come here."

Stoney's arms came around her again. She lowered her chin. Whimpered. Kept it up.

"What can I get you?"

"Nothing. Anything. Whatever."

Callie stayed bent over. Cocked her head up to see him walk away. Mind on overdrive.

He walked back over with a glass of scotch. "This will help."

She took a sip, downed the rest. Smiled at him. "I need…"

"Take the day, no problem."

"Call me if you get more news. Promise."

"I will."

"When will you tell the crew?" She watched him. Every expression. *This motherfucker betrayed us all. Almost got Trevor killed.*

Callie wasn't a fan of Jack Stone. The way he treated Trevor infuriated her.

"I'll wait until you're gone."

"You need more info, Stoney. The full story."

He turned away from her.

This is not good. He can't look at me.

She walked to the door. After she shut it, Callie saw Stoney stare out of the window again. He looked down on his teams.

She exhaled. "What has he done?"

The emotion was pure fury.

Present Day: Late Saturday Afternoon

The phone rang twice. "Yes."

"Duchess?"

"Hello, Lily."

"Do you have time today?"

"Always, for you."

"I'll be by in a half hour." She made another call. "Dr. Winter, please." On hold.

"Kate Winter."

"Hello. I'm Lily Cates. Got your message."

"Oh, Lily, thanks so much for the call. Do you have a few minutes to talk? In the middle of an investigation on what happened at Riverbend Road. Found your necklace."

Her hand came up to her throat. "Yeah. I'm naked without it. It must have happened that night."

"Can we meet? Where are you?"

"I've got an appointment this afternoon, but I can meet you at the Riverbend house afterward, around 7:30 p.m."

"Can we meet in Bethesda, perhaps? There's a nice bistro that would..."

"You've got questions, right? Need answers. So, if you want to talk, that's the place."

Kate didn't respond. Why did she pick the Riverbend Road house to meet? Kate didn't understand. She'd need more on Lily Cates before they met. The young woman was on a different wavelength.

Lily waited. "Hello?"

"I'm here. Okay, I'll see you there."

Lily didn't say goodbye.

Lily drove toward Mechanicsville, Maryland. It was a trek from the cabin, but she derived pleasured from long drives. Time to think. Her life had spun out. She needed information. First, she had to center herself.

Her friend, Duchess, lived alone on five acres of land in rural Maryland. Lily had gotten a recommendation on her from a man who had introduced himself as a warlock. Worked in a little shop near Solomons Island.

The early loss of both parents had marooned Lily. Inconveniences began early. Trust came hard. When a kid becomes an island in life, there is no backstop, which means no boundaries. Guardians can't mold a person they don't understand. Advice from adults was slanted toward traditional choices. The opposite of Lily's instinctual voice.

She didn't trust elders. Never sought guidance. She trusted her gut, her instincts, and her intuition. It began on YouTube. Mystics flourished on the platform. Where crackpots and charlatans mixed with gifted coaches, astrologers, and new-age guides to seekers. The necessity to hone these unconventional life skills became her obsession.

The journey led her to Duchess, a metaphysical guru. Translated, it meant psychic medium to Lily. A gifted woman who tapped signals from the wider world and the cosmic universe. They met on Lily's 16th birthday. The meeting changed her.

Until Duchess, she'd floundered. Tried religion. Looked for answers but all the dialogue came from men. Through traditional structures they had built. What could men share about a woman's experience?

It was a foreign concept to Lily.

There had been no men in her life when she was young.

She had been on her own from the start. Learned through experience. Life depended on her actions alone. Her gut became a satellite dish. But only if she got quiet enough. It didn't take long before her mind and her thoughts betrayed her. She searched for answers. Found a guide.

On MD-5 South, the turnoff wasn't far. The early fall brought mud across the roads. Fun to drive in her truck. By the time she'd landed on the porch, her boots were caked. Two kittens were balled up on the sofa outside, underneath the front window. A blue jay was mad. He landed with a thud on the SquirrelBuster birdfeeder. No squirrels. Cats were on guard.

Knock on the door.

"Get in here, young lady."

Duchess opened the door. She was tall, slim, with thick, lustrous silver hair. "Come here, gorgeous." Lily disappeared in her embrace. The folds of the bright aqua, gold, and black kaftan enveloped them both.

"What's that smell?"

The mystic looked at her. "Guess."

"Chocolate-chocolate chip." A smile spread across Lily's face.

"Your favorite."

"Yay. I'll light the candles."

"All new ones on the fireplace mantel."

They walked into the large room, which had two oversized chairs, smaller couches, and a gorgeous Oriental rug in the center. A hand-carved coffee table doubled as a dining table, as long as you liked to sit on the floor for dinner. Two overstuffed leather chairs stood on one side of the room, in front of the massive fireplace. In the center of the room, pillows were stacked and strewn across the cushions of a sectional sofa. A monstrous chandelier crowned the high ceiling, its lights on a dimmer, threw a glow across the main living area and the open kitchen. Bar stools stood along the demarcation between the two rooms, a spectacular marble countertop.

She'd been here many times. The two women sat on the sofa. They had customs they honored. Lily munched on a warm chocolate cookie. Duchess watched her.

"What happened?"

Lily shot her a glance. Chewed her cookie.

"Oh. That bad this time, huh?"

Another glance. More chews.

"Woman or man?"

"Man-baby."

"Explains why I haven't seen you for so long."

Lily put the half-eaten cookie down. "It wasn't about you."

"Oh, darling, it never is." Duchess smiled. She intuited first. Before others had a sense. "First, your meditation."

Lily groaned. "Can't we…"

"No. *You* can't." She waited. No response. "Do you prefer music?"

"No."

"I'll get out the crystals. Begin when you're still." She walked from the living room, through the kitchen, into another room.

Lily began. The incense obliterated all odors. Crept into her senses as a reminder. She batted away messages from the tape playing in her head. Rolled one shoulder, then the other, next her neck.

An image popped up. It shook her.

Duchess walked back into the room in time to see Lily react from across the room. She stood still. Watched. Her friend was in a struggle. Turmoil was lodged deep.

Lily broke from her meditative breathing. Stood up, stretched. Shook her arms, one leg, then the other. Grabbed two more pillows to put around her before she sat back down on the sofa.

The mystic smiled.

Good. She leans into it. Shakes off tension when it arises. She's meditated since we last spoke. It's part of her now.

"I'm ready."

Duchess walked in. "We can begin."

Present Day: Early Saturday Night

"Do you want cards?"

"Not sure."

"Your choice."

"Maybe I'll pick one card."

Duchess picked up the overstuffed deck. She shuffled. Handed the cards to Lily.

"What?" Lily was puzzled. They'd never done it like this before.

Duchess took the cards and put them in front of Lily. With a nod of her head and a look, she sent a message of certainty. "Play with them as you desire. It's your energy. I'm the net. Power up as makes you comfortable."

The cards were embossed with an emblem. A white tiger following a woman walking over a gentle stream, an eagle in a nearby tree, all encased in a golden swirl. The painting from which Duchess drew this emblem hung above the massive fireplace across the room from where they sat. A consummate artist and painter, Duchess had dropped out of the competitive New York art scene decades earlier.

The choice of the mystic arts had been made for Duchess at birth. It had taken years to respect the voices channeled through her. They were imprinted on her soul. Wisdom she ignored at a young age to survive. In her teens, she took ahold of her gifts. Now a master of unexplainable realms. She never talked about her gift. Not even to her apprentices.

When Lily shuffled, cards flew out of the deck. She didn't stop.

"Wait," Duchess said. "Do you want to check the messages on the three cards that jumped out of the deck?"

"No. I wasn't concentrating."

Lily picked up the three cards, separated the large deck into two, shuffled again. Held the cards in her left hand, and with her right hand, drew the cards from the bottom to the top. Over and over, she shuffled.

Duchess placed her hand over Lily's. "Stop. What's wrong?"

"I'm afraid. What if I pick a wrong card?"

The laugh from Duchess rolled through the room.

Lily stared down at the cards.

"Get out of your head, my darling. There is no 'wrong' card. You can tap in through any of them. Remember what you first learned. There is no right or wrong. No good or bad message. Feel through your center, your heart." Duchess reached across. Touched Lily's solar plexus with her palm.

"Got it. Right." She shuffled. Stopped. Laid the cards down. "It's time to tell you." Lily began. The story in her head had twisted her in knots.

The mystic knew before a word was said. No woman's energy gets this loud unless a man is in the picture.

It was not an original tale.

"We met when I interviewed for a research job at Ransom Center. Nothing happened for weeks. One Friday night, a bunch of us decided to go for drinks. Callie, one of the team leaders, pushed Jack Stone – we call him Stoney – to join us. He never did, but this time we talked him into it."

Duchess watched her.

Lily looked down after the last line she spoke. Her eyes in a half-squint. Regret pasted across her face.

"How long have you been dating?"

"Ha. 'Dating.' We work at the same place. We fell into it."

"It worked for you?"

No response. Lily looked away. Considered the question. "I'm thirsty."

The mystic smiled, moved into the kitchen. She came back with a large tumbler of water. "Here. You've stalled long enough. Out with it. When you come here, you must do the work."

Lily didn't look up. Closed her eyes. Duchess would wait her out. They'd done this before.

"It worked until he wanted more."

"Aha. You didn't."

"It was convenient. Didn't expect him to get serious." Paused. "There's more."

She smiled. "There always is."

"His daughter is... was my best friend."

"The plot thickens..."

"It's nuts now. Amanda found out about us. There's this house where we partied this summer. We both ended up there one Friday night."

"We've talked about her before. The intense one."

Lily nodded. "I can't go into it all, but she's had a rough year in and out of rehab. She got fucked up at the party. Freaked out and called her father. When he arrived, he saw me there. It got crazy. He followed me outside and..."

"Stop. Nice babble, but I don't need the cast of characters. Only how you feel. Okay? He wanted more, so you wanted out. Is that it?"

"Yes."

"That's all of it?"

"I talked to Amanda. Tried to tell her my side. She hung up on me."

"Her loss." The mystic smiled. "And?"

"It's a dead zone." Lily looked at Duchess, who said nothing. "Say what you're thinking."

"What do you want?"

"For real?"

"The truth."

"I have to get out of here." Lily stood up. "I don't fit in." Took her glass into the kitchen. Walked to the front door, walked outside.

After a few minutes, Duchess picked up her cards, shuffled them. Placed them down in front of where Lily had been seated.

"Break is over." Duchess uttered it as a command.

Lily walked in, sat down, stared at her.

"Shuffle the cards, cut them, pick out three. Set them in a line."

"Yeah, I remember." Lily began. After two shuffles, she paused. Shuffled again. This repeated three times.

Duchess reached across the table, touched her hands again. Lily looked up.

"Sweetheart, you're in a manic spiral. I repeat, there are no wrong answers, one card isn't better than another. Center your mind on your challenge. The thing that drove you away and brought you here."

She didn't move. Stared across at the woman who had become her guide. "I'm scared."

"Of what? The cards?"

"The truth."

Duchess chuckled. "The answers are clear. Face the truth. Step into your power."

Deep breath.

Lily picked up the cards, shuffled, laid the deck down, cut it.

"Pick three cards. Lay them here."

The first card Lily picked was The Tower. She looked at it. "Bad news. What else?" She picked up a pillow, threw it.

"What's bad about liberation?" The mystic would not overload the young woman with details of the ancient iconography that would play into her fears. "You may have experienced this stage."

"What do you mean?"

"You dumped the man-baby. And Amanda found out about you and her father, correct?"

Lily nodded.

"What happened?"

"She hung up on me."

"But how did you feel once it was over?"

Her face brightened, her mouth opened. An "aha" moment. "Relieved. Felt like shit, but no more secrets."

"A start. What else?"

"Terrified what people at the Center would say. Social media pile on. They'd flame me. She looked down. "I'd lose my friends."

Duchess nodded. *She won't admit it yet, but it's close.* "Choose another card."

The next card was the dove clasping three swords. The Three of Swords.

"Shit. This can't be good."

A chuckle. "What does a dove signify to you?"

"Peace."

"Okay, what else?"

"Couples release doves after people get married."

"Anything else?"

"Two is company, three is a disaster."

"Is it for you? Who's the third? His wife or his daughter?"

"How the hell do I know?"

Duchess smiled. "Breathe, then pick one final card."

Lily did as instructed. She laid the next card down. When she saw it, she freaked. "Oh, fuck me."

The Death card.

"I'll be back in a second." Lily walked out the back door into the wooded area behind the mystic's home. From outside she heard a roar of laughter. She ran back inside.

"I'm fucked, and you laugh about it? What's wrong with you? It was a mistake to come here." Her footsteps banged across the floor. Lily retrieved her purse, turned to walk out. Stopped. She was at the door. "Thanks for nothing."

The mystic stood up. "When the truth displays itself it's a miracle. Don't be harsh because you can't see it. Won't face it. You have the answers. It takes courage to accept what's in your heart."

"None of it makes sense."

"You are in the eye of a cognitive maelstrom."

"Whatever the hell that means."

"The brain protects us from our mind."

"The brain is the mind."

"Is it? Perhaps. But what if they are two separate parts of ourselves?"

"When you get into mumbo jumbo, you lose me."

"Do you want to stop? I refuse to force a conversation you are not ready to have."

"It's my fault. I'm unenlightened." Lily plopped down on the sofa.

"You, my darling, are the opposite. What scares you is your differences. Three steps ahead of your peers, the fight against flight is about liberation. Didn't you say you wanted to get 'far away'?"

"Yes." A whispered reply.

"It's what you want, correct?"

Lily didn't respond. Her eyes darted around the room. Stood up.

"Sit down." Duchess waited.

Lily looked across at the older woman. Her mane of hair. No tension in her presence. Relaxed a bit. Did as she was bid.

"When you think about freedom, your personal independence. Does the journey to manifest this life sound easy or difficult?"

"An ordeal. It costs a fortune to move. I'd need a new job. And where would I go?"

"Okay. Now, close your eyes. Imagine you have moved away. You are independent, found a job, a place to live away from here. How does that make you feel?"

"I can't."

"Why?"

"Too good to be true. It's never been good here for me. I'm not like my colleagues."

"No, you're not. The Tower came through because when you break free those still connected will want to hold you tight. Your emotions will be pulled in a million directions. Your current world crumbles. What you no longer want becomes the foundation to a future not yet manifest." She paused. "Difficult decisions set you free. It doesn't mean the change is easy."

Lily looked up at Duchess, her mouth agape.

"What?"

"Did I want to confront Stoney, with his daughter? I never thought about it before."

"I doubt it. You're a seeker, so you aren't malicious on purpose. The choice not to inform your friend, however, must have led to one hell of a confrontation on the phone call you had with her."

"Is that why the three of swords came up?"

"You tell me." Duchess saw her look away. *What is going on with her? It has nothing to do with why she came here.*

"I'm scared."

Duchess waited. *She's in her first battle.*

"But I'm not ready to tell you yet."

"Okay."

"You sure? I don't want you to be pissed."

Her head tilted back, Duchess laughed. "A waste of my energy, don't you think?"

Lily moved towards her. Their arms came around each other in a hug. "Thank you. I'm not sure why, but I'm relieved. Ten pounds lighter."

"Oh, my dear. Just wait."

Present Day: Early Saturday Night

On the way to the car, her cell phone rang. Caller unknown. Kate let it go to voicemail. Before she pulled out, the ping sound of a text message. Texted back. The call came in a second time.

"Hello."

"It's Clay."

She straightened up. *WTF?* There was no reason for his call.

"Hey."

"Can you talk?"

"Yeah. Shoot."

"Privacy?"

"Alone in my car. Make it quick. I've got a rendezvous at Riverbend Road."

"What do you mean?"

"Nothing, failed attempt at humor. What's up?"

"So, you haven't talked to anyone at Ransom Center today?"

"This morning, not since. Tell me. I don't have time for Q&A right now." Her phone buzzed. "I've got an incoming call from the Center."

"Don't take it. I can fill you in."

"On what?"

"Trevor's missing. The police aren't involved yet."

"Stoney will freak."

"He may, but not for the reasons you think."

Her mind spun. Kate turned her car off, put a window down. "Why aren't the police involved? What aren't you telling me?"

"Trevor is okay, banged up, that's all."

She waited.

"He works for me." Clay waited for her reaction.

"What do you need with a nerd?"

"That's not why I recruited him."

"So, now he's recruited. You said you don't work for the bureau anymore."

"Correct."

The conversation came in bursts. Clay doled out tidbits. Kate played sponge. The full picture in the distance.

"You don't want to say what you have to tell me. But I don't play these games with you anymore, remember? Tell me about Trevor, or I'll hang up and call the Center back."

"He's undercover on a case my firm has worked on for months. Maryland State's Attorney's office is out for blood. Money-laundering case, but Trevor's blind to that part. He's on part-time. I hope that changes."

Kate's meet with Lily was at 7:30 p.m. She'd be there after 8 p.m. Would she wait? If not, she'd have to track her down again.

"Money-laundering case?"

"I contacted Trevor after they abducted his brother."

"Wait, what?"

"That's the tip. You won't like the rest."

"I don't like this part." Kate paused. "And a brother?"

"Lives with his mother in San Francisco. They picked him up off the street. Van, no markings. Threatened to send him to Thailand."

"Sex trafficking?"

"If Trevor works off the price they'd get for his brother. They'll set him free."

"Bullshit. Nobody goes to those lengths for this. There has to be more. And they'll never let him go."

"They hit Trevor to get to Stoney."

Kate's mood sank. Stoney had been off his game for months. She'd thought it was the divorce. It was the Center. "Oh, dear god."

"When you have time, we'll talk. You said you have a meet on Riverbend Road? Don't go there. It's not safe."

"I work where it's not safe. I've got to fly to get there before she leaves."

"Who?"

"You don't know her."

"Lily, right? The woman with the necklace."

She stopped. "You'll tell me how you discovered it was her sometime."

"No mystery. I read the police report. We work with law enforcement."

Her thoughts kicked into gear. She didn't need the distraction. "I have to go."

"Kate, wait. You won't be alone there. The Riverbend house changed owners several months ago. An off-shore outfit has control. We suspect the man responsible for Trevor's disappearance, Straker Kent, is the owner. Riverbend became an emergency drop-off after D.E.A. raided one of his stash houses."

"So, bust them."

"We'd rather watch them. There's more to it."

"Where is Trevor now? Shit. Has anyone told Callie?"

"Trevor's partner called her. He's still inside."

"Partner?" She was so far outside the loop, Kate felt like a civilian. "Thanks for the call about Trevor. Have you called the Center? They need to be told. If the police tell them about Trevor it will explode on social media."

"Stoney cannot know Trevor is alive and in hiding."

What does that mean? "Stoney's in trouble." Said under Kate's breath.

"Six exits past fucked. But he hasn't accepted it yet."

Trevor's brother was Straker's insurance policy with Stoney, who had gone to Straker for a high-interest loan. Loan-sharking was a mainstay for Straker. He had trapped Stoney into laundering his drug money, without a way out for him, although Trevor was ignorant about Stoney's financial problems. Trevor thought they took his brother to keep him in line and supplying Straker with new clientele.

Clay Zach's team had surveilled Straker, put a veteran former undercover agent, Tack Marin, inside. When Trevor appeared at Straker's compound, it provided Clay with an opportunity. It also gave Trevor a way out. Help with saving his brother. An option to get even with Straker.

"Caught up in a scheme or a victim of his own greed?"

"Straker Kent is a habitual criminal," Clay said. "He's at the center of this. We're on him. If Straker and his men were aware Trevor worked for us, he'd be dead for real..."

"I had no idea."

"The case has turned into a monster. We've got bad actors using real estate for drug parties. Makes our job more difficult. They regret it. We seize their property, they move on. It starts all over in a different state."

Exhale. "I have to meet Lily."

"She's the one sleeping with Stoney. He's involved with a woman at the Center and she fits the description, according to witnesses."

Another bombshell.

"I have to go." Kate hung up.

On the drive, she mulled what Clay had said. At least Callie was wise. She and Trevor were tight. The last tidbit about Lily and her boss was good to have before they met. Stoney's daughter was Lily's age.

Self-destruction. "Criminal. What did you do, Stoney? ...And how much will it cost us all?"

Willful blindness.

He'd acted odd long before the divorce, but Kate had ignored it.

Nothing touched the powerful man in the windowed office. The creator of the international firm that law enforcement officials, homeland security, and the Pentagon looked to when social media storms, criminals, and greed merged. When trolls, hackers, and bot farms squeezed companies, government agencies, and private firms, their leaders called Jack Stone's Ransom Center.

Answers would have to wait.

Present Day: Early Saturday Night

Distracted.

Callie couldn't get her mind off Trevor. *Where are you and why haven't you called me?*

Her phone buzzed. A text message. Answer to a prayer. She texted back. Picked up her desk phone.

She saw Stoney up in his office. He didn't pick up. His choice. Short message from her. "I'm out the rest of the day. See you tomorrow."

It was a promise Callie wasn't sure she'd keep.

Grabbed her purse, laptop case, and walked.

It surprised one member of her team to see her on the way out.

"You never leave early."

"Right? See you tomorrow." She didn't stop to chat. Didn't check to see if Stoney watched her leave. He'd get her message. Didn't care about anything but Trevor.

Outside, she walked to her car. Sped off, as he'd said to do.

A car pulled in behind her. It was Trevor.

She slowed.

He passed.

Callie followed him across the bridge and into Virginia. Stayed close. Didn't recall the exact address of his condo, which had to be where he was headed.

The purchase was a two-bedroom condominium. It had happened in early spring. A gated property along the Potomac River in Old Town Alexandria, Virginia. It surprised her. Trevor made more money than she did, so the price tag of the address wasn't an issue. But he had talked a lot about moving home to San Francisco in the last months.

They had gotten close, but not tight enough for him to tell her what he was doing. He always had more than Ransom Center on his plate. Restlessness drove him now. Callie didn't understand it.

Their relationship grew as they worked together. It happened one night. They'd been alone at the Center during the last Thanksgiving holiday. Skeleton crew, they slipped away. They had been inseparable since.

Trevor turned off the highway and followed the short route toward Old Town. Callie followed. Several turns took them near the Potomac River. He used his keycard to open the gate. She followed behind.

He opened her car door. "It's okay to park here?" Callie grabbed her purse and the other items.

"Yeah, I've got two spots," Trevor said.

"Lucky for me."

He kissed her.

"You'll have to do better than that." Callie stopped and smiled up at him.

Trevor grabbed her arm while walking.

"What are you—"

"Not here. When we get upstairs."

Callie's phone buzzed. The call went to voicemail. They walked into the building in silence. Neither spoke in the elevator.

Views of the wide Potomac, a wall of windows. Small but impressive space. The view mesmerized her.

"Can't appreciate this place until you're up here. It's beautiful."

"Yeah, I'm never here."

"I still don't understand why you bought it."

"We're safe here. Only one person besides you has the address. I want to keep it quiet."

She stared at him. "Safe from what?"

Trevor didn't answer her. No walls in the main room, the living area flowed into the kitchen. "Water or wine?"

"You're kidding? Wine."

He walked over to the sofa, close to the windows. She joined him. Took a sip of the red wine. Watched Trevor rifle through messages on his phone. He held up one finger.

"Be right back." He walked away.

Callie drank her wine, looked at the view. Her emotions roiled.

"I had to call my boss."

"You called Stoney?"

"No."

"Didn't think so. What do you have to tell me?"

"We need to talk."

"I'm right here. Talk."

"Several months ago, four men grabbed my brother off the streets."

"In San Francisco?"

Trevor nodded.

"Now I get it."

"No, you don't. I'm being blackmailed."

"What?"

"It's a long story."

"So, tell me."

"My mother called the cops. I got a name from one of the S.F.P.D. detectives on the case. A guy who runs a private outfit here. Used to be F.B.I., part of the Behavioral Analysis Unit. The people who kidnapped my brother wanted to get to me."

"For what? I don't understand."

"I didn't either, at first."

Callie stared at him.

"It's…"

She moved closer. "What are you scared to tell me, Trev? It's okay. I'm on your side."

He looked down. "It's fucked up."

"What is?"

"The Center."

"What does Ransom have to do with your brother's kidnapping?"

"No idea."

"You're not making sense."

"I can't tell you what I don't know."

"Huh?"

"What I've learned... You won't believe."

"Tell me anyway."

Present Day: Late Saturday Night

A truck in the driveway.

No lights on inside.

Kate parked. Dug into her bag for her night vision binoculars. Anyone on watch would see her. She didn't care. Lookouts always left clues behind.

Scanned the area, saw no one. But Clay wouldn't bullshit her about this. They'd made an awkward peace and he wouldn't risk it.

On the porch, Lily's voice. She was inside.

Opened the front door. "Hello, Lily."

No answer.

"It's Kate."

Walked into the main room.

"In the kitchen."

Kate walked toward Lily's voice.

The first step she took into the room made her stop. Kate gagged. The stench. "What's that smell?" Coughed. It turned into vomit. Kate on her knees.

"You okay?"

She looked up and saw Lily. Only her torso was in view.

"It didn't smell like this last time I was here." Straightened up. Lily was on the opposite side of the massive island from where Kate stood. "What's in the air? It's weird." Walked in her direction.

"Stay where you are."

"We need to talk."

Screamed. "Stop."

"Calm down. What's wrong?" Kate moved toward Lily. Past the edge of the island.

"Don't come closer."

"Let's sit at the table." Three steps forward, Kate froze. The island had blocked the full view of where Lily stood.

Kate's mouth dropped open.

A milky-colored cloud encased Lily.

Neither woman spoke.

Kate reached out to touch what surrounded the woman. "It's cloud-like. You're in a fog." Her hand closer.

"No. Don't."

Kate's hand got nearer. A bolt. Charged energy pierced her right palm. It threw her back into the kitchen counter. She recovered, didn't move.

Lily's response was immediate. "Marie, don't."

Looked at her hand. Kate watched Lily. *Who is she talking to?* Analytical mindset kicked up. Nothing made sense.

Blindsided.

This was new territory for Kate. She excelled in her field because she anticipated events, placed a high value on instincts and intuitive perception. But she had walked into this house like a newbie. Guard down, senses asleep, and her mind on Clay Zach.

"Nothing is out of bounds." Kate whispered to herself. *An unknown force is in this room. Don't doubt it.* Her hand stung from the experience. *It's real.*

"How long have you been like this?"

"I got here an hour ago," Lily said. "I tuned up before I arrived. She sensed it."

"Tuned up? What does that mean?" *She? A spirit? Buckle up.*

"Meditated and opened channels with a guide. I was desperate. Things are out of control. First time I came here, this happened. But not with Marie."

Oh, lord.

Lily turned to look at Kate. "You felt it, right?"

No answer.

The second time, Lily's voice was stern, and it wasn't a question. "The force, you felt it."

"Yes."

Lily leaned in. Whispered. Stopped. Whispered again.

Kate peered around the corner of the island. Lily was the only other person in the room. But the silences between her voice replicated a two-sided conversation.

"You can sit down." Lily pointed to the breakfast nook.

Kate's plan was toast. A normal interview with Lily was impossible now. Whatever this was, she'd be wrecked afterward.

"Who were you talking to?"

A look toward Kate. Her breath caught when she saw Lily's face. Eyes like glass. Her face was tan.

"Her name is Marie."

A shiver crawled up Kate's spine. Took root in her gut. Her mouth was like the desert. Tried to speak, nothing came out. Cleared her throat. "Marie?"

No mention of a "Marie" in the old case file of the murdered parents. Dred replaced curiosity.

"Yes." Lily shook her head.

Kate stared back.

A smile, but it wasn't at Kate. "You can sense her."

It was a statement of fact.

Remember the multiple personalities you've worked with. It's about what they experience, not what you see. Things hidden in plain sight. Accept the terrain, question later. Kate reached down where her purse had dropped when the entity's energy pushed her back.

"Don't move."

"I need my recorder. My phone for video."

"She won't allow it."

"Okay."

Lily leaned over. Her whispers started again. Silence in between her bursts of dialogue.

Kate watched Lily in conversation. The milky cloud was the source of the sphere of energy. Where she sat was outside of it.

"The stench is gone."

Laughter. "It keeps people away."

"How many parties have there been in this house over the summer? A lot."

"She doesn't care about that. When people come, she leaves."

"How do you know?"

"She told me."

"How did you meet?"

"I came here after the daughter murdered them."

"Curious?"

"I wanted to see if the energy lingered. The hatred mustered to kill her parents. I never knew mine. I became obsessed with what the daughter did."

Such viciousness against people who brought life to a child. Kate had seen it before. But what drove a child to such an act? Something amiss in the little girl's brain?

Psychopathy was a rabid beast. No cure.

How could Kate reach Lily? She stayed in the moment. It was an opportunity.

"Many psychologists believe we react stronger to negative information. It's doubtful Marie got where she did alone." Kate took a breath. "The daughter's separateness from those who raised her may have struck a chord with you."

"Never thought of it."

The room was quiet.

"It was her alienation," Lily said.

"Careful with overidentification. It can linger if you let it. Become a trigger for what lies deeper and issues of post-traumatic stress syndrome."

"I was drawn here. Can't explain it."

"Compulsion."

"Is that what you meant?"

"Depends on the effect it has on you."

"I'm comfortable with it. Took a long time."

"How does it work?"

Lily stared at her.

"You don't know?"

"It only happens here," Lily said.

"Have you tried it in other places?"

She didn't answer.

"What happened the first time you tried to… connect?"

Silence.

"Are you going to answer me?"

"No. Duchess warned me about questions. Said civilians will use the answers against me."

Change tactics. Validate her experience. "Did Marie confide in you a while ago?"

"Yes."

"She doesn't appear?"

"Depends on what you mean."

"You feel her presence now?"

"Oh, yeah." Lily chuckled. "She knocked you on your ass."

Kate listened but didn't understand.

"Says she's lost. Fled from her husband when he deserted. He surprised her when he returned home. Found she and her lover in bed."

"Huh?" Kate shook her head. *'Deserted'?*

The subject had shifted.

"He was a soldier under General McClellan at the Battle of Antietam."

"Civil War? Oh, my..." Words came out in a whisper. Goosebumps. Her mouth dropped open. Kate slid down the counter. Sat where she had stood.

Bent over again, Lily listened. "She's upset. Said you look like someone."

Tried to speak, nothing came out. "Give me a second." Kate had to adjust before the moment evaporated. "Explain more, please."

The information was impossible to grasp. The watery cloud remained. No denial would destroy what she had seen in this kitchen.

No ghost.

Energy in its rawest form.

A presence.

What it meant was unknowable.

"Marie was sure her husband would die in the war. She'd fallen in love with a young man who hid after the Civil War began. Her husband caught them."

"Okay." Paused. "He survived the Battle of Antietem?"

"Is that a big deal?"

Uncomfortable laughter. "I'm no historian. But I believe it was the bloodiest single-day battle in American history. It took place in Maryland."

"Wow. Intense."

The sound began as inaudible. Familiar, yet not.

"What's that noise? The... Sounds like scratching?"

"I've never been able to bring it in," Lily said.

"Um... What?"

"Channel it."

"Okay." Kate's gut was at odds with her mind.

The two ideas collided like shooting stars on the night's sky.

In conflict with how she was raised. Warned about the dark arts by her pastor. Out of her depth. It was as if Kate was being confronted with all the questions of her life.

Holy versus unholy was what she'd been taught. Her upbringing clashed with what she'd seen this night. At a loss. Her honest questions were all she had to offer.

"How did you get entangled in the psychic arts?"

Lily ignored the question. Leaned over again instead, became animated in a conversation.

Kate's brain was in shock. She was awake, but it seemed like a dream.

The further she delved into behavioral motives, the more of a crap shoot life became. She had lost God in the horrors of blood-splattered crime scenes. The terrors of human cruelty on a scale only a deity could solve but didn't.

Crazy. This young woman is captive inside an energy. I see it. Can't hear it. But... It's nuts. Who will believe me?

Was Kate sure of what she saw?

Hand in her purse, she grabbed her phone. Pulled it out. Eyes on Lily, who engaged again with the force she said was named Marie. Kate tried to move without notice, while she prepared to capture a picture. Brought the phone up, still unseen, she believed, clicked a shot.

A gust of dirty wind.

A wave of energy blew across the room.

Dirt and sand granules within the gust stung. The windows above the breakfast nook cracked. A contagion of energy worked across the panes and left a spider web effect on the glass.

When the event was over, Lily lay on the ground, Kate close by. The milky-colored cloud had been swapped for darkness.

Two women motionless.

Present Day: Late Saturday Night

Neither woman spoke. They looked at one another. Kate stood, turned on the light above the stove.

"Is this why you wanted to meet here?"

"No." It took effort for Lily to stand. She leaned against the kitchen island.

"It would have been a good reason. Wild." Kate attempted to shake off her tensions. Failed.

"She's gone."

"Yeah, I gathered. When did this start?"

"Met Marie last year, around Thanksgiving. She caught me in tears."

"Why here? When I have a good cry, it's alone at home."

"I was born in Frederick, Maryland. Grew up with bizarre stories. Unexplainable things. A haunting in this house in the summer of 2017 made news. But no one has kept a record of events here."

An unhelpful answer.

"But why here?"

She shrugged. "In 1950 there was a murder here. A woman killed her husband, then disappeared. Police never found her. Legend is she crossed over. Haunts the place."

Suspend your disbelief. Rational thought is irrelevant. I saw her in a conversation. Or is she troubled, unstable? A force knocked me back. It's unexplainable. The stench I first smelled wasn't gas. Like nothing I've smelled before.

"Have you ever been trapped?" Lily looked at her.

The question stopped her. For an instant, Kate faltered. Didn't speak. The answer to this question paralyzed her. "Trapped?" Her voice sounded like a squeak. Coughed to clear her throat. "Why do you ask?"

Lily's face clouded. Her brow wrinkled. "What's wrong?"

"Huh?"

"You're white as snow."

She rubbed her hands together. Cold flesh. An innocent question threw her into another moment. What had happened years before. *Shake it off. No time to lose yourself.* "Sorry."

"It happened here to me."

"What did?"

Lily squinted, doubt across her face. "You're acting weird. What's wrong?"

Kate needed information from Lily, which is why she agreed to meet her at Riverbend Road. But 'have you ever been trapped' lingered in Kate's mind. She pushed fraught emotions aside. They boomeranged back into her head. Like a tape you can't stop playing in your brain.

Concentrate, Kate. Bring it back to what you need. The evidence she may have locked inside her head. "You lost an item the night of the party."

"My necklace."

"The Stratford police have it. You will get it back when they're finished."

"Don't want it back."

"How come?"

"Bad energy attached to it. I'll need a crystal instead."

"It was a gift?" Kate guessed.

"Yeah." A whispered reply.

"A guy you broke up with?"

Lily's eyes darted. Locked with Kate's.

"I have questions to ask you. It's why I called."

"You're not the police."

"Correct. Our company works with law enforcement. We were tasked to connect events from the Friday night party." She wanted to excavate the entity's force but had no time. She had a job to do. "Who provided the drugs?"

"Never seen them before."

"Lots of parties here this past summer?"

"Pop-ups."

"Excuse me?"

"Word goes out, address, it's on. Social media does the rest."

"Drugs?"

"Always. Not my scene."

"What about police, the neighbors?" *In L.A., pop-up parties were the rage for a while. But it was in a warehouse or vacated building. Cover charge and controlled.* "It's a sure bust when people trespass in vacant homes. I don't get it. Why is the electricity on? The rental sign is gone, too."

Lily ignored her.

"You saw the men who brought the drugs?"

"They were obvious. An Asian guy at the party was friends with them."

It had to be Trevor. "Handsome, thin guy?"

"Hot, too. Never met him. Oh, but Amanda had."

"Friends, maybe?"

"Nah. Too formal with him."

"Can't be sure. But sounds like a man from Ransom Center."

Lily's body stiffened.

Kate noticed her reaction when she mentioned the Center. She kept at it. "The night of the party. Why'd you run?"

"I don't have to talk to you." Lily looked away.

You've lost her. "I need your help."

"I don't think so."

"Why?" It came out louder than intended.

"Tell me why I should talk to you."

"The suppliers laced the drugs with fentanyl. If it happened once... Next time it will end worse."

"Good reason. But I can't."

"Won't, you mean."

"What's the difference?" Lily smiled. Looked Kate up and down. "Hmm..."

"What?"

"Nothing." Lily smiled.

"No, you don't. I'm here because we need answers. I'll call the Stratford PD if you'd rather talk to them."

"No, you won't."

Kate scratched her forehead. Stayed silent.

Lily chuckled. "You're uncomfortable. You like to control situations, but you don't have any control here."

"Do we have to do this now?"

"Relax."

Kate detested being told to relax. It was an insult. Like saying "calm down."

Don't react. It's what she wants.

"It's okay I know more than you," Lily said. "I won't tell anyone."

What Lily said hit her. *You're pissed because you're not on equal footing.* It made Kate smile. Surprised she hadn't seen it quicker. *Let go of your ego.* Deep breath.

"You're right. The mystic arts aren't my bag. But I live and work through my instincts. It's a job requirement." Thought for a second. "When I found your necklace in the mud on the hill. No one had to tell me the woman tied to it was important. You saw more than you will admit. It's okay. I'm patient."

Lily eyed her. "What is it you do again? Doctor of what?"

"Psychology. People's behavior, the actions of psychopaths. Events in the real world."

Lily drew back. "What happened here wasn't real?"

Shit. Don't alienate her. "Oh, it was real. Unexplainable, let's say."

"Not to me."

"So, tell me."

"Marie got lost. She has no memory of how she got here."

Speechless. Resignation set in. An official case required documentation of an interview. *How do I make this believable for hardcore skeptics? There it is, my Achilles' heel. Ignore the crutch of other people's opinions and approval.*

A Wayne Dyerism. Part of Kate's new age excavation after the church had failed her one too many times. It dawned on her.

Maybe I was thrown into this situation to force a confrontation with powers I use every day but can't explain.

Both women were quiet. Both working to understand what they'd experienced together.

"I have no fucking clue how to report on..." A deep exhale. Kate stared at the cracked glass above the breakfast nook.

"I'm thirsty." Lily walked toward the kitchen door.

"Don't leave." A yelp. Kate winced.

Lily stopped. Turned back to Kate. "Fucking *chill.*"

She watched Lily exit the kitchen. Heard the front door open. When she didn't come back, Kate walked out of the kitchen.

Lily was on the porch, a bottle of water in her hand. Looked through the screen door. "Let's talk outside."

She joined Lily on the porch. "Tell me more about Marie."

"It won't help. She's uninvolved. And I'm not a spiritual tutor."

"*Spiritual?*" Surprise registered across Kate's face. "You aren't serious."

Lily walked over to a small wicker couch, dusted off the pillows, sat. Stared at Kate. "You still don't understand, do you?"

"No, I don't."

"Aren't you from California? You meditate, right?"

She laughed. "That's funny." It made Lily smile, but she stayed quiet. Deep in thought, Kate struggled to make sense of what had happened in the kitchen, and why she was in this house. Moments passed in silence. She couldn't extrapolate the meaning.

"What do you want to ask me?"

"Why did you run?"

"A man I didn't want to see showed up."

"Who's that?"

She smiled. "None of your business."

No reason she should tell me a thing. I came at this all wrong. I'm on her turf, out of my comfort zone. She's got the power. I wanted to make her comfortable. Assumed she was wounded, a victim. This woman doesn't need my help. Surrender your authority. She has to trust, or it's a dead end.

"I'm out of my element here."

"You're repeating yourself. You're pissed because you got played."

"What?"

Lily looked at her. "You're kidding, right?"

"About what?"

"Come on."

"I'm lost."

Kate sat down in a chair across from her.

"You don't understand?"

"That's an understatement. I thought if we discovered why you ran it might help us fit pieces together."

"Why does it matter?"

"Amanda got..."

"Oh, please." Lily got up, walked to the end of the porch.

"Wait. What do you mean?"

"Nothing happens to Amanda she doesn't orchestrate."

"That might be said about you, too. All of us. Our choices create our reality."

Lily stayed quiet.

"You ran, but from what? Did he threaten you?"

Lily turned to face Kate. "I'm no victim."

"Didn't say you were. How did you lose your necklace on a muddy hill above the creek?"

She turned away. "It's cheap, doesn't matter."

"It matters that you were chased. It matters you're hidden away. What you know will matter to a lot of people."

"You can find out from others."

"No, we can't. Talk to me, please. What happened at the party that made you freak out and run?"

"What are you asking?" Lily looked away. She fiddled with her hair. Played with the ends.

God, help me. I'm serious. I need guidance. Closed her eyes. Said a silent prayer.

She had no choice but to follow Lily's story.

"What happened to Amanda?"

"I didn't see anything."

"Did you know the guys she hooked up with?"

"No."

"They were strangers, party crashers?"

"No." Lily played with her nails. Index finger in her mouth. A hangnail occupied her.

"When did Jack Stone arrive?"

This got her attention. Shook her head.

"Nope. Not doing this." Lily got up and walked down the porch, away from Kate.

Pay dirt. Don't let go. Push her where she wants to go. "It's okay if you're afraid. I understand." Kate turned and walked toward the front door. "I can't make you talk."

Kate's play worked.

Lily rushed toward her. Stood in front of her.

"What?" Kate waited.

Tilted head. Lips pursed. Annoyed. "Why did you ask me about Stoney?"

"When did he arrive?"

"Ask him."

"Doesn't work that way."

Deep exhale. Lily stomped over to an outdoor chair. Plopped down on it.

It took work for Kate to keep a smile off her face. They were both strong-willed. Being accused of fear pissed Lily off. But the young woman was nobody's fool. Resisted the subject of Jack Stone, which confirmed what Clay had said.

She is the woman involved with Stoney. Locked down her shock. Waited for the explanation.

Lily's voice was soft when she spoke. "I was standing over by the big window in the living room when I saw him." She fiddled with her hands. Closed her eyes.

What sounded like the crunch of a branch distracted them. Lily stood, walked to the far end of the porch again. Kate stayed put, watched her.

"What happened next?"

Lily turned to look at her. "I split."

"Out the back door."

"Yeah. The second I saw Stoney, I was out." She turned, in profile to Kate.

"What happened next?"

A moment. A whispered response.

"Sorry, what?" Kate said.

Cleared her throat. "He followed me." Lily looked into the distance. Regret plastered across her face.

Patience. Wait for it. She wants to tell you. Kate rummaged in her bag for a bottle of water. Took sips. Remained quiet.

"We talked on the lawn." She bowed her head. "He was pissed."

"What was he doing here?"

She chuckled. "Amanda."

"So, why was he chasing after you?"

Lily glared at her. "Why the fuck do you think? Need instructions?"

Kate's face lit up. Confirmation she needed from the woman at the center. *Jack Stone is a fucking idiot.*

"Ah, the doctor gets a clue." Sarcasm dripped from Lily's voice. The smile on her face wasn't happiness.

"How long?"

"It's over, who cares?"

"Stoney."

A burst of laughter echoed out among the trees. "Fuck him."

The information about Stoney and Lily wasn't a consideration when the investigation began. She'd confirmed Lily had run and from whom. Kate had a lurid lens into Stoney's troubles. If his daughter was aware it foreshadowed layers of hell to plumb.

"I still don't get why you wanted to meet here tonight."

"It's not important."

"Maybe. I've learned a lot from you here." Kate looked out over the front yard. Smiled. "I'm overwhelmed. This stuff that happened tonight. It's..."

"Hard to believe?"

"Yeah. My parents went to church every Sunday. I was, *am*, an Episcopalian. This stuff doesn't translate."

Lily laughed. "Tell me about it. I was raised Catholic."

"Oh, you win."

Shared laughter on a deep-rooted subject. They were sisters of sorts. Two of the millions of women who fell in love with their church. To discover it was another realm ruled by men. The one that mattered most.

"I haven't won squat. This is beyond choice, my mentor says." A different smile from Lily. She stared at Kate. "This house. Come back all the time. I needed to be here tonight."

"Needed? You were drawn here?"

"It's complicated."

"You're gifted, I assume."

"It's weird put like that, gifted. My guide…"

"What would you call it?"

"A burden. Most times."

"Intelligence is a gift. It comes in many forms. Knowledge is weight. It comes with responsibility."

Lily perked up. "That's it. The responsibility. I didn't ask for it."

"Didn't you? You ask by interaction, by your actions. Like tonight."

"No one talks about this stuff. If I hadn't found Duchess… She's the mystic I mentioned. It would be over."

"See, you asked for it. You engaged."

Lily didn't respond.

"When you follow your instincts, the door of secrets flies open. Your choice to probe mysterious events, portals, even, demanded a response. We all have the gift. Few use it. Even fewer tap the world beyond to infuse their life with deeper meaning."

"The nuns at Saint Mary's would have wrapped my knuckles if I dared say that."

Kate smiled. "Oh, forgot to warn you. Episcopalians are blasphemous."

"It won't end well."

"Excuse me?"

"Prepare."

"For what?"

"Death."

The air turned ice cold.

"Lily. Hey, Lily?"

She stared forward, no response.

Louder. "Lily. Hey."

Lily shook her head. "What?"

"Where did you go?"

"It happens when I'm here."

"You said, 'prepare for death.' What do you mean?"

A shrug. "It's channeled. I hate it." Lily walked past her, off the porch and toward her truck.

Kate moved to the center of the porch. She could see Lily's license plate. Made a note. Dialed.

"Hello. Dr. Kate Winter at Riverbend Road. Lily Cates was here. I need a tail on her now. The plate is…" She waited. "Don't engage. Report where she goes. Thanks, officer."

Kate got into her car. Hit the address book on her tech console, pushed the button for Ransom Center. "Yeah, it's Kate. Let me speak to Callie." She listened. Her brows knitted together. Shook her head. "Okay. Tell her I called."

Callie must be with Trevor.

Sped away from the house, didn't look back.

Present Day: Sunday After Midnight

"Clay Zach."

It's so weird he's back. Kate collected herself. "You were correct. Stoney's girlfriend is Lily. *Was* her, she's done."

"People don't say hello anymore."

"Sorry. I'm shook."

"It's okay. So, Stoney didn't get her message."

"Shocker."

"Glad you called. We picked up two men in the orbit of the people who own the Riverbend Road house. Does the name Tucker Jensen mean anything?"

"No."

"The man with him called him Clint."

She perked up. "Wait. Stocky guy, twitches a lot?"

"You've met."

"Caught him inside the library. Nervous guy."

"He's been chatty since I brought him in."

"Outside your purview, aren't you?"

"Who's he going to tell? He was in the house to pick up drugs. It's why you caught him in the library. A war is coming. D.E.A. will get him when we're done. What did Lily say about her necklace and what happened?"

Fatigue hit her. Kate had been at it for days.

When did I last eat?

Hard to concentrate.

"Let me pull over." She turned off the nearest exit. "Better. Long day." She rolled her neck around. Tension had crept into her shoulders. She listened to Clay.

"... What do you think?"

"Huh? Sorry. What did you say?"

"Are you okay?"

"Of course. Wanted to confirm your hunch about Stoney's girlfriend. That's all."

"You sound funny. You're sure you—"

"For fuck's sake. It's been a long goddamn day, okay. Why do men ask women if we are 'okay'? What if I said no?"

Clay didn't answer for a moment. "What's wrong?"

"Everything. I need to go."

"Call if you..."

Dial tone.

"Mistake. Why did I call him?" She was beaten. Her thoughts came in spurts. *This case. Clay... and the necklace.* Closed her eyes.

She had pulled off, then driven to a park off MD-301. A dull ache had moved from her neck to her forehead. It had intensified in the last thirty minutes. She took out a pillbox. Swallowed four aspirin with water. Closed her eyes again.

Minutes passed.

A loud crack.

Kate jumped.

Surroundings unfamiliar, she forgot where she had driven.

A strong odor wafted through the window.

Fetid and malodorous.

The stench jettisoned her mind backward in time. She was in the kitchen at Riverbend Road. The Lily necklace zipped through her thoughts.

She touched her neck.

Her mind took off.

A necklace.

A memory.

The instant life changes.

Kate couldn't breathe.

The odor again.

Inside her car.

Tried to banish the next thought. It commandeered her brain, body, and senses before she could shut it down. Clay's voice over and over in her head. The mantra from long ago. *You are okay… You are okay… You are…*

But Clay wasn't near, and Kate was not okay.

The aroma tripped the lock on her mind's vault. A place where she stored remnants of dead cases, memories long banished. No good would come from a revisit.

Not her choice.

In her head, Lily's necklace had morphed into a pendulum. A piece of jewelry Kate cherished. The black tourmaline crystal pendant torn from her neck one wicked night when evil broke in and drowned her defenses.

Fought back.

Lost.

An image of Raymond Drake oozed out of the locked vault. Banished images and events had resurfaced.

The tabloid headlines which had haunted her scrolled across Kate's brain. "Psychic Solves Serial Killer Crime Spree" plastered across supermarket gossip rags after the case ended.

The mind of Raymond Drake was a cobwebbed trap. Once Kate looked inside, it wasn't easy to escape. What was worse is she didn't want to.

A security guard had haunted her. Bleakness reeked from his demeanor.

Kate had met Raymond Drake out of the blue. She and Dr. Bridgette Carlisle discussed blood-soaked crime scenes, bad men, and her overwork and lack of self-care. Anyone who delved into the minds of serial killers benefited from regular sanity checks.

Raymond Drake had slithered into the hole left by so many serial murderers who got away. Handsome, masculine, and gruff, Raymond had lit up Kate's instincts the day they met.

He bothered her. Had lingered in her mind. The detachment she got from Raymond was a warning. His avoidance technique set off alarms. What she'd learned about the so-called Chesapeake Slasher from Clay Zach confirmed the worst of what her gut was screaming.

It had taken work, but Dr. Carlisle had gotten ahold of Raymond Drake's employment file. The health care facility required a physical and a background check. They didn't verify his out of state employment history. It puzzled Kate how Raymond got through it.

Psychopaths can be as intelligent as they are lethal. Some are charmers, talented manipulators. The level of control they practice when on the hunt prepares them.

Kate thought about what had happened one time she walked into the Bridgette's building. Coming on to Raymond would work. But she and Clay had argued about it.

She walked in and flirted with him. Kate had asked Raymond if he'd like to get coffee with her. He'd looked at his watch and said, "How about now?"

Maybe Raymond had dreamt about her since the last time he saw Kate. She had been close enough for him to touch. Fantasies fueled men like this. The desire to replicate a rancid dream in blood and skin was a psychopath's pattern.

They had coffee for 3 consecutive weeks on Tuesdays in the summer. The challenge was, nothing ever progressed. Raymond didn't ask her out. Kate couldn't push any harder. She suggested walks. He went along. The dialogue was stilted between them. And he never once tried to kiss her.

When Kate talked about her work, Raymond spaced out. She talked about men who couldn't get close. Disinterest was his prime reaction. Mentioned that a lab tech at work had lost her dog.

"Animals are dirty," Raymond had said. No interest, no empathy.

Then two women disappeared. Both women had participated in a speed-dating event that had been held in an upscale restaurant near Baltimore, Maryland. Neither woman had returned home after the event.

Kate and Raymond had met for late coffee on the same day, so he was clear.

She wasn't done. Kate's suspicions were confirmed when she dropped by Raymond's home. Another thing left out of Clay's briefings. There was a sign in the window about a pop-up store, and the date it would appear, where Raymond's loft was supposed to be.

Called Clay. He dropped a bomb. Told her Raymond had followed her moves. Every errand, he trailed behind her. He watched her.

"You tailed me?"

"We're on *him*. You walked into the middle of our investigation after I warned you."

"I can investigate whatever I want in my role at Ransom Center."

The call ended with Kate and Clay further apart.

She had gotten into Raymond's head. His warped mind trapped him. The vision of her tortured him. This was the pattern with psychopaths.

Clay cooled off. Resurrected their idea. Reminded Kate they could work together to bring Raymond in. His team would have her back.

No danger would keep Kate from the punishment she wanted to mete out. She would handle whatever was required. Except for the borderline choice she had made to lure a psychopath into a seduction to catch him. One of the reasons she preferred her position outside official channels was the independence. Kate put her revulsion aside and ramped up her plan.

She manipulated Raymond like a sugar baby played a benefactor. Cheap thrills, no emotions, stoked his ego, always available.

It had been a breeze.

Past events rolled through Kate's mind. She relived it as she sat in her car unable to move. She recognized the post-traumatic stress disorder she'd fought against since the night everything changed.

No connective tissue between them, no plans, no normal talk of the future worked on Raymond. She had made certain he was secure with her. A temporary state.

Home from work after 11:00 p.m. one winter night in 2011. Her mind whirring over a case at the Center. She had walked into her house as usual. Turned on the foyer light as she did every night. Walked into the kitchen for a snack.

The television tuned to NBC News. A report rolled.

In July 2011, there had been multiple murders in a city near Acapulco, Mexico. Four women on holiday had been no-shows on their flights home to the U.S.

Kate was back in a bleak memory. One of the four women who had disappeared in Acapulco was also the sister of the governor of California. A dear friend. The women were colleagues.

NBC News now reported the governor's sister had been found alive. The chyron on her television read, "Governor's Sister Found Naked and Bound, Clings to Life."

Thoughts collided. Muted the television. On her phone, Kate had searched for details about the woman she'd known for years. Checked her emails. Made calls. The only news was breaking across cable channels. When she called Clay, they had told her he was out of reach on a case.

Nothing made sense.

The news on her television preempted the next MSNBC show. An odd picture was shown on the screen.

The word "orchiectomy" sped by on the chyron.

She had lost her breath for a second. Unmuted the sound. Stared at the screen.

The governor's sister had remembered a detail about the man who'd brutalized and tortured them. Killed her three friends, whose dismembered body parts hadn't been found. The perpetrator had a distinct difference from other males. An orchiectomy left a nasty scar where one of his testicles had been removed. No reason was given. The newswoman ticked off a description of the man.

Triggered memories came in a contagion.

A necklace. *Her* necklace this time.

Kate was not in her car. She wasn't in Maryland, 2018. She had fallen backward in time.

It was the winter of 2011 again.

Before the headline, "Psychic Solves Serial Killer Crime Spree." Spurred by a comment from Clay, who was overheard by press saying, "Dr. Kate Winter was psychic about Raymond Drake." Talked about Kate's "gut," and how she followed her instincts to catch him.

It's Raymond Drake, she had thought. *He's the Chesapeake Slasher.*

She had chastised herself for staring at his scar when Raymond changed his clothes one day after a hike. Kate read what had been described on the documents Clay Zach had given to her. The records had prepared Kate for what she might witness when alone with him.

The startled look he had when she had asked him about a trip.

Then it happened.

One teeny-tiny detail.

The MSNBC report Kate had watched stated the governor's sister would never forget the tune the man whistled. It would get quiet. The women would relax. Then he'd start again.

Raymond Drake had taken one woman at a time, over many hours. He would come in whistling. They'd try to talk to him. He would stare at them, smile, and keep whistling. It wouldn't stop until the door to the garage attached to their bungalow had closed.

The screams would start.

Stop.

Return louder, more desperate.

All quiet came next.

When the whistling started again, the women knew he was coming back for one of them.

NBC talked about *Kill Bill*, the movie poster plastered on Kate's television. It wasn't the original movie associated with the song, the news anchor said.

Then they played the tune.

The whistle played in Kate's head, from a memory, as she sat in her car in the present. A prisoner to the past. The tune Raymond Drake whistled when he loaded his trunk one day.

Pictured the poster to the original film, "Twisted Nerve." A replica framed in her office to remind her of what happens when you're reckless with savages. The words off the movie poster from 1968, she had memorized.

But she couldn't remember them now.

"Twisted Nerve." Her own voice. Amid a flashback, powerless to hold back what had happened.

The Bernard Herrmann tune played in her head. Kate's personal American horror story.

It was the night the profiler became the hunted. The evening Kate was confronted by the Chesapeake Slasher. The man she'd tried to seduce to capture.

"Hello, Kate," Raymond Drake had said.

Long ago, now.

She hadn't responded.

Didn't move.

Raymond had appeared behind her. Nothing Kate could do. Stayed silent. Waited. When would he move? Take her. She had closed her eyes to sense him better. Sense his movement. Had been ready for what came next.

He grabbed for her.

Kate had been prepared. Anticipated his movements.

Reached for her neck.

She had felt his ragged nails on her skin.

He had caught the chain of her black tourmaline pendant.

Kate had bolted forward. Ran.

The single item of jewelry left behind on the kitchen floor had saved Kate's life. She flashed on the night she'd found Lily's necklace. Her lunatic lover had been stopped for an instant which had allowed Lily to escape. Two different circumstances, the same impulse had tied her to Lily for a reason Kate hadn't yet discovered.

Left behind, Kate's black tourmaline pendant had become a talisman for Clay Zach and his team until they had found her. He held on to it as his lifeline to a woman who'd been taken on his watch. A profiler, his colleague.

Raymond had abducted Kate in a stolen van from a local carpet cleaner.

For three days Clay and his team tracked them.

Manic. Raymond had gotten sloppy. Needed supplies but wouldn't leave her unattended. When he'd stopped for gas, Kate had been seen through one of the van windows. A woman with a gag over her mouth. Her eyes screamed terror to a driver pumping gas when he happened to look in their direction.

A contagion of calls led Clay, local police and the F.B.I. to a stolen vehicle report on the van. There was no security video from the gas station. The license plate found, they had tracked them through a network of law enforcement, civilians, and surveillance cameras.

Kate couldn't get out of the time warp. Touched the black tourmaline pendant around her neck. Repeated a mantra. "I am protected. God is here. I am safe."

A meditative prayer to bring her back.

Anxiety coursed through her body. Dry mouth. A formidable migraine had taken hold. She saw wavy lines in her sight of vision. An arc started at her temple and arched above her right eye. A distorted line of vision. Driving would be unsafe, impossible.

PTSD had been part of her life for years. Controlled it more often than not.

"Lily's necklace triggered this. And chaos at the Center." Kate chastised herself for what she took for granted. Sanity. The clean edge of thought where nothing touched her. To keep from the pull of the edge, she had to perform stronger self-care. Be disciplined in her thought patterns.

She began with deep breaths.

I can't call anyone at the Center.

Few options. One smart one. Hit speed dial. Waited.

"Hello."

"Hey." Her voice was low and an octave deeper than normal.

"Who's this?" Silence. "Kate?"

"I'm in Regent Park, MD-301, close to…"

"What happened?"

"Raymond Drake."

"Tell me where in Regent Park. Southside or west?"

"Near the swings on the southside. The Fort Washington exit. Sorry, I can't see to drive."

"On my way," Clay said.

They were two A-type personalities who both worked 24/7, traveled on a whim, and lived with death. Intangible emotions lay between them. But Kate and Clay couldn't find space for each other.

Kate turned on her car. Punched the button to a jazz channel on satellite radio. Anything to soothe her torn nerves.

Present Day: Sunday After Midnight

A car window rolled down partway.

A knock.

"Step out of the car. License and registration, please."

Kate opened her eyes. Disturbed from the calm she'd mustered. The look on her face quizzical. *Where am I? Wait. Oh, right.* She looked up.

Clay smiled.

She opened the door, stepped out. "Thanks for this. I'm better now, but I don't think it's wise for me to drive."

A brow of worry lines. His face serious. "What happened?"

"You won't believe me."

He drew back. Head tilted. "That's harsh. Who was with you when the Drake case exploded?"

It took a second. "Sorry. I'm not good with headaches. Takes me time to recover."

A chuckle. "Have you looked in the mirror?"

"No. What?" She ducked back into her car. Black smudges underneath her eyes. Her hair matted on the side. Stuck straight up on the top. "Holy hell. I look how I should after what I saw. Wild night."

"Hey, Clay. Okay if I split? My flight is in two hours."

Kate hadn't seen the woman. A swift sense of embarrassment flicked across her face. *Oh, no. Of course, he'd be with a woman.*

Clay walked over to her. She was shorter than Kate, petite. Cropped platinum hair, and older than Kate. Or maybe she had lost the ability to be objective.

Turned away from the goodbye, Kate turned back at the moment they kissed. The woman's hand came to his face. She made out "good to see you" from the woman. The ability to read lips was a curse.

The woman got in her car and sped off.

Clay came back, leaned against Kate's car. Arms crossed at his chest. "How long have you been here?"

Looked at her watch. "About an hour."

"Not the best place to park and sleep. Your house would have been safer."

"Couldn't drive."

He doesn't have to explain, and I won't ask. Doesn't matter. Well, it shouldn't... She continued the debate with herself.

"Hey. Kate."

"What? Sorry."

"A migraine? Last time you had one of those was... When? What triggered it do you think?"

"Have you ever dealt with psychics, mediums, channeled spirits? Those sorts of elements in a case?"

Shook his head. "The bureau is centered on conventional law enforcement. Traditional methods. The occult world is out of their purview."

"A bunch of babble. You didn't answer my question."

"All I can say is, I'm curious. Never engaged with a psychic or medium for a case. But, since the last time we worked together, I've done research." He stared at her. They had history, so he sensed she'd get to the point.

"Curious? You used to call it hocus pocus mumbo jumbo."

"Before Raymond Drake."

"Whatever." She paused, looked away. "I met with Lily tonight." She gazed away from him.

"I warned you."

"Needed to interview her. Stoney's distracted."

"Nothing new. Okay, what happened when you talked to her? What led to you asleep in your car in a park after dark?"

Looked at him. "When you put it like that it sounds awful." Kate walked on to the grass. Stopped, looked around.

Clay watched. She'd left important details out. Waited for it.

"It happened inside the house at Riverbend Road." Her back was to Clay, so she didn't see his reaction.

"There's a shocker. You're not an amateur, but that's a newbie move if ever there was one. Still don't get why you did it."

She turned. "I followed my gut."

"You and your damn gut."

Her lips tightened. Her eyebrows bunched. She glared at him.

He returned the stare. "What?"

"I'm sorry I called you." She walked back to her car. He moved to block her way to the door. "Move." He didn't. "Please."

"No."

She exhaled, turned and sat on the hood of her car. Head in her hands.

Neither spoke.

"Okay, this leads nowhere. Do you want me to drive you home? Tell me what you want me to do."

There was no way out. She had to tell him what happened. Hadn't figured it out yet. But the events with Lily and Stoney... Amanda... and Trevor, too, were connected.

"You won't like it."

He shrugged.

"I want you to follow me back to Riverbend Road."

He kept eye contact. "Why?"

"Because of what happened tonight."

"Is it related to Stoney?"

"Unrelated to anything."

"I'm not interested in a wild tangent. Don't have the time or the patience anymore."

Kate didn't flinch. "My headache is better. I can take it from here." She hopped down from the car. "If you want a further explanation, we have to be in the house. You cannot talk me out of it."

Shook his head. "I won't even try." He walked around, opened the passenger side door for her.

Clay got in and they drove off.

Present Day: Sunday, 1:00 a.m.

"You've reached the Stratford County Police Department. Please hold, an officer will be with you in a moment. If this is an emergency, hang up and dial 911."

It took a few moments.

"Hello, this is Clay Zach. Patch me through to the team at Riverbend Road. Thanks."

"Officer Benchley here."

"Hey, Charlie. When did your shift start?"

"We've been here a little while, after Dr. Winter called it in. There was an officer-involved shooting in Baltimore. All hands situation."

"I'm sorry."

"Both officers had a vest on. Dead if they hadn't."

"Good news. So, no officers have been at the house tonight until you and your partner?"

"Correct. All's quiet."

"Thanks. Didn't want you surprised. Dr. Winter and I are on our way." Clay drove the winding trek toward Riverbend Road.

Kate had ruminated on how to explain what had occurred there. She had to walk Clay through it.

They walked up the stone path. Stood on the outdoor porch.

"I don't want to go in," she said.

"Fine with me." Clay walked over, sat down in a wicker chair on the porch. "There's a team here. The place wasn't guarded for hours tonight. No one saw you or Lily."

"I didn't see anyone here earlier."

"So, now what?"

"Where to start?"

"Tell me about Lily."

No way to get around it. He won't believe me, but he'll listen. "She's a mystic."

He scratched his forehead. Tussled his hair. Stood up. "Where are you going with this?"

"Nowhere. I stated a fact."

The wind picked up. The contagion rustled through the forest around the house. A thousand chattering branches sounded as they blew in the breeze.

"So? Lily is a mystic. Means nothing for my purposes."

Clay wouldn't give Kate an inch on this subject.

"Right. It means nothing."

He nodded. "I'm a show-me-the-evidence, produce-the-proof type of guy. You wanted to come here. We're here. Now what?"

"I didn't understand it at first, either." She walked to the end of the porch. Walked back.

"Start from the top. Was Lily here when you arrived?"

"Yes, but I didn't see her at first. She was in the kitchen."

It dawned on Kate she was doing this wrong. He'd never care about the energy she experienced. No way to reproduce it. Lily would sound unstable if she recalled the details of the event she'd seen.

"Wait, stop. It doesn't matter where she was tonight. It's what she told me about the night of the party."

"Finally, info that matters."

She walked to where he sat. "You've got to stop. There are unexplained phenomena normal people experience, which you'd benefit from by not doubting. I saw it with my own eyes tonight. Experienced it myself. I'll leave it aside, however, because I don't intend to justify these events to you. I met Lily on her turf and learned a valuable lesson."

"Why did you need to come here to tell me?"

A lift of her shoulders, and a quizzical look on her face. "I can't explain it. But I want to walk through what she said while inside this house. I need an investigator tonight. You fit that bill."

His body relaxed. It made sense to him. "I get it. Lead the way." Clay walked toward the front door. "Where's the lockbox?"

"Huh. You're right. It wasn't here when I met her, either."

He pushed the door open. Kate walked into the unlit room. She glanced over toward the kitchen which was dark.

Forget what happened tonight. Recount what Lily said happened at the party. "Lily said the night of the party, she was standing over here." Kate walked toward the picture window. "Right here."

From where Clay stood, he could see her silhouette.

"Stoney came in through the front door."

"Okay, I'm Stoney."

"Ew, but okay."

"He saw Lily. She bolted out the back door." Kate walked to her right, down a short hall, and out a door of the house.

"This is a nice piece of property. No neighbors would hear music or a party. A lot of space."

"They had the fight out here. She ran to the edge of the lawn."

Clay watched her.

Kate turned around when she got to where the grass and the forest met.

"Oh, my gosh." She walked back to where Clay stood.

"Has anyone interviewed Amanda?"

"We're caught up on another angle."

"Trevor, right?"

"One thing at a time. What about Amanda?"

"She was here that night, too." Kate walked toward the house. The far side where she'd exited earlier. "I'd bet Amanda saw her father and Lily going at it from inside. It's why she hooked up in a threesome."

"Father dates your best friend. I'd say that's a good reason for any woman to act out."

Standing beside him, Kate smelled his cologne. The energy Clay emitted.

"Thanks for this. After what... Sorry. I needed to be here again."

Clay walked on and into the house. She lagged behind until they were in the main room.

"What happened at the party is nothing, right?"

He turned. "What are you asking?"

"The necklace focused my attention for obvious reasons." She'd lose him if she started on the energies. "The Center was brought in to dissect the social media side. Who texted what and how everyone converged. The personal stuff is one dynamic. Then there's Trevor and whatever is up with him. You said we could talk."

"Are we done here?"

"Almost. I'll be right back." She crossed in front of him. Walked into the kitchen. He stayed put. Looked around. "You need to see this."

He noticed the instant he walked in. "Those windows weren't cracked the first time my team walked through the crime scene. Wonder how that happened?"

Kate's smile lit up her whole face.

"What?"

"I can tell you, but you won't like it."

He took out a recorder. Set it on the kitchen counter. Turned it on. "I'm at Riverbend Road with Dr. Kate Winter." He logged the date, time and other incidentals. "The windows above the breakfast nook are cracked. Whatever hit them didn't break through. But it totaled all the windows. Dr. Winter, what did you see?"

"I came here to interview Lily Cates. The woman whose necklace I found. She refused to meet unless it was at Riverbend Road. When I arrived, the one light on in the house was in the kitchen. When I walked in, a milky-colored white energy field encased Lily. I tried to take a picture of the scene, but dirty wind, an energy, blew through the room. When it was over, we were both on the floor, and the windows above the breakfast nook were cracked."

Clay didn't move. He looked at her. Cleared his throat. Turned off the recorder.

"And that's why you ended up in a park with a migraine?"

Kate nodded.

"I'll add it to the case file when I get back to the office." Clay turned and walked out of the kitchen.

"No questions?"

He shouted back to her. "Outside, please."

They stood on the porch. Neither said a word.

"So, Trevor, what's going on with him?"

"You surprise me all the time," Clay said.

"Sorry?"

"You told me a story about an apparition—"

"It was not a ghost."

"An energy? Whatever. But now you're all business. How am I supposed to react to what you said happened in the kitchen? What is my team supposed to do with the information?"

Oh, no. Not this time. "That's not my problem."

"No, it's not. It's mine."

"What do you want? Me to lie? Want me to ignore what happened and what I saw? What I experienced in the kitchen with Lily, a witness to what happened at the party? All because your delicate sensibilities can't handle what lies beyond the world of logic? It happened. I saw it. Deal with it."

"It's that simple for you?"

"Oh, I haven't told you everything and I won't. Take it as testimony from a witness. Confirm it with Lily Cates. You don't always believe witnesses, but what they tell you makes a path to answers."

"If this gets out, you'll be disgraced."

Her eyes wide-open. Mouth, too. "Are you serious?"

"This stuff might work at the Center."

Kate's reaction was immediate. She tried to slow her breathing. Gritted her teeth. Jaw locked. Before she spoke, Clay did.

"Wait. Came out wrong. Social media is driven by emotion and unaccountable power of the mob. I have to deal with what can be proven. Conventional evidence, which is different. I cannot present this in court. Agree?"

"Forget it and tell me about Trevor."

"I won't forget it. We get stuck on this every time. As for Trevor, not here."

"Where?"

"There's a bar nearby. Keys, please."

"Oh, right. Your car isn't here. Almost forgot."

"What's on your mind?"

Shook her head. "Not a thing."

Clay turned. Kate behind him.

CLAY ZACH

Present Day: Sunday, 1:30 a.m.

Clay pulled out a key card. The door buzzed open.

"Where are we?"

"Private club."

"You mean men's club."

He smiled, but she was behind him and couldn't see inside. The corridor was long. It led to a gigantic open space that was longer than it was wide. At one end was a stage, a dance floor in front. The bar was centered in the room, spaces on each side for tables and booths.

The Allman Brothers' "Midnight Rider" played.

"Let's sit at the bar." Kate sat on a stool in the middle of the bar. She watched two undercover cops walk in. They headed to a corner where a group of men sat around a large round table. A waiter walked by with a bottle of Scotch and seven glasses on a tray.

The bartender nodded.

"Club soda, please."

Kate stared at him. "You're kidding?"

"Nope. Don't let that stop you."

"Oh, it won't. Shot of tequila, Corona Light, too, please." The bartender poured her shot. Set it on the bar. Kate downed it. Tapped the top. She side-eyed Clay. "Don't you dare."

His hands went up. "Not me. I don't advise people on their vices. Waste of time."

They sat in silence. The Allman Brothers in the background.

She looked around. "What's the story with this place?"

"Former military and intelligence, other patriots and civil servants of our great country pooled resources to have a place to relax, get drunk and not worry about who did what when and have it all posted on social media. I don't suggest the poker table. Murder squad."

"All law enforcement types?"

"You serve, you are welcome to join. Came in one day and a former ambassador walked in with a senator."

Kate nodded. "Dues?"

"Oh, yeah. Initiation hurts, but it's not bad afterward. I can see what you're thinking. You have to be sponsored." He batted his eyelashes.

She laughed. "I've never seen a man flutter his eyes like a girl. It's terrifying." A sip of her beer. "You still need to tell me about Trevor."

He stared at her. "First tell me more about what happened with Lily."

"Already have, so I better be quiet. I might be ruined." Raised her hand to flag down the bartender again. Pointed to her shot glass.

"Disgraced is what I said. When did you start with hard liquor?"

A glance in his direction. "Don't worry about it."

"Not me. I'm curious. I want to…"

She turned to face him. "It's the same shit. It never ends well when we talk about what's beyond evidence. You're not evolved enough to consider what cannot be proven."

His jaw dropped. "Harsh." Shake of his head.

"It's the truth. Let's move on." She winced. Moved her head to one side. Rolled her shoulders. "I don't have the energy to educate you. So, Trevor?"

Clay's mood had shifted. She stared at him. Raised eyebrows. Waited.

"It starts with Stoney."

"Let me help get this started. It's about money. What did Stoney do?"

"Discounts to law enforcement hurt his bottom line. The reach out to private firms solved it. The buzz brought outside interest. Things were good."

"His divorce?"

"Nah, that's an excuse."

"The expansion?"

"It's never one thing. Ransom Center got hot. Can't blame the guy. But he never hired a C.F.O., and Stoney is not a good manager. He's sloppy."

"An understatement. He's worse with money."

"Over time, a lot of expenditures. He couldn't pay his bills. Froze you out. Things got worse. He chose the dark side."

"Translation, please."

"He started spending. His donors weren't enough. Got under water. Needed cash. Turned to a loan shark. It morphed into money laundering for people he can't handle."

Her mouth dropped open. "That was the trigger. He leveraged the Center." It all made sense, and it hit hard. "Watch out. Stoney's got a wicked mean streak. Don't underestimate him."

"Minor league. These guys kill your family if you don't pay them. And send the body parts to prove it."

Kate looked at him. He was serious.

"Stoney's a pussycat compared to Straker Kent, a criminal scumbag with a long reach."

"Where does Trevor come in?"

"Got a call from a colleague in San Francisco. A young Asian male, early twenties, had been kidnapped. Trevor's..."

"Brother."

"This colleague and I go back to the bureau. He told me about Trevor's brother, so I would break the news in person. Trevor's an impressive guy. Checks all the boxes for me."

"In undercover work?"

"Right."

"You're mysterious about your work since you left the F.B.I. It's weird. You sound like a spook, but that's not it."

"No, it's not." Clay laughed. "Has Stoney mentioned a guy named Straker Kent?"

"Doesn't sound familiar."

"Didn't expect it too. Stoney's too proud. He wouldn't want you privy to his nefarious arrangement. Straker Kent has kept Ransom Center's lights on for the last year."

"Wait. What? I don't understand. I'm his fucking partner." *This is a new nightmare, worse than I imagined.*

"We were tasked to watch Straker, not Stoney."

She sipped her beer. Stared straight ahead. Tangled in her mind's panic, Kate had realized she might lose it all. Her money, her reputation, and her company. All the people, all the hours, their employees had trusted them.

Clay looked at her. "You still with me?"

"Huh? Yeah, sorry."

He repeated what he'd said, then continued. "Straker is a sex trafficker, pushes bad dope, and has a reputation for torture when his people go rogue. Counterfeit narcotics, and a network of black-market pill manufacturing, too. Makes the mob look manageable. When people disappoint Straker, he posts his corporal punishment on the dark web. Stoney came into the picture when I got the call from San Francisco."

"And Trevor?"

"I saw him walk into Straker's compound. Had a man on my team follow him when he came out, which led them back to the Center. What made me reach out was a team on Straker saw Stoney meet with him at Straker's place. I called it into other partners we work with because it was out of the norm. What came back was news of a Financial Crimes Enforcement Network investigation. Jack Stone and Ransom Center have the attention of the Treasury Department. Their message was short. 'Back off.'"

"I need another shot."

Clay looked at her. "It won't help."

"Can't hurt." She put her hand up to get the bartender's attention. She refilled her shot glass. Kate downed it.

"The fact Trevor was close to both Straker Kent and Jack Stone was good for us. We told him we'd find his brother. Informed Trevor he should not count on a happy ending."

"So, what's the deal with him now? No one has seen him."

"Trevor is stressed to the hilt. No word on his brother. The pressure on Stoney gets passed down the chain. From what Trevor told us after he went into hiding... Oh, about that. Callie is with him."

"Figured. Does Stoney know?"

"He knows about Trevor, not that Callie is with him."

Kate smiled. "I can't wait to see his face when I confront him."

He watched her. "Nothing about me, got it?"

A frown covered her face. "Give me some fucking credit."

He smiled. Smart-ass, badass Kate was the persona he loved most about her.

"Keep going."

"Trevor didn't have a chance finding his brother without help. It was incentive for him to help us with Stoney. But Straker is an old-school villain. He pushed too hard. Said shit about Trevor's brother and it set him off. One of my men, Tack Marin, helped get Trevor out alive. He's my eyes and ears inside the compound. Trevor is dead until this is over."

Kate stayed quiet after Clay stopped speaking. It was important news about Trevor, but she remained distracted. What had happened at Riverbend Road hovered over their conversation. She needed to rehash it. Make sense of it. He was not the person who could help her with this. She changed the subject.

"How long have you been back?"

"Never left."

Slack-jawed, she stared at Clay. "And you didn't call?"

He looked at her. Said nothing.

"Right. I told you never to call me again."

"Your exact words were, 'don't you ever fucking call me again.'"

"Ouch. Sounds horrible."

"It felt worse."

Quiet.

"I'm glad it hurt. You deserved it." She looked at him.

"Deserved what?"

Head tilted, a harsh glance. "You don't respect what I do. Never asked you to agree with my methods. But the breakthroughs I've manifested speak for themselves, except with you."

He looked down. Deep breath. "I was wrong."

She drew back, chin down, surprise written across her face.

"We have to go into court with facts. But I admit. We need to consider everything. There can be signs before a build-up to mania. Opportunities for him to strike that don't make sense. Intangibles."

Kate looked at him. "When I talk to career law enforcement to encourage them to use their instincts, consider unprovable signs, their initial reaction gets in the way."

"Most think it's bullshit. I get it. It's institutional."

"It's also a waste of time."

"Investigators need proof. We're not psychic."

"They make a judgment on my expertise based on prejudice. It's hard to convince them to open their minds to the unexplainable when it's been grilled into them that instinctual aspects are irrelevant."

"You're talking about what happened with Lily."

She nodded.

"Police will not take paranormal events at face value. It's not personal."

"A split second wasted on doubting what I've proven has wider repercussions. My instincts are far more accurate than an agent's or police officer's ego."

Clay tilted his head back and laughed.

The tension between them released.

"I'll be back." Clay walked across the room. Stopped at the packed table at the other end of the private club.

Kate watched him. Got lost in thoughts.

He sat down. A young man walked up to him. They talked for a few minutes. Clay came back to their table.

She was tired. The shots had kicked in. Curiosity won.

"Who's the blonde?"

He stared straight ahead. Didn't say a word. Kate stared at the side of his face. He didn't engage.

"Don't worry, I'm not jealous." *Am I jealous?*

"Whew, I was scared for a minute."

She leaned in, nudged him with her body.

"What is this, high school?" He chuckled.

"You aren't going to tell me about her?"

A glance in her direction. "No, I'm not."

The question written on her face. He didn't take the bait. She would have to vocalize it.

"Why not?"

"It's none of your business."

"Okay, but—"

"Leave it alone. You're not interested."

The bartender walked by.

"I'll take the check."

Kate was speechless.

He stood. Dug into his back pocket. Took out two twenties from his money clip and laid them on the bar. He walked toward the exit. Kate followed and was still talking as the door shut behind them.

She quit walking. "Please. Stop a minute."

"Come on, it's late. You need to take me home."

"Oh, right. Keys, please." He tossed them to her. "I'm not leaving here until you understand."

"We are not doing this."

"I hate when you're like this. We need to talk—"

He shook his head. "Sweetheart, *I* don't."

His answer, the way he said it, shook her. He wouldn't be able to tell she was crushed. The look on her face displayed pissed off.

Kate started the car and pulled out without a word.

"On second thought, take me to my office."

She simmered as she drove. Silence the entire drive. Kate arrived at the loop to his compound. Pulled up to the gate. A nondescript building beyond the electric fence. Two security guards stood outside.

"Thank you for..."

Clay looked at her. "For what?"

"Being there."

"No problem." He opened the car door and walked toward the building.

Emotions flooded through her body. Questions Kate had asked herself for months.

Why can't we get past our differences?

A picture of the blonde who'd dropped Clay off floated through her mind again.

The blonde has nothing to do with us. Don't be… that woman.

JACK STONE, aka STONEY

Present Day: Monday

Stoney closed the blinds on three walls of his windowed office. Collapsed into his expensive, high-backed leather chair. He sat. Head in his hands rested on his luxury brushed-steel desk.

Phone buzzed. Pressed one button. "Hold all calls." His thoughts roiled his mood. Too much had happened. The news from Straker about Trevor had crushed his resolve.

"How did it happen?"

He talked to himself a lot these days. Walled off his world from others who wanted answers.

He'd betrayed his partner.

Fucked his daughter's best friend.

Lost all of his money.

The wall behind him was filled with photos and news clippings of Ransom Center publicity. The headlines glowed about Jack Stone. What he had created was a game-changer.

"I've ruined it."

He reached toward the credenza behind his desk and took out a bottle of moonshine. Unscrewed the cap. Didn't bother with a glass. Took a slug of the clear, oily mixture. Got it down. Coughed. Gagged and wiped his mouth. Another slug of the homemade concoction.

"That'll take you off the ledge."

Stood. Another slug. Didn't stop.

The laughter began. Louder. He staggered around his desk. Walked to his office door. Opened it. Walked out. Stumbled over to the rail where he could look down on the bullpen. The place he had given the speech of purpose to his team. To young people who looked to him for leadership, guidance, and a career with future potential and power.

Ransom Center would change the landscape, he had preached. Led the way and had shown corporations there was a positive way to make social media work for their bottom line.

Stoney didn't mention the corporate raiders and the men he'd enabled, or the celebrities, and foreign clients, for whom he had pushed the legal limit. Saudi money, a fetish of the Washington, D.C. think tank class, cloaked his sins. Transparency was embedded in the company's mission, but it didn't apply to the Center's delicate private clients.

It was all about money, which is how Stoney had ensnared himself. He couldn't exorcize his demons.

What we don't make peace with inside ourselves can destroy dreams.

Stoney's executive assistant saw him too late. She'd looked up from the phone call as he walked up to the railing.

Kate walked up the winding staircase to the second floor. Her eyes on Stoney. Several employees walked by and stared. He had the bottle of moonshine in his hand.

On the first floor, one by one he got their attention. People stopped their work to watch the spectacle.

The founder and president of Ransom Center was drunk.

No one said anything. Eyes riveted.

"Stoney." Kate's voice echoed through the Center. All movement stopped.

He saw her. Reached out to her. "Dr. Kate Winter to the rescue."

She walked over. Reached for the bottle. He swung it around behind him. She grabbed for it with both hands. He arched back. Ducked out of her reach. Stoney attempted to go downstairs, but Kate rerouted him. He skulked back toward his office. She guided him inside. Closed the door.

He tripped on the tip of his area rug. Did a header into his plexiglass coffee table. A loud crack. He lay on the floor on top of the pieces. Eyes closed. He laughed. Drool trickled down his chin. Kate watched.

"Stoney." She walked closer. Looked down at her business partner. "Hey." His eyes flickered open.

"Go fuck yourself. Don't you judge me." He turned over on his side. Tried to get up. Fell over on his face.

Arms crossed, Kate waited.

He didn't move. Snoring.

"Unbelievable."

Kate poked her head out of Stoney's office. His executive assistant was on the phone. Shut the door. Walked over to the phone on his desk. Dialed. "Hi. I'm in Mr. Stone's office." Waited. "Yeah, again. Let's do a super B-vitamin shot, please." Listened. "Whatever you think."

She looked down at him.

Stoney hugged the bottle to his body.

"Jack Stone, you are pathetic."

A knock on the door.

"Come in."

The woman was dressed in light yellow animal pattern print scrubs. She had a medical bag with her. Saw Stoney asleep on his rug. On top of the fragments of the table he'd destroyed. Eyes squinty, her face scrunched up. She was surprised.

"Is he... drunk *again*?"

"Yep."

"You want me to give him a shot like last time?"

Kate nodded.

The nurse began her work. Cleaned her hands with packaged antiseptic from her bag. Put on latex gloves. Continued her preparation. A 1-milliliter syringe and a 25-gauge needle.

"Help me with his pants."

Kate hurried around. Got down on her knees. The nurse kept Stoney on his side, her body against his back. Kate worked on his belt. Pushed his pants down so the top of his left hip was exposed.

"Great. Got it." Swabbed the spot with alcohol. Far away from his sciatic nerve. When the needle went in, he stirred.

"Thanks so much. I'll take it from here."

The instant the nurse moved away from his body, Stoney rolled over on his back. Snoring...

"Good luck." The nurse left.

Kate looked down at the drunk she'd trusted with her money and her career. Walked over to the fridge. Reached in the cabinet for a large bowl. Filled it half-way with ice from the freezer. Cold water from the faucet washed over the ice. Walked back over to Stoney. The bowl in both hands, she tipped it, frigid liquid dropping onto his face. Waited.

No response.

"Screw it." She threw the rest of the ice-cold water on his head. The splash covered his face, his shoulders, soaking him.

Stoney coughed. Brushed the water off his face. Shook his head. Drenched. He looked down at his unbuckled pants. Stared up at Kate, who snapped a photo of the spectacle.

"What am I doing on the floor? I'm soaked."

"You're drunk."

"Not." He looked around. Next to him. Behind him.

"This what you want?" Kate held up the bottle of moonshine, which was over three-quarters gone. "Sorry, the Stoney show is over for today. We'll be lucky to have a staff by tomorrow. I doubt if twenty-somethings want to put their future in the hands of a blackout drunk."

An inaudible sound came out of his mouth. "I don't."

"Huh? Don't what?"

He hung his head. A groan slipped from his mouth. "Get out. I don't need your moralizing."

"Tough. Since you're pissing on my career and our partnership. I get to decide what's moralizing and what is my fiduciary responsibilities to our investors, our clients, our employees, and your partner."

"He's gone."

"What?"

"Trevor."

"It's terrible. Tragic." *He bought it. Thinks it's real.*

Stoney perked up. "Who told you?"

Stick with the plan.

After she'd dropped Clay off, he'd called her. Woke her up early. He'd given Trevor orders to disappear for a while. He had mentioned a trip to San Francisco to see his mother. It was a good idea, Clay thought. Trevor said Callie would travel with him. Sounded like a plan. So, Clay supplied two tickets to San Francisco.

"Callie called. She's broken up." Kate waited for a reaction.

Stoney stared into space.

"Hello?" No response from him.

It was easy to see it from where Kate stood. *Maybe I should have left him with the hangover.*

"What did Callie say?"

"No idea how it happened. Police found him near the Potomac close to National Harbor. His neck was broken."

Stoney grunted. His expression dark, brow furrowed. Upset.

He bought it. Clay had been sure he would.

"Trevor was a hotshot. Too smart for his own safety."

Kate clenched her jaw. Forced to take a breath. She wanted to strangle him but had to keep it together.

"Nobody better."

No reply.

The slow boil inside her chest choked her. Fury hard to hold down. *The son of a bitch feels nothing.*

"It's our fault."

And, he's back. The blame game jolted him into reality. "What? What did you say?"

"Trevor is on us. We let this happen." Stoney tried to get up. On his knees, he swayed. Stood with effort.

"You said his death was *our* fault. *We* didn't kill him." She walked up to him. Looked in his eyes.

"Didn't we? Trevor, gone. Callie is next."

"She gave me her notice." Kate watched his reaction.

"I need to lie down."

Stoney slow-walked to the couch. Sank down into it. More snoring as Kate walked from his office and over to his executive assistant.

"You can program his office line to go to my cell, right?"

"Sure."

"Do it."

"Done."

"You work for me now. Tell no one."

The woman looked relieved. "Okay. Sure."

"Call if Stoney says anything useful. Keep this between you and me."

She nodded.

"Reach me on my cell."

Kate had hoped to make Stoney admit the affair with Lily. Force him to face himself. But when she saw him drunk and out of control, she had no desire to save him.

Jack Stone's relevance vanished in the vapor of his inebriated belches.

Present Day: Monday Night

Home. Kate dropped her bag, case, and purse at the door.

Straight to the kitchen. Poured a big glass of Pinot Grigio.

Walked outside to her expansive porch. Windows locked tight. The air had chilled. She turned on the gas fireplace.

First breath was deep enough to reach into Kate's tired muscles.

So much had happened, and it was the first chance she'd had to mull the noise in her life. A leather-bound journal was on the cocktail table. Reached for it. She wrote.

Thoughts a jumble.

My world has shifted.

The past collided with the present and I can't make sense of it yet.

Stoney has fucked up. Fear I'm dumb on the worst of it. Forced me to make a move against him to protect the Center. It's the first of many.

Owe him a lot, but... What I didn't expect is the dangerous financial situation he has put us all in.

I will fix it. He will accept his reality. The Center will be safe.

I'm dug in. All the way. The loss would be a financial catastrophe. After all the work...

Part of what troubled her was a cinch to decipher. Other issues were lodged deeper. In places few others tread.

Lily's necklace worked as a trigger. Brought the Raymond Drake case back with a vengeance.

Thought I'd closed it down. How weird to find Lily's necklace and have it lead back to an event in my own life.

Kate fondled the black tourmaline pendant around her neck. Sipped her wine.

Coincidence? No. It's clear what I thought I'd processed, I hadn't. Confronted. Can I let it go?

Events converged in a way I couldn't ignore. For whatever reasons, I was meant to be a witness.

But what does it mean?

It threw me back into the worst moment of my life. I was there again. But it all began days earlier when I found her necklace. And I called Clay to rescue me.

Rescue me.

Kate scooted down to the area rug on the floor. A space large enough for meditation and stretching.

Touched the soles of her feet, with her knees relaxed. Felt her hips open.

Breathed deeper. Her spine lengthened with each breath.

Moved her feet forward. Arms beyond her feet. Her head between her knees.

Oh. Tight.

Released and came back to where she began. Deeper breaths.

Rolled her neck one way, then the other. Slowed down the motion. The stretch in her shoulders became more intense. Returned to the couch.

Clay's words bounced around in her brain. But he was not at the center of what was on her mind.

She continued writing.

Did I step over the line with Lily? There was no reason to meet her at Riverbend Road. So, why did I? She wouldn't budge. No choice.

It's not the same as what happened with Raymond Drake. Being thrown back to the moment brought up so much emotion.

Clay's tied up with it. He reminds me of my choice to get close to RD.

Do I resent him because of it?

When I spun out tonight after meeting Lily, I needed to be rescued. I'd made another decision that put my life in danger.

Clay was never on board.

And he was right.

The risks tied Kate in knots.

The ethics were untenable.

Another deep breath.

Clay came back into her head.

He is not the problem.

Do I blame him instead of myself?

Clay calls me on my shit. Confronts me when he disagrees with my choices. When he says it's dangerous, he means life-threatening.

He is everything Stoney isn't.

Clay has hunted the worst murderers on the planet. I live inside tormented minds. Much in common.

It's not like there's an abundance of males who understand the work I do and the demands of my job.

The thought brought Lily to mind again.

None of it seemed coincidental.

Synchronistic instances when a person's choices collided with a fated event. When the unexpected happens and people are pulled together.

When a door you've closed opens again.

Jump or retreat?

The memory came in a flash. She'd forgotten it. A vivid recollection.

Hiking one afternoon, she'd stepped wrong on a large boulder. Next instant, she tumbled down a treacherous hill. Jabs from rocks hit her torso.

Out of nowhere.

Kate found herself above her body as she watched herself fall.

Saw her body hit rocks.

She had separated from her physical self. The definition of an out-of-body experience. No serious injuries afterward.

I'm guided. Accepted most of it. What I have to reconcile is my strengths aren't enough to convince institutional players, foundations, and others who have all the money.

What mattered was all she'd risked.

The new Ransom Center. How to keep the doors open after Stoney?

Tighten up the budget.

I partnered with Stoney because of his institutional ties. White male power still runs the world.

Could Clay play the traditional investigative role? Would he want to?

Can I change? My intuitive streak is formidable but not without the investigative, and scientific aspects of my work.

Clay showed up for a reason. Can I make peace with whatever it is about him that hits a nerve? We can't keep going 'round and 'round.

Our chemistry is a bonus and a blaring horn.

See it as an opportunity.

It's time. If I want a personal life.

Present Day: Early Tuesday

Hungover.

He ached from head to toe.

Stoney's first attempt to stand made him dizzy. He hadn't eaten in hours. The liquor had soured his stomach.

No recollection of Kate or the B-12 super shot he'd been given to mitigate his alcohol binge.

Staggered to his desk. Inside a locked drawer were prescription pills. Filled a large glass with water from a pitcher on his desk. Drank it down with pills from each of the three bottles which came with warning labels on drug interaction.

Acute alcohol poisoning was an excuse. Enhanced high was the goal. Damn the final results which might be fatal. Pills to cure his malaise would make things worse.

Lips curled, nose scrunched up, one pill got stuck. "Don't try this at home." A croaked command. Stoney took another swig of water.

A bottle of moonshine drained to the last drop rolled around on his desk.

But he wasn't as out of it as he thought he'd be.

Hand shook as he reached for the pitcher again. Noticed the tremor. Wrecked, but he had no time for it. The bullpen was dark.

Walked to his office door, peeked out. He was alone. The few hours between the night's activity and when the Center opened for the day.

Walked back inside his office. Put water in the Keurig and added a pod. Slumped down into one of his overstuffed leather chairs until it was ready.

The cell phone on his desk vibrated. Reached across to snag it to see who called. It had been Amanda.

Better return the call.

She picked up after the first ring.

"What's up, sweetheart?"

"I woke up, and it was too quiet."

"No need to worry. Slept at the office."

"You sound weird."

"Woke up after… a long nap. Coffee will slap me awake."

His voice gave him away. His words elongated, not crisp. Hungover. He'd started the pills again.

"What's wrong, dad? Tell me."

"Nothing, sweetheart. Overworked, nothing more."

Bullshit. He'd been distant, distracted, and his depression was back. *He will never let me help him.*

Amanda had no power to influence her father. Nothing she did or said got through to him. Thoughts trolled her.

I'd bet it's about Lily. Ask him. Pictures of what she'd witnessed churned through her mind. "Is this because of Lily?"

"What?" He paused. "No." Quiet. "I'm... She's..." His voice trailed off.

"So, it is about her."

This wasn't a conversation he was prepared to have with his daughter. He changed the subject.

"When do you go back to work? Bet you're tired of living with your old man."

Amanda had been forced into a sabbatical by the institute where she worked. Her health issues and successive absences gave them no choice. The plan was for her to return after therapy and drug treatment.

The coffee didn't kick in. The fog in Stoney's head remained with no chance to escape it.

"You changed the subject. Why don't you want to talk about Lily?" Amanda hadn't waded into the quagmire of her dad's personal life before.

"We can talk about it. But not right now. You haven't told me why you called."

"Wanted to talk."

"Let's have dinner soon."

"When?"

"I'll call you later, so we can set it up. I love you, sweetheart."

She didn't answer.

"Talk to you later."

"Bye, Dad."

How does a daughter tell her father he doesn't know her at all?

Present Day: Late Tuesday Night

Kate arrived at the Mechanicsville, Maryland address.

Lily had called to ask if she'd meet her there, without explanation. She'd provided an address without a hint of why.

Sounds of a car. She walked out to greet her guest. "Hello, I'm Duchess, please come in."

"Kate Winter." She held out her hand. Duchess took it in both of hers. They walked inside. "This is cozy."

"I think so. Can I get you anything?"

"It's been a long day. Whatever you're having."

"Have a seat. Give me a second."

The fireplace was in view. The enormous painting above the mantle riveted Kate. Duchess came into the room carrying a tray.

"I assume you're the artist?" Kate pointed toward the fireplace.

"A long time ago. Seems like another life."

"Impressive."

A nod of her head, a sly smile acted as a thank you.

"Guess I should tell you. Lily begged off. I got a call about fifteen minutes ago."

Kate stared at her. "You're kidding? I apologize."

"I'm glad you're here."

"I appreciate it, but I'm at a loss. No clue why she wanted to meet here. Lily didn't say."

Duchess laughed. "Oh, Lily." Looked at her guest. "She wanted us to meet, I assume."

She sat down.

Kate watched Duchess prepare her tea. Didn't ask how Kate liked it but put no sugar in her cup. Added a healthy squeeze of lemon. Handed it across to her. Prepared her own cup.

"Is it okay?"

A nod. "Mm. This is delicious."

Duchess smiled.

"Did you guess I take lemon, no sugar?"

"It's not rocket science."

"Don't most people prefer sugar in their tea?"

"You don't."

Kate stared at her.

"Welcome into my world, Dr. Winter."

"Call me Kate. Lily told you about me?"

"You are well-known. People remember the Raymond Drake case." Duchess looked at her. "You, my dear, are a brave woman."

"My colleagues call it reckless."

They sat in silence.

"Does the painting have a back-story?"

"It does."

"May I ask what it is?"

Duchess lowered her head. She didn't reply. Kate let the silence sit. Waited.

"It's the original art that adorns the back of my personal tarot deck. The rest of the story is mine."

Kate's eyes widened. Her mouth opened wider. "Ah, so you're Lily's guide."

Full-throated laughter filled the room. "My, lord." More laughter. "In my experience, Lily needs no guide."

Kate eyed her. "That's not an answer to my question."

"Whatever the young woman needs, I'll be."

"Well, she needs someone."

"She does." Paused. "We all lean on our guides."

"True. But my so-called guides have been of a different variety."

"Are your parents religious?"

"Yes, they are. Church every Sunday." Kate took a sip of her tea. "I joined the Episcopal church after college, but I don't practice anymore."

"Organized religion is difficult for modern women. Lily was a Catholic."

"She told me."

"At this point, her beliefs have changed because of what she's experienced. Her own power led her in another direction."

"It's difficult for people whose spirituality is traditional. What I saw the other night with Lily?" Kate shook her head. "Whew."

"Uh-oh. Sounds like you speak through an event with her."

No reply.

Duchess eyed Kate. "Received an email from her late one night not long ago. Lily described a channeled event inside a house. Were you there with her?"

"I was."

"What was it like for you?"

A simple question. But Kate's body tensed up. "Unexplainable. It shocked me, which was a first."

"A first?" Duchess let the moment widen. "What about Raymond Drake?"

For the woman who'd endured the confrontation with a psychopath, the reminder trod on a trigger. But Kate had locked Raymond Drake away, compartmentalized the trauma since the night of Clay's recent rescue. A conversation about Drake wasn't why Kate came here.

"That wasn't anything like what happened with Lily. Not close." *What's with the look on her face?*

Scrunched brow, Duchess nodded her head back and forth, then shook her head no. "You have blocked it."

Kate reared back, a look of disapproval across her face. "No, I haven't. I've never channeled a message from...*beyond.*"

"Oh, that may be true. I don't doubt."

Difficult territory for Kate. She sat back. *Stop. Take a breath.*

"Why do you think Lily wanted us to meet?"

She saw my reaction. Changed the subject. Okay, Duchess understands.

"Lily sees me as an ally which I am," Kate said. "Raymond Drake did not attack a Doctor of Psychology and a veteran criminologist. He attacked a woman because I crossed a line to let him into my personal space. Offered him an invitation."

"You intuited the man's nature, which is why you're still alive." Duchess paused. "You put yourself in the bull's eye of his homicidal mania because of an advantage you had. And because of your ego."

Kate's laughter filled the room. She looked down at the floor. Shook her head. "You nailed it. Can't deny it. I let my ego overtake my common sense. Part of it was because of the team behind me." She sat back.

"Yet you trusted yourself in the most intimate quarters with a killer. Why?"

"No answer for you. But it was unethical, for starters."

Duchess stared at her, head cocked. "I'm sorry, darling. That's bullshit." She shrugged. "Finish your tea and then we can adjourn." She got up and walked from the room.

Kate stood up and walked over to the fireplace mantle. The detail of the painting above it was spectacular. The iconography was different, but it reminded Kate of tarot cards she'd seen on an online crystal shop.

I will not share that with her.

"Release your fears."

The words came out of utter silence.

Quick intake of air. Kate whipped around. Took a breath, sharp exhale. "I…"

Duchess's hands came up on Kate's shoulders. Her eyes riveted on Kate's.

"Stay with this fear."

Kate nodded. "Okay." *Don't resist. Fear is correct.*

"Where would you be without your instincts? They led you to trust you'd be safe. Gave you the courage to bring Raymond Drake into the open."

"It isn't channeling. It comes from my…"

"Gut?"

Kate shook her head in agreement.

"A portal to more miraculous possibilities. Once a person relies on her or his instincts. It's a leap of faith to open yourself through meditation. Results are immediate. An instant response when you walk into a situation. A channeled source of a different variety. The force."

"I've never heard faith mentioned in context with 'channeled source.' It's hard to untangle."

"For whom? You understand it, maybe even accept it."

"No, I don't. It... Collides with my rational mind."

"Because you're a behavioral scientist?"

"It's a big part of it."

"And yet you call on your intuitive self every day in your work. You don't want grief from your colleagues. Your fear is not about the intelligent guides we all have at our disposal. It is about tangling with the traditional structures with whom you interact. People who are unevolved. Locked in the approval of their peers they are paralyzed."

"Sounds like a Wayne Dyer-ism."

Duchess shook her head, a silent "ah" on her lips. "Always appreciate agreement with a strong spirit."

Kate looked at her. "I... This isn't... Never expected..."

Duchess waved her off. "Mania and lucidity teeter on the edge of the cliff of sanity. A channeled voice lives outside both but can only be reached through one. Mania locks out such divine messages."

"Psychosis and clear thought are on separate wavelengths. The latter unattainable when the former exists." Last sip of her tea. "My rational mind pushes against the notion of a channeled spirit."

"Is it your 'rational mind'? You were raised in organized religion's orbit, which has no relationship to the powers of the force, whether you call it God or not. A woman's full powers depend on a divorce from this structured and systematic separation from the divine."

"I can't decipher what that means." Kate looked away.

Duchess watched her. "You're uncomfortable with the subject. I bet this doesn't happen often."

The exhale came as relief. A chuckle. No other verbal response.

"I guess Lily was aware of why she wanted you to come here. You need to believe her. Trust the process."

"Trust what I saw, you mean."

"What did you trust the night you found out what and who Raymond Drake was?"

"I didn't come here to dredge up the past."

"Yet, it continues to stop you."

"How so?" Clay came into her mind. She cut off the thought.

"Why did you risk your career over Raymond Drake?"

"Trust me, the answer is ugly."

"Why would I be afraid of a person who has no power to harm me?"

Eyes wide on Kate's face. Surprise registered across it. "Images are hard to erase once seen. People are spared the horrors for a reason."

Furrowed brow as a response. "I understand. It doesn't explain why you think I'm too delicate for the truth."

"I recognized the type of man he was the minute we met."

"How?"

"His so-called 'mask of sanity' was easy to see through. I sensed a suppressed personality far more diabolical."

"You couldn't prove it."

"Which is why I risked my safety." Clay popped into her mind again. He wouldn't go away.

"When we listen to our inner voice, what you call your gut, it teaches us to live beyond our brain. To allow our mind to consider options. To interpret signals. The force from the universe. We sense when something is wrong before we have the facts. Our brain trains us through what we are taught and remember from elders. Our mind deduces the risk-reward quotient. It is our entry into the collective consciousness if we dare to suspend our fears and *dis*belief."

"When I met Raymond Drake, I sensed a fake persona. No way to ignore it."

Duchess nodded. "Take it further and you have Lily's brilliant mind at a time when women are stepping into their power."

"Did Lily tell you what happened in the house?"

A nod.

Kate rubbed her hand. The place where she'd experienced the energy that had thrown her back. "A milky-white cloud, sudden frigid temperature, the shattered windows. I'd experienced nothing like it."

"How to explain the invisible force?"

Kate chuckled. "I haven't written the report on what happened yet. Not certain where to begin."

The truth was deeper. Colleagues would read about what she had experienced. It mattered if her peers considered the event with Lily as an important aspect of the larger case because of her involvement with Stoney.

"I understand your emotions."

"Reduce it all to emotions?"

"A scientist documents, as does a criminologist. Emotions drive us all. Why can't you document what happened?"

Silence.

"Where's your restroom?"

"Behind you, down the hall." Duchess pointed in the direction.

Kate walked out of the main room. Duchess got up and walked into the kitchen. When she came back into the room, her guest was seated again.

"Did you help Lily break away from Catholicism?"

Duchess turned. "No, I did not." Shook her head. "A person's religion is sacred territory. It was her decision. Since it came from guardians, not her parents, it might have been easier than what you have faced."

"What makes you say that?"

Duchess took a moment to think. "I've talked to many women over many decades. Few have been spared the cost of traditional religion's grip. But we're in a new era. Thank heaven. Treachery exposed through the Catholic Church's pedophilia scandal. Lack of respect for women's role in the church, whatever the religion. Women are as divine as any man. It makes no sense to younger generations of women to be deemed unfit for service to a god who places one gender above another."

Kate looked up at the painted swirls of color above the fireplace. "I remain an Episcopalian, but I haven't been to service in years. I miss the rituals around Christmastime. My principle form of soul connection is through meditation. But the church was my gateway. Without it, I wouldn't have discovered... The tangible beyond the doubt."

"Ah, good for you."

"It has changed my life. My work, you wouldn't believe the difference." Kate laughed. "I'll always be tied through ritual to my church. But the hierarchical strictures suck."

"Amen."

She sat back. Kate's body relaxed for the first time since she arrived. She stared at Duchess. Through all the pretense, the rebuttals and the inner monologue. She needed to surrender.

"You're right. I can't let go. Won't, I mean."

Duchess laughed. "I'd bet you've learned through meditation that spirit guides are there to tap."

"I have."

"You don't need a penis to receive divine guidance."

A guffaw from her gut. Kate watched the mystic. Saw a halo effect. An actual glow surrounded the woman before her. It was the first time she had witnessed an aura.

Neither woman spoke.

Duchess slipped into another state, a trance.

Kate took out her phone. Turned on the recorder to capture any voice commands, without video, which she expected would be a no-no.

Nothing happened for several minutes.

"The danger is… not Lily. She is safe. A person is in the way. You won't be involved." She stopped. Duchess blinked, looked at Kate. "Oh." Shook her head and smiled. "Awkward. There is never notice. What did I say?"

"You don't remember?"

"It's not for me. It comes through me for another person."

Kate rewound the audio track, hit play. The two women listened.

Duchess shrugged. "It's an unhelpful message. I don't control the content." A drink of tea.

"It's helpful to learn Lily is safe."

"I agree. But who's the person in the way?"

"I need something stronger."

"Good idea." Duchess walked over to her open kitchen. Came back with a bottle of wine. The pour was a deep red elixir with a pungent aroma. The stuff of earth and patience.

She held up her glass. Kate joined it with hers. Neither offered a toast. There was more each wanted to say, but the moment had passed.

"Ah, wonderful. Sangiovese?"

Duchess smiled. "One of my favorites."

"The... invisible world. It has thrown me for a loop."

"It's what most women who cross my threshold say."

Kate looked down, rubbed her thumb over the wine glass stem. Deep in thought.

"What?"

"Can I come back to talk again with you?" Kate was surprised by her own request.

Duchess grinned. "Of course." She took the phone from Kate. Put in her number. Handed it back.

"Maybe you can help me decipher all of this, so I can explain it to others in a more approachable manner."

"Lily must have sensed you needed me even if she didn't understand why."

Both women connected to a shared mystery, which began with Lily Cates.

"The guides discriminate on whom they bestow messages." Duchess paused.

"Lucky me."

"Microphone, I am." Duchess winked at Kate. "Most Yoda types are women."

"I'll drink to that.

Present Day: Wednesday Night

Kate pulled out her tablet to make notes for the report she hadn't yet written. The conversation with Duchess opened her mind. A factor which animated her conclusions. She had filled in details.

It began with Lily, who demanded their meeting take place at Riverbend Road. On she wrote, picayune tidbits before she got to the spirit entity who had revealed herself to them both. Plunged into the deepest doubts about what she saw. When she wrote about the energy that pierced reality to blow out the windows, her fingers flew across the keys. Momentum built as she typed. The drama, the spectacular power of the force. Facts tumbled from her brain. Her mind sculpted the story through the awe she remembered. The experience of an invisible force, the chilled air, and the moment the windows cracked.

Human powerlessness in the face of an energy capable of dismantling reality. All the words Kate hadn't found before spilled out.

Duchess had empowered her to trust herself.

The risk was taken to explain the truth she'd seen. All down in a report, she'd once ducked out of fear. More details needed, but Kate had captured the nuance of the craziness she'd witnessed. Relief coursed through her muscles, her mind relaxed for the first time since she'd found Lily's necklace.

Wind picked up outside. The remainders of a storm that had made its way to the mid-Atlantic. Rain pelted the windows. Loud noise in the vicinity of the backyard. Got up to look. Nothing.

Must have been next door.

Typed away, careful not to miss a detail of what happened, what she had seen with Lily. Explained in detail the milky-white cloud, which never formed as an apparition. The channeled entity, Marie, with whom Lily conversed.

It liberated Kate to write the details. Put the swirling thoughts down into a narrative. No speculation or defensiveness.

A loud knock on her front door.

Looked at her watch. "Who the hell?"

She didn't trust it. Walked into the kitchen and opened the pantry door. Tucked on one shelf, it disappeared like an old shoe box might. Unlocked her gun safe. Pulled out the HK 9mm. Held it down at her side.

No peephole, she looked out the kitchen window. Saw a coupe in the driveway. Stymied at who might be at her door.

"Kate, it's me, Clay."

Stopped in her tracks. "Just a sec." Walked over to unlock the door.

Hands up. "Don't shoot."

A smile. "What are you doing here?"

"Can I come in?"

Unlocked the screen, Clay entered. Walked into the kitchen to put her gun away. "Can I get you anything?"

"Alcohol, please." Clay sat on the couch. Saw her work notebook. "Did I catch you in the middle of your work?"

"Yes, but that's okay."

"Came by earlier but you weren't home."

Kate handed him a glass of white wine. Sat down in the chair across from him. "So, this is a surprise."

Nodded. "Found myself driving and ended up here."

"Twice?"

Locked eyes. Clay shrugged. Neither spoke. Kate picked up her tablet. Put in her password again.

"I want to share a report with you. It's not finished, but I'd like you to read what I've gotten down so far."

"Sure."

Held up her hand to stop him. "First, I need to explain it."

Headshake, quick response. "No, you don't."

Pause. "Yeah, well, I do, but not how you think."

"Okay."

"I've had a breakthrough of sorts tonight." Held up her hand again. "Please, listen."

A nod from Clay, he understood.

"It's about what happened with Lily at Riverbend Road. She asked me to meet her at a house in Mechanicsville tonight. She didn't show. That was the plan because she wanted me to meet her spiritual guide."

Clay raised his hand. "Okay for me to ask a question?"

A nod.

"What do you mean by spiritual guide? A minister, a priest, a…"

"I would call her a clairvoyant, a psychic." Pause. Kate licked her lips. Pushed her hair behind her ears. "Others more knowledgeable would say she's a… medium." *I'll leave it there. See how he reacts before I go further.*

As Clay listened, he saw Kate for the first time. "Don't edit yourself. I can handle it."

She smiled. A chuckle and a deep breath. "She channels messages from entities beyond the visible world. Connects to voices beyond the earth plane."

"Don't get pissed, but how does this help you with the Riverbend Road case?"

"Oh, it doesn't. We're past it for the sake of this discussion. It's about what's going on with Lily, which ties into Stoney, and Amanda, too. The emotional states of three people who made awful choices, which collided at Riverbend Road."

"Behavioral impulses drove them?"

"On a collision course."

"They've already collided."

"Agreed. But Lily's choices are so dramatic because of the gifts she's cultivated. Aided by Duchess, the name of the woman I met tonight. Separate from Stoney's colossal fuck-ups. His need to be validated as the world he built fell apart led him to her."

"Maybe because she was there?"

"Could be."

Clay took a sip of his wine. "When you've got a riddle wrapped in a dramatic event, pick the simplest answer to explain what happened. Go from there. It's the way we work."

"Stoney was desperate, and Lily was unavailable. The ultimate aphrodisiac may be power, but its complement is the challenge of an unattainable woman."

"Doesn't hurt she's gorgeous."

"True." *Enough chatter. Let him read it.*

Kate flipped through pages on her tablet and then handed it to him. "Read from the top of this page. It's not done, but this is the part you need to see. I'll be out on the porch. Take your time."

Spectacles out, he began.

Refilled her wine glass. Walked out to the porch. She'd made progress. Judgments of colleagues far from her mind. Kate had deciphered random events with a wider view. A human hurricane of emotions, guilt, desperation, and an opened door. Dark forces allowed to enter and manipulate the petty brains of people on the edge of disaster through their own poor choices.

"A perfect storm." Whispered to herself. Movement from the other room. *He must be done. Here we go.*

Clay stood in the doorway of the porch.

"Well?"

"Your mind is a marvel. It's what drew me to you the first time."

"What did you think?"

"It's data. An event you witnessed with the young woman who's at the center of events she can't explain. It would make any sane person seek a guide who delves in the unknown."

"That's it?"

A guffaw. His head tilted back. "Hell, no. You will rock their world, Dr. Winter. No one will look at you the same way."

"Will I be a disgrace?" Kate had used his word.

Winced. "No. It's a flawless report."

Chills in her legs ran up to her chest. "You think so?"

More laughter. "Don't look surprised. You've waited your whole career for this moment. Own it. It's all yours. Followed your gut about a necklace because of what had happened to you. It's fucking freaky."

"Happened to *us*." She looked at him.

A nod. "Yes, it did. All the way back to Raymond fucking Drake. Had no idea what you experienced. Now, I do and so will everyone else."

"I looked into his eyes and saw through him."

Clay smiled. "More than a bit psychic." He paused.

Kate waited. He had more to say.

"No wonder you never quite fit with my crew, traditional law enforcement. The usual jobs for people like us strangled you. I never understood it before. Still don't but I accept the ground you've broken on your own."

Kate couldn't contain her euphoria. She walked over and hugged Clay. Beyond herself, their embrace lasted more than it would have between two platonic colleagues. They held tight to each other. Buried her head against his chest.

She looked up at him. "It doesn't sound crazy? You're sure?"

"To rigid, black-and-white investigators, it might sound nuts. No way it's crazy. Not the way you've written it. No one can strangle your voice of reason. Amid the challenge to rational thought, you explained the entity Lily channeled as a spectator to the event. A witness to the phenomenon."

"Duchess validated it."

"She sounds wild."

The look in her eyes stirred him. A door had opened to the most impossible subject imaginable.

Clay's hand came up to her neck. A tug of her hair from him. Her face tilted upward.

"I'm going to..."

Before he finished the sentence, her lips reached his to smother the words in a kiss.

Hips and legs, torso and heart, it was the moment. Clothed, their lust ignited in an all-encompassing instant.

Discovery through their wait for one another.

One kiss.

"Whew." Kate stepped back.

Grabbed her hand, pulled her close. "No, you don't."

"Think I will escape?"

"Not this time."

She took his hand. They walked through the house until she stood at the threshold of her bedroom. Her top dropped first. He stood and watched.

"You can come in."

"I like the view from here."

It was the first time she had stripped naked in front of a fully clothed man. One item at a time. Clay watched.

Kate wanted him to see her.

Wanted Clay Zach to see all of her.

Nothing held back.

They had waited long enough.

Present Day: Early Thursday Morning

"You're sure?"

"I'd like to help you, Kate."

"We'll send a car for you."

"Unnecessary."

"No arguments, please. It's a long drive from Mechanicsville. Besides, I've learned to prepare for what happens afterward. These events can drain an athlete. We'll meet you there at 11:00 a.m."

"See you then."

A phone call made to the Center's car service. Kate called to check on Stoney. "Has he come in yet?"

"No, Dr. Winter. Mr. Stone called to say he wouldn't be in today."

"Thanks. You can reach me on my cell."

A half-dressed man walked into Kate's kitchen.

"I cannot believe I slept here last night."

Her smile came from inside. "It's a rare sighting in this house." They embraced. "What's on your schedule today?"

Skeptical look. "My gut tells me to say I'm flexible. Did I guess right?"

"Yes. I've made plans."

"Oh, okay."

"Get dressed." Walked past him toward her bedroom. "French roast in the pot."

He yelled at her as she walked away. "Don't I get breakfast?"

"We'll stop at Starbucks."

"That'll work."

The bustle between them to get ready to leave wasn't coordinated, but they arrived at the front door at the same time.

"What's the plan?"

"You can come with me or follow. Doesn't matter. I'd enjoy the company, but I'll go straight to the Center afterward for a few hours."

"Figured, so I'll follow. Where to?"

"You'll have to trust me."

"So soon?"

Smiled before she leaned against his body.

Clay looked into her eyes. "Anything you want. I'm a goner."

"But I should warn you."

"It's Riverbend Road, right?"

The look on Kate's face made him laugh. "And you thought men never used their intuition."

"Am I that easy to read?"

"Not at all. You let me in last night. Least I can do is let you prove your theory."

"Good answer."

"Learned the lesson. Won't repeat the mistake."

"Let's get to it."

The drive seemed to take forever. Kate was not sure what Duchess would add to what she'd experienced but needed to trust her hunch. Clay had to meet her. Since he'd read part of Kate's report, it was more important. Duchess was direct, so she could take Clay the rest of the way.

Close to Riverbend Road, the butterflies in Kate's stomach wouldn't quiet. It was an epic moment for her. The mystic world was about to meet a formidable immoveable force, Clay Zach, former F.B.I. behavioral guru, now private sector profiler. If the two of them could coexist, Kate would have her dream team.

One thing mattered today. Make sense of what she and Lily had experienced. Expose Clay to it all. Duchess would either tip Clay to her side, or Kate would find out the gulf between them was unbridgeable. She wouldn't go back to self-censored assessments to keep people appeased.

Kate's worlds were about to converge.

After she saw Stoney inebriated and out of control at the center. After she shared part of her report about the night with Lily at Riverbend Road. And after Kate had been introduced to Duchess.

None of what happened had been a coincidence.

The last turn onto Riverbend Road.

A driver stood outside a Lincoln Navigator.

Laughed to herself. "A mystic, a lawman, and a behavioral scientist walk into a haunted house."

Kate would have to wait for the punch line.

Present Day: Thursday Morning

The phone call with her dad had pissed Amanda off.

He was a dick.

She'd had it with his lies.

A thought of her mom floated up, and it depressed her. Amanda's mother ignored her most days. Spent her time in malls or out "with girlfriends." She was absent, so Stoney was stuck with her. Different babysitters came through her life. It wasn't an event when they divorced.

Amanda wondered why her parents had a kid. Neither of them had been interested in her when she was young. Sat her in front of the television. She was their burden. An angry girl. Mood swings masked the deep-rooted nature of her fury.

Jack Stone and his ex-wife had no clue about the daughter they ignored. Their story differed from hers. It didn't matter anymore.

Two days ago, she'd sat and waited. Hoped her dad would call back. *What the fuck was he doing? Waiting for Lily's call? Her summons?*

Took a swig of her water bottle. Filled with vodka. It was a simple thing.

Put vodka in a water bottle and I can drink all day.

Her alcohol tolerance had built up over years of sneaking booze from her parents' liquor cabinet. She'd started young. No need for physical exams and blood tests. After she turned 18, she didn't care who found out.

The one time Amanda had put herself in jeopardy of being caught was the night she saw her dad and Lily together. One year ago, as she remembered.

Parked in this same parking lot, she'd seen her dad walk out. Drove toward him until she heard a honk. Pulled over, looked around, couldn't see anyone. Her dad had waved. Then her dad's car pulled up near him. A woman driver.

Amanda ducked down as they drove around the circle which led them by where she had waited for him. Tried to identify the woman driver but couldn't. Her dad had told her he had to work late and would not make it home.

It was a constant refrain.

Divorced, it didn't matter who he screwed anymore.

What bothered Amanda was her father never choose her first. Mother the same way, but she'd dispensed with her in another way. Never talked about her. Referred to her mother as dead.

Mother absent through her adolescence. When Amanda became a teenager, it got worse. "You're a young woman now." What her mom had said the day she turned 16-years-old. Any pretense of motherhood became something she wanted to forget. "I'm too young to have a 16-year-old daughter. We'll pretend we're sisters."

Car keys meant freedom to Amanda. To her parents, it meant they'd done their job. Their daughter was smart, so she'd figure the rest out on her own.

The day her dad was picked up by a woman. Amanda drove a loaner because her car was in for service. He'd never identify it.

She had caught her dad in a lie for a reason. It was fate working with her. Amanda was in sync with the universe.

When the two of them had gotten out of the car, the woman her dad was with shocked her. It was treachery of a magnitude she couldn't digest.

Amanda watched as he grabbed Lily. She laughed and ran toward the entrance to the upscale hotel. Stood and waited for Stoney to catch up. Threw her arms around his neck as they kissed in broad daylight.

The flashback played out as Amanda sat and waited for her dad to exit the Ransom Center. Unlocked sore places stoked her venom. Scenes of betrayal spiked her rage. She'd kept it all tucked inside until this moment.

Never allow them to see your true thoughts.

Emotions and fantasies riddled her mind. Horrific outcomes she would conjure up for her enemies to endure.

No one would ever suspect her, a woman. Society hadn't accepted the rage women swallow. Women weren't killers was society's ultimate denial.

Amanda welcomed people's ignorance. Never thought of consequences because nothing matched her invincibility.

Unknown.

Identity became hers to craft. A world controlled through her whims. She would shape destinies. Get even through actions no one would consider.

It wasn't until Stoney had chased Lily outside Riverbend Road that the public saw what Amanda had discovered before everyone. What upset her was being a witness to her dad's pathetic weakness, his neediness, and vulnerability. Amanda had witnessed Lily's relationships with men. Connections out of convenience. Her best friend was allergic to commitment.

The moment had fed Amanda. Made what came next easier.

Lily was no bargain. A wild child.

Amanda had her own foibles. If her dad paid attention, it would force him to see her ugliness. The moment she craved. Her grandiose thoughts birthed from mania. Led to violent acts to soothe wounds that remained raw.

Time ticked by.

Stoney walked out of the Center with an item under his arm. Drove around the circle and past Amanda's loaner car, which he didn't notice. Followed him once he'd turned left, out of the lot.

They traveled at a quick pace. On MD-301, Stoney turned off and took back roads, then the freeway entrance and headed east. Exited and drove back roads until he reached a gated compound.

Amanda had kept pace. Pulled up near where she'd seen her dad drive up to a gate. Pressed a button. She noticed a security camera above the gate which took footage of anyone entering the compound.

Security cameras. Not good. Her mind took off on ways she might get around being filmed.

A smile crept across Amanda's face.

Then a whisper... "It's good to be seen."

Present Day: Early Thursday Afternoon

Stoney parked his car and walked to the door. Looked up at the security camera. Buzzed in.

Tack walked up to him. "What are you doing here?"

"I need to speak with him."

"About what?"

"I'll tell him."

Tack didn't move.

Stoney stared back. "We can stand here all night. I will not do this with you."

"When was the last time you showered?" Tack turned and walked toward the double doors. "You stink."

The wait wasn't long.

Straker strode through the double doors. He walked up to Stoney. Tack had followed him but stood back.

"We need to talk."

"You have something to say? Say it." Straker's jaw muscles pulsed. His stance ready for more than a conversation. Watched Stoney pace in front of him. "Hey, man. You need a Quaalude?"

"The man's wired." Tack took a step toward Straker.

Stoney stopped in from of him. "I'm out. I paid you back. It's over. I'm done."

"I'm sorry. I must have misheard you." Straker crossed his arms. Dared Stoney to repeat himself.

"I said, I'm out."

A nod from Straker over his shoulder.

Tack walked back to the double doors and exited. Checked his phone. No text. Nothing he could do about what might happen on the other side of the door. *Maybe they'll kill each other.*

"You should rethink your decision."

Stoney shook his head no. Didn't speak.

Straker's ventriloquist dummy smile came across as maniacal. A cheesy grin meant to warn. It terrified, instead.

Stoney closed his eyes, tried again. "It's gotten too dangerous."

Mouth open, head back, malevolent laughter followed. Straker's amusement rose the more he thought about Stoney's inability to accept what came next if he defied him.

"Trevor's death. It's too much, Straker. I didn't sign on to murder."

"You asked me to save your precious Center, which I did."

"The hell you did. You turned me into a money launderer. You won't—"

One hand held up, his head cocked, eyes down. His lips tight. Straker was livid.

Stoney didn't speak.

Words in staccato. "You begged me for cash. Said you'd do anything. Ransom Center would have been shuttered without me. Your reputation destroyed."

"But I've paid you back every dime. That's what I agreed to."

Back and forth he shook his head. "No, no, no." Eyes locked on Stoney.

"You went too far. Killed Trevor. The loan paid, I'm out. No way anyone can tie me in with what you did. My people would mutiny."

Straker walked over to his cabriolet desk. Opened a chest, took out a chubby cigar. Cut the tip off. Lit it. Puffed until a red flame pulsed at its end. Blew on the flame.

"It would be a mistake to test the point."

Stoney wasn't finished with him yet...

Present Day: Early Thursday Afternoon

Kate walked up to the Lincoln Navigator and opened the rear passenger side door. Clay wasn't far behind her. The mystic exited the vehicle.

"Duchess, I'd like you to meet Clay Zach. He's a renown former F.B.I. profiler and criminologist."

"Hello, Clay. You wrote the book about the cycles of serial killers. I'm fascinated by your hypotheses. So many possibilities."

"Ha. You bought the one copy sold outside the law enforcement fields. Appreciate your kind words."

"People in traditional jobs don't admit when they've been out-thought. Ego is protected as a life force. Don't take it to heart."

"How will I keep up with two such accomplished thinkers?"

Duchess touched his arm. "Remember, we're the strongest bullshit detectors you've ever met. Now escort a woman inside, will you? I'm not as steady as I once was."

Kate watched them. *I'd put my money on Duchess in any fight. It's a tactic for her. She disarms men. They relax. She uses her age and gender to neuter fear. Death knell for her enemies.*

"My pleasure." Clay took her hand, put it on his arm. "You lead."

She walked forward with purpose. He shuffled to keep up. The door was locked. "Let me get it." Clay punched in a code. Twisted the lock off and tossed it on the porch.

Duchess was through the door and into the main room before Kate could catch up.

"No, you two wait behind me. Let me get familiar with this house first."

They complied.

"Okay. Come in and close the door behind you."

"What's going on?" Clay looked at Kate.

Finger to her lips. Kate pointed to the left of where they stood. A small couch nearby. They walked over and sat down.

Whispered in Kate's ear. "What is she doing?"

Held up one finger. Closed her eyes. Clay stared at her. Said nothing.

"You may talk. Quietly, please."

Kate opened her eyes.

"Did she...Did you?"

"I asked her if we could talk."

Clay whispered to her. "In your mind?"

Kate nodded.

Eyes wide, Clay looked at her. "She heard you and replied?" He couldn't wrap his head around this concept. "Okay."

Duchess turned toward the kitchen. Walked in that direction.

Does she remember what happened in there? The question in her head made Kate laugh.

"What's so funny?" Clay's brow wrinkled up. He looked confused.

"I'll tell you later."

Sat back into the couch. They waited. Minutes multiplied, with Duchess out of sight.

"What's she doing? Can't we go in?"

Kate mouthed the word no. "Be patient. She'll call us."

Minutes ticked by.

"Come see this." Duchess's voice was animated.

Clay led them across the room. The first through the door. He stopped. Kate came around to see.

Duchess held something in her hand. A long chain attached to an odd item. It swung in a small circle clockwise.

"This fascinates me," Kate said.

Duchess looked in their direction. "Come in and sit." Motioned toward the breakfast nook. "This is where it happened, right?"

Kate nodded.

"Sit over there near the cracked windows."

"Is it safe?"

Kate gave him a gentle nudge. "Hush. Go."

"This room is alive with psychic energy."

"What's in your hand? The thing on the chain?"

Duchess walked over and put it in Clay's hand. "It's a bloodstone crystal pointer. My favorite item when I tread places where death has visited."

Quiet.

"This is the room where Lily and I experienced...whatever happened."

"A psychic event with a medium is a phenomenon. It was a nod to you. Spirits don't reveal themselves to disconnected humans. It's a waste of their energy."

"So, you're saying Lily is psychic or a medium?"

Duchess looked at Kate. "She's a rare person who is both psychic and a medium."

"What's the difference?" Clay stared at them both. They smiled back at him.

"Great question." Duchess put her hand out. He laid the crystal pendant in her palm.

"A person can be both. But a psychic is not a medium, who is a person who can channel spirits no longer alive. Lily is both and more. Her gift is one of the strongest I've experienced. A formidable human presence."

"Using the stone, what's it telling you about this space?" Kate had innumerable questions for her.

"No doubt you and Lily had a mystical experience in this room. Compared to the main living area, which is a dead zone. When my back was to you, I brought out another crystal of black tourmaline. It's special. Never fails as an instrument. I'm grounded in this room. Powerful forces here. Not all angelic."

"I feel like a country western hick at a Lady Gaga concert. Crystals, energies, and clairvoyance. Kate's report explains what Lily experienced. How do you explain the milky-white cloud she stood inside?"

"I cannot."

"Can I be honest?" Kate looked at Duchess. "The description came from desperation to explain the difference between the air around Lily compared to the atmosphere in the rest of the room. While Lily was encased in what looked like a cloud. There wasn't a definite border like clouds in the sky. It was more amorphous. Is it clearer what happened if I explain it this way?"

"It doesn't matter. What do you say, Clay?"

He looked at Duchess. Hands up, he shrugged. "I'm a witness. A silent observer. None of this makes sense. Except that I believe what Kate wrote. I understand she wants her investigators to use all of their senses. It makes sense when you're immersed in the elusive business of behavioral science."

"What are you..." Kate stopped speaking. "How to ask the question?"

"Don't edit yourself. You want to understand your psychic gifts. We might as well begin here. Be blunt."

"Can you sense an energy centered in this room?"

A broad smile across her face. Duchess pulled another pendant out of the small satchel at her side. Dropped the crystal pointer down. Closed her eyes.

"It's selenite," Kate said.

Clay looked up at the ceiling and shook his head.

Kate nudged his side. "Shh... Say to yourself, my mind is open. If nothing else, don't judge. Watch."

It took time.

Whispers from Duchess. Silence. More whispers. The selenite pointer swung back and forth. Stopped dead.

The next instant, the temperature dropped. Not freezing, but it was cold. Yet, no air conditioning was on.

Mesmerized, they watched her. Duchess closed her eyes, stood still.

Minutes passed. It was a process.

Kate motioned for Clay to come closer. Cupped a hand to his ear and whispered. "This happened with Lily. A woman talked to her at the same spot where Duchess now stands. She might be in a conversation."

"What? How?"

Kate shrugged. "When it happened with Lily, I was... catching up the whole time. It was my first experience like it."

"This is unbelievable."

They continued to watch Duchess. She removed her shawl. It dropped to the ground. A long sheath over pants tucked in short, flat boots. There were scarves around her neck and a long belt that draped down the front.

"Oh, my lord."

They looked at each other.

Duchess touched her chest. "Awful." She shook her head.

Clay was lost. "What's going on?"

"She's talking to someone."

Whispered question. "Who?" Kate shook her head, shrugged.

"So much suffering and pain."

They watched her waver. Stumble backward.

Clay lurched toward Duchess.

"No." A whispered yelp. Kate tugged on his arm. Shook her head.

He sat back down, but Clay was uncomfortable. His face contorted.

They watched.

Duchess nodded her head. Hand over her heart. Tears ran down her face. She put the selenite pointer around her neck. Her head swiveled in their direction.

Kate gasped.

Clay's mouth dropped open.

"You need to go outside now." Not her voice. Her eyes trance-like, Duchess was in a channeled state. An entity talked through her.

Kate hugged herself as goosebumps rippled down her arms and calves. When she looked at Clay, he was awash in disbelief. Eyes riveted on Duchess. Kate didn't think the plea for them to leave had registered.

"Clay … Clay … Hey."

"Huh? What?"

A nod toward the door. "Follow me." Kate got up and walked through the kitchen, into the main living area. Picked up her steps until she was outside.

Clay hadn't followed.

Kate sat down on a chair on the porch. Waited. Walked to her car to get a bottle of water.

Minutes ticked by.

Clay remained inside the kitchen with Duchess.

She'd turned away from him.

He couldn't take his eyes off of what was happening. Took out a small notebook he carried with him at all times. A pen clipped to it. Kept close for crime scenes. If he didn't write what he was a witness to in this moment, he feared he'd remember it as a dream or a complicated nightmare of unexplained phenomena. An event he'd shrug off and refuse to document.

A nod of her head. Hands before her in a prayer gesture.

Clay noted it all.

The way Duchess's eyes stared forward. Eyeballs like glass orbs.

He saw it with his own eyes. But Clay couldn't imagine ever putting it in a report to his peers before this moment. For the first time, he understood Kate's angst. The confusion. Rational thought doing battle with the unexplainable.

The scene before him continued.

A spirit had commandeered her body. Clay watched, wrote, and waited. Duchess reacted to what the entity told her. Notes scribbled on a page. He hoped he could decipher them afterward.

A force is in control of the mystic's mind as the conversation between the entity and Duchess progresses. The mystic, Duchess, listens to the story the entity is recounting to her. She reacts to what her mind is receiving. But will she remember this?

I'm less than six feet away from Duchess. Before this began, the temperature of the room had dropped at least twenty-five degrees.

He stopped. Duchess whimpered.

"After they took your husband. It must have been torture to be separated from your daughter." Duchess's reaction revealed deep empathy.

A woman is the entity. The mystic, Duchess, is crying.

I'm a witness to an unexplainable event but it's real.

Clay shook his head. "I'll never doubt Kate again." The words came out as a prayer.

A gasp.

Duchess had collapsed on the ground.

Present Day: Thursday Afternoon

Clay ran toward Duchess.

She was breathing, in and out of consciousness. Grabbed a kitchen towel on a hook attached to the island. Slipped it under her head. Stayed quiet. Waited. The fear of waking this woman squelched his impulse to yell for Kate. Duchess needed to come out of it herself.

Stirred, looked at him. "Water. Please." Her eyes closed shut again.

Found a glass, filled it. "Here you go." Held it out.

Scooched up onto her elbows, Duchess sipped the water. Looked at him. A smile. "What happened? Did I say anything?"

Clay didn't understand. "You don't remember?"

"I never do. But I'm so sad." The face of a woman stricken. Close to tears.

"You were upset when you spoke."

"What did I say?"

"I don't have an exact quote. She talked to you, and you responded." Clay checked what he'd written down. "You said it must have been 'torture to be separated from your daughter.' The last part is a direct quote."

Another deep inhale, Duchess touched her chest. "Oh, I remember what she told me."

Clay had taken out his iPhone. "Can I record this?"

She nodded yes.

"They'd been shackled by a white Marylander whose house was used as a storage place for slaves being sold south. On the way to Baltimore, this woman had broken away when the slave wagon stopped to let them urinate. She was desperate to find her daughter, who'd been ripped from her arms when they'd separated her family at the Marylander's farm."

Duchess looked at Clay. Her pallor gray. She was weak.

"Are you okay? Do you want to stop?"

"No." Duchess grabbed his arm. "People like to forget, but many white Baltimoreans were pro-slavery." A bitter smile. "Anyway... The woman was captured later and accused of being a runaway slave. Insisted she was a free woman. They didn't believe her, so they took her to the Baltimore County jail."

Duchess took another drink.

"Please, don't stop. What else did she say?"

"A man who was friends with the warden of the jail advertised about the slaves for sale. Described them in advertisements before they took them down to the wharves in chained gangs. Where they'd be loaded onto boats.

"It's when she saw her. The woman's 16-year-old daughter in chains. They'd taken her to the jails on Philpot Street, she said."

Duchess paused. "Her child lost to her for eternity. It's unimaginable. The cruelty."

Her chest heaved, tears flowed down Duchess's cheeks.

Clay put his arms around her. Held her while she sobbed.

Noise behind them. At the door of the kitchen.

"I waited for..." Kate stopped mid-sentence.

The scene she walked in on was difficult to grasp. An open wound. Duchess crying in Clay's arms. It was beyond her ability to comprehend. She didn't move or make a sound.

"Is Kate here?"

"Right here."

"Good. Come close, please."

She knelt next to Clay. Looked at Duchess, who nodded.

"This house. ... This house." Closed her eyes. "Help me up. Get me out of here, please."

They helped her up and walked out of the kitchen, into the main living area.

Duchess shuffled along. Kate shot Clay a look. The weight of Duchess was on them. She couldn't hold herself upright.

"My legs are about to go."

"No problem. Get the door, Kate. I've got her." Clay held her up. "Put your arm around my neck." His shoulder into it. Arm around her waist. "Ready? We're going straight out the door to a chair on the right. Okay?"

Duchess nodded.

"Let's go."

Swift walk across the main floor, over the threshold, outside. Quick turn right. Duchess found the chair. Kate had a bottle of water ready.

"Please get my purse. It's in the car." Kate took off. Brought back her purse. "Thanks." Duchess opened it and took out a plastic bag of crackers. "I'm okay. Give me a second."

A nod from Clay, Kate followed him. Space for Duchess to recover.

"I waited, but..."

He shook his head. "Remarkable." Looked back at Duchess.

"Are you okay? You look like you're in shock."

"I am. Oh, I am."

Duchess was on the walkway. Her movement was slow motion forward, one step at a time. "Well, that was a first."

Laughter.

"Sir, you look like you've seen a ghost." Duchess smiled.

"You must tell me what I witnessed. I'm not sure." Clay scratched his head. "But you made me a believer."

Kate looked at him. Her eyes wide. "What the hell? Tell me what happened."

Silence.

"Your man there can fill you in." Duchess turned back to the house. Shook her head. "A white Marylander used this house to hold slaves being sold south. Well over one hundred years ago. They traveled from here to the Baltimore jail." Looked at Kate. "There is so much psychic energy held in this house. The center is the kitchen which you found out for yourself."

Duchess looked at Clay. "Thank you. You stayed with it, with *me*. I'm grateful."

"Any time. I mean it." A nervous chuckle from Clay. "I have a lot to learn."

Duchess walked by them toward the Lincoln Navigator. They followed. Stopped at the car door. Embraced her two new friends. Another gaze back at the house.

"Pain comes through the walls in wails and cries of agony. It's not a haunting. This house is a portal. Where tortured souls in the throes of unspeakable grief convene. Desperate to find those they loved and lost to a living death."

Kate reached out, touched her arm. "Clay will fill me in, but I can't thank you enough for showing us the way."

"I thank you for insisting I experience it myself. Did you know?"

Kate stared at Duchess. "Yes, I did. But also wanted to see if it was Lily or the house."

"Don't think about it. Let your answer reveal itself." Duchess smiled.

She touched the mystic's arm. "I had faith you'd give me the answer."

The women laughed.

"Hmm… Faith. There is something perfect about it. Yes?"

Kate shook her head yes.

Clay looked at Duchess, then to Kate. "What did I miss?"

"You'll catch up." Duchess smiled at him.

They helped her into the SUV.

Clay took Kate's hand.

Neither spoke a word.

Present Day: Thursday Afternoon

The worst of Clay's suspicions about the Center wasn't proven. His team on lookout at Straker Kent's warehouse had not yielded what he had hoped.

But the situation had spiraled beyond anyone's control.

Stoney had never done an illegal act in his life until the Ransom Center became insolvent. He had one hundred regrets. He could keep laundering Straker's money or go to the police. The latter was not an option in his mind.

Curls of cigar smoke wafted from Straker's lips.

Thoughts of exposure paralyzed Stoney. People had trusted him. *I should have gone to Kate. Told her about Straker before I first approached him. How can I get out of this without the Center being destroyed?* It was over for him there. But his ego wouldn't relent. He couldn't let go.

Stoney was beaten. He choked back tears of fury. Emotion strangled him. Walked up to Straker. Got in his face. "I will burn you down."

A shrug. Straker pursed his lips. Kissed the air. "Move along. You've got a new side job."

"Are you high?"

The men eyed one another.

"The bags are by the door."

With a glance, the message hit. Stoney didn't speak.

"You're down a man by my count." Straker wasn't smiling. But he was pleased with himself. "Sorry about Trevor."

Stoney controlled himself for once. Walked out of the compound with three black duffle bags. Inspected them when he got to his car. More money he was expected to launder through Ransom Center for Straker.

Amanda spied her father's car leave the compound. She ducked down. Waited. She was in no hurry. Drank, listened to music.

Clouds over the sun close to sunset.

Amanda pulled her car down the road. No one noticed. Did a U-turn down the street from Straker's compound and stopped at the side of the road. Grabbed her purse. Freshened her lipstick. Unbuttoned two buttons. Her push-up bra provided the perfect tease. Pulled up to the gate underneath the security cameras.

She wanted them to see her face. Pushed the keypad. A crackle noise came from the old speakers.

"Yeah?"

No answer.

"Name."

Looked up. Coquettish smile. "Amanda Stone."

The gate opened, and she drove her car inside.

Straker stood at the front door and watched Amanda walk toward him. A lopsided sneer spread across his face.

What a douche bag. Amanda wet her lips. Flipped her hair. Swung her hips as she walked. *No man can resist. It's the same every time.* Tugged on her purse at her side. Amanda had a plan.

His eyes traced her body.

Stopped in front of Straker. "Satisfied?"

He grunted. His tongue licked his upper lip.

Head down, cocked up, she looked at him. "Aren't you going to ask me in?"

Stepped back from the door. She sashayed inside.

Straker's fantasies spun in his head. "Your dad was here earlier."

Turned. "Oh?"

A nod. Tack walked through the double doors. When he saw Amanda, he froze. For a brief instant, his expression gave him away.

Amanda looked at Tack. "What's up with him?"

Straker laughed. "Take a walk."

Tack didn't move.

"Yeah, we've got business." She hoisted herself up on a bar stool near Straker's cabriolet desk. "Oh, bartender."

A nod in Tack's direction. Straker quit walking when he didn't respond. "What?"

Two hands up, Tack turned. Walked out of the room.

Present Day: Early Thursday Night

The team Clay had assembled months earlier, when they'd discovered Stoney's financial situation, had eyes on Amanda the instant she drove her vehicle up to the compound gates. Her license plate had identified her. The unforeseen development complicated their mission.

"Hey, get in here. You need to see this." A man tasked to watch Straker Kent's compound was stunned seeing Amanda Stone.

A woman dressed in jeans and a t-shirt entered the van and walked over to where her partner sat in front of monitors.

"Holy shit. Is that...?"

He nodded.

She hit speed dial on her cell phone.

Clay picked up after the second ring. "What's up?"

"Stoney left the compound a while ago. Peeled out, so he's pissed."

"That's it?"

"Well, you won't believe this. Amanda Stone drove into Straker's compound after her dad left."

Paused. "Anyone with her?"

"Nope. What do you want us to do?"

"What's up inside?"

"Tack is quiet. No word. This will freak him out."

"Okay. Hold on a second." Clay pushed mute on his iPhone. Walked into the kitchen where Kate had laid out a snack. "What's the story with Amanda, Stoney's daughter?"

Her brow furrowed. "Mean, narcissistic woman. Hates her parents. I wouldn't meet her alone."

"Sounds like a piece of work. Boyfriend?"

"No. But she sleeps around. A lot."

"Does she hate her parents enough to hurt herself to get to them?"

Kate laughed. "Oh, she's capable of a lot of mischief. But hurt herself? No way."

A nod. Back to the call. "Amanda isn't our problem. I need you to take down this address." Clay relayed the address in Mechanicsville where Duchess lived. "Watch the house. We still haven't talked to Lily Cates. She has more info about Stoney's situation, I'd bet."

"The Cates woman lives there?"

"She's close to the woman who does and might make a stop there. If she does, don't wait. Arrest her and bring her in so we can talk to her before someone else finds her. I don't want to alert anyone, but we need to question her first."

"What about Tack?"

"I'll make the call."

"Got it, boss."

Call ended. The agent continued to watch the entrance to the compound. The van parked a block away.

What does Amanda Stone want with Straker Kent? The female agent on Clay's team couldn't make sense of it.

Clay and his team had done a full rundown on Amanda Stone, which told them she was a troubled woman. Her tastes in men, terrible. The last boyfriend was a convicted felon. He and Stoney had gotten into a fight at a local restaurant. Police were called, but they kept it out of local headlines.

People in the area had become accustomed to Ransom Center and the good they did in the community. Stoney was a big donor to the Baltimore police. Respected throughout the law enforcement community. No one wanted to make an example out of him because he was one of the good guys. He also had deep pockets and liked to spread his money around to keep his friends loyal.

None of it mattered anymore.

"Clay pulled the surveillance. Wants us at an address in Mechanicsville."

"What about Stone's daughter?"

"She's on her own."

"Tack?"

"Clay's on it."

"Okay." The man at the monitors turned off the equipment.

The woman looked at him. "Stone's daughter and Straker Kent. Odd couple if there ever was one. Too bad we won't be here when she runs out for help."

"*If* she comes out."

Present Day: Early Thursday Night

Straker eyed her. "What would you like?"

"Vodka martini, please." Amanda crossed her legs. Her sweater stopped short of her waist. Leggings tight on her body.

"Good idea."

A smile. Straker looked at her, his eyes lingering.

"What?" She intended to make him wait for it. *Patience. He wants me.*

The martini glass was filled to the top. She sipped it. "Mm. Is that lemon vodka?"

"Yep."

"I like it." She followed him over to a couch. Straker sat in the middle.

He's done this dance before. Amanda sat down next to him. "To new friends." Her glass held up. A toast. Clinked her glass with his.

"So, how long were you outside?" Straker looked at her, stone-faced.

"A while."

"Why are you here?"

The best way to get him interested was to stay close to the truth. Dangerous men weren't stupid.

"Saw my dad was pissed. I followed him here. Wanted to see where he was going. He's got a girlfriend he hasn't told me about." A lie. Delivered straight into Straker's eyes. *The way he looks at me. He's all about sex. Won't be interested once it's over.*

Straker set his martini glass down. "Come closer."

Mimicked his movement. Sat her glass down, scooched closer to him on the couch. His hand came down on her thigh. Looked at her. She didn't move. He moved his hand higher. A smile spread across her face. He glanced at her.

"What's so funny?"

"Funny? No. Hot, maybe."

Flipped her hair back over her right shoulder. Saw his eyes move over her body. Suppressed a shudder.

Careful. Don't underestimate him.

She saw the knife sheath on his belt. No gun on him.

Have to get his belt off.

The French doors were closed but Tack could see the scene from the back room. Amanda complicated the hell out of things. She was Stoney's daughter. It was enough to worry him. The team outside had to have seen her enter.

Amanda inched closer to Straker. Her arm on the back of the sofa. She pushed her breast against him.

A light touch across his bald head. "Sexy." Merciless flirt, her directness worked.

In one swift move, Straker brought his hand around and grabbed her hair. Pulled her into him and kissed her hard. Her hand came down on his thigh.

A little groan escaped Amanda's lips.

Tack's phone rang. He winced. One ring. The signal he'd waited for from Clay. He watched Straker, his view clear enough that he saw him stop.

Straker cocked his head and turned around.

There wasn't a second ring.

"Hey, where'd you go?"

He turned back to Amanda. "I'm right here, baby." The second kiss was harder. His grip on her tighter.

From behind the French doors, Tack watched for another minute. He had to make sure the one ring hadn't alerted Straker. A man notorious for his distrustfulness.

"Thank you, Amanda Stone." Tack ready to split.

But the door to the back of the compound squeaked when it opened. So, he had to wait until Straker was preoccupied. It would take more than a kiss to commandeer his attention. Tack walked back to watch them behind the doors.

"Tack."

Pushed the door open. "Yeah, boss."

"I'll be..." He looked at Stoney's daughter. "...busy for a while. Handle things. I'll be in the loft if you need me."

Tack nodded. Closed the French door.

"Come with me." Straker stood, walked over to the stairs to the loft. Amanda stayed seated. "I said, come on."

Tack saw Straker make his move on her. It wouldn't be long. But he had to wait until they were both in the loft.

"Where are we going?" Amanda didn't budge. *Ooh, he's pissed. Not used to women who don't jump when he calls.*

No answer. Stared at her, his face hardened. "I won't ask again."

"Why so serious?" On her knees, her hands on the back of the couch. She looked at him. "Bossy men are a turnoff. Chill."

"Whatever game you're playing, I'm not interested. You're here to piss off your dad. So, let's piss him off." Walked toward her.

Amanda stood. When Straker got close, she threw her arms around his neck. Pushed her body against him. It happened in increments. Kissed him on the mouth. His body relaxed. Another manufactured kiss. He responded with fervor. The hardness of his body pressed against her.

It wasn't her charms. Straker was into conquests.

His desire escalated each time her tongue lapped his lips. It was the moment. She had him. Hands on her ass, he pushed into her. A moan escaped her lips.

"You like that, baby."

Eyes bored into his. "More. I want more." Another wet kiss.

Hands came up on her shoulders. He nudged her in front of him. "Up the stairs. Go." A swat on her derriere.

Amanda grabbed her purse. Slung it across her body.

Giggles. "Ouch." Turned to look at him. Wagged her finger. "You're a bad boy, aren't you?"

Head tilted back, he let off a guttural laugh. "Get up there." Wiped his mouth.

Tight ass, strong legs. The look from behind revved Straker up.

Amanda rushed to the top of the stairs. Flaunted herself, posed, turned. Wagged her butt. He rushed up the stairs behind her. She ran into the loft space where there was a large platform bed. A small chest to one side with liquor bottles on top. A mini-fridge next to it.

Straker walked into the room. Stripped off his t-shirt. He was ripped.

Not bad. She smiled.

Tattoos down his arms were visible to anyone. No tats on his chest or back.

Muscles. Nice.

Amanda walked over to Straker. In front of him, she threw her purse on the floor next to the bed. Grabbed her top and pulled. She wore a strappy red lace bra. A smile on his face. Stepped out of her heels. Moved closer to him. Hands on his belt. She undid it.

"I got to piss." Walked away from her and through a door across the room.

Footsteps on the stairs. They were in the loft.

When the toilet flushed, Tack opened the back door. The sound from the hinges screeched. He waited. Nothing. Slipped out the back door. Left it ajar.

Two rings, a man picked up.

"I'm out," Tack said. "But Stone's daughter is still in the complex with Straker. They're both upstairs in the loft."

"Clay made the call. Didn't want you anywhere near Amanda and Straker. Not a good scene for us."

"She's either crazy, brave or wants to screw with her dad."

"Yeah, I'll pick all the above. Clay pulled us from the site. You're close to MD301. Hang out at the service station near the turnoff. Our people will pull in to get gas."

"I'll figure it out." Tack hung up. Jogged toward the station. It was a relief to be out of Straker's orbit.

Amanda had to work fast while Straker was in the bathroom.

Opened her purse. Pulled out the syringe. Hid it behind the bed platform on one side of the bed. Stripped off her leggings. Took off her bra. But left the cheeky panties on and hopped into bed.

The look on Straker's face when he saw her topless was what she'd hoped to see. His one-track mind played into Amanda's plan.

"Did you hear something downstairs?"

"My mind is on something else." She bit her lower lip.

A lop-sided leer. Straker stripped off his pants. No underwear. His naked presence a formidable sight.

An intense glare from him. He joined her on the bed.

Callouses on his hands were like sandpaper on her skin. His breath was foul. A mixture of cigar and alcohol. No cologne.

This guy is a cretin.

Amanda turned over on her tummy. Up on her knees. Stared back at him. Wagged her butt. Flipped over on her back and spread her legs.

He reached for the lube on the side table. Stroked himself. "Are you clean?"

"What?"

"I don't use condoms. You aren't diseased or anything?"

"What do you think?" No one had ever asked her this question.

Straker wasn't worried.

No finesse in his movements.

Amanda held on tight to his back. Shut her eyes. Took him without a whimper. His lust escalated with every thrust. It was what she needed to fuel her fury.

It's all about him. No thought at all about me.

"You like this, baby?"

Rolled her eyes. "Oh, yes. Don't stop." She shrieked for effect.

It took longer than she thought it would. Every second was torture. What got her through it was the finale she had planned for this pathetic excuse for a man.

A final gasp, Straker fell off her. They lay together, both in deep-breathing mode. His was real. She faked it.

Men are clueless. Amanda moved closer to him. Saw his chest rise and fall in a rhythm. Laid next to him. Stayed quiet.

It didn't take long before he was asleep.

Careful. No sudden movement. She eased over to the side and off the bed. He didn't budge.

Syringe in her hand, she crawled along to the foot of the bed. His legs sprawled apart. Bare feet splayed. Body was relaxed.

What if he woke up when she touched his foot to insert the syringe between his toes? She couldn't fight him off.

This won't work.

Improvise.

Crawled back to where her purse was and put the syringe back in it. Her second idea was worse, but she wouldn't leave without payment. Straker represented what Amanda hated about men. About people who thought they had power over her.

Moved to where his pants lay on the floor. Popped the clasp to get to his knife. Pulled it from the sheath. Inspected it. The weight of it in her hand. Touched the tip to her thigh. A light touch. It sliced through her skin without effort. Blood dropped to the floor. Swiped her index finger across the cut. Licked off the blood.

Turned to look at Straker. He was out.

In cat-like motions, she crawled back on the bed.

A groan. She stopped. Quiet again.

Amanda sat on her knees. Looked down at him.

Straker's eyes shot open.

She smiled.

He closed his eyes. "Lay down." He was oblivious.

Her breath quickened. Images in her head. Others who fell to her spell. The knife on his flesh. His panic. Her breathing got louder. If he caught her, he'd kill her. It was worth it.

"I'll show them."

"What? Did you say something, baby?" Straker's eyes were shut.

The knife slid into the right side of his throat with ease. As his body reared up in reaction, Amanda threw her weight forward, behind the next thrust. The blade ripped across the front of Straker's throat.

His eyes opened wide. Shock. It registered too late.

Gurgles.

The noise a body makes when air, blood, and death collide.

Amanda jumped back and off the bed. She watched her prey writhe on the sheets. His eyes transmitted what his voice couldn't. Grabbed his throat and reached for her at the same time. Failed to do both. His formidable body strength was no match for the precision strike she'd made on his vital arteries.

When Straker moved, arterial spray doused the side wall and the bed with his blood.

Rivetted. Her pulse raced. Watched him. Excitement bubbled up with each gasp of air he tried to breathe.

Straker dropped face first on the bed. His head to the side.

In a rush, she dropped to her knees to watch him. His eyes. The flutter of his lashes. Amanda had never seen the life go out of a man.

The blood drained from Straker Kent's face.

Breathing had stopped.

No sounds.

The knife in her hand. Amanda walked into the bathroom. Washed it off with hot water. Wiped it clean. Took a towel and wiped down everything she had touched.

There was no reason for Straker to believe Amanda Stone was lethal.

The naivete of men and society's blind spot benefited her.

Men like Straker believed any woman could be handled. He'd been schooled the hard way.

Vigilante justice, Amanda-style.

But she hadn't cared about surveillance cameras. Daddy had always come to her rescue. Never considered being caught. She got dressed and walked out of Straker's compound, the knife used to kill him in her purse.

Bloodlust satisfied, Amanda thought about what came next.

Find Lily.

Present Day: Friday, 5:00 a.m.

"Yeah."

"Dad, it's me."

"Huh? What time is it?"

"Early. Or late... Wanted to tell... I fixed things for you."

"What do you mean?" Tried to wake up. Hungover, Stoney's head clanged. Turned on a light on the nightstand. "Where are you?"

"It doesn't matter. But you don't have to worry anymore."

"I'm not in a mood for your bullshit. I'm going back to sleep. We can talk in the morning."

Dial tone. Amanda stared at the phone. "Bye, Dad." Inside her condominium, her favorite outfits were snug in a sturdy suitcase. Looked around, the last check. One more phone call.

"Hello."

"Wanted to say goodbye."

Lily turned down the radio in her car. *Amanda.* "Where are you going?"

"Away from here."

Lily pulled off at the next intersection. Drove into a nearby service station and parked. "What's wrong?"

"From you, the question is hilarious."

"I tried to explain, but you wouldn't listen."

Amanda stayed silent.

"Can we meet? You can yell at me, hit me, if you want."

A chuckle. *She thinks it will go away with words.* "Been there, don't want to go back. I'll be in touch." Amanda hung up.

No explanation was good enough.

It was Lily's turn to wonder. Closed her eyes. Worked to interpret Amanda's words. The phone call was out of place.

"What are you up to now?" Dread crept into Lily's mind. Old memories wafted into her brain. *I've gotten on Amanda's bad side. No way I can trust her. What she might do.*

Lily drove out of the station and back onto the road to Mechanicsville. She'd made a decision before the call from Amanda.

No reason to change her plans.

Present Day: Friday, 5:00 a.m.

Tack waited a long time inside the mini-mart.

He glugged a large drink and wiped his mouth with his forearm.

A sports car turned into the service station. Parked near where the air for tires was located. The lights blinked off and on.

Caught Tack's attention.

The driver's side door opened. Clay got out, waved his hand in the air. Tack jogged over and got in the passenger side. Looked at his boss. "What's up?"

"Not sure." Clay hit a button on his console. "Hey, it's me. Anything new from your end?"

"Center is quiet. It's too early. But everyone is curious about Stoney. Scheduled a meeting."

"That'll be... eventful. Listen, I'm headed back to Straker Kent's place with a man from the team. Not sure what we'll find."

"What aren't you telling me?"

A chuckle. "Damn. I've got to get used to this. Your knack for reaching into my brain."

Kate waited. "It's about Amanda, right?"

"Bingo. I had a team on Straker's compound before the Riverbend Road party. Amanda showed up there last night after her dad. After what happened with Duchess, I pulled my team and sent them to Mechanicsville. We need to find Lily and she might go there. Also, we have to pull the cameras we've got inside Straker's. See what Amanda was up to."

"I don't like the idea of a team on Duchess. A lot of pieces connect to her, not all legal."

A smile stretched across Clay's face. "I see your point. Be in touch after we get into Straker's place."

"If you don't object, I'll meet you there."

"Sure." Clay gave her the address. "I'll pull the team sent to Mechanicsville. Have to make a stop by the office."

"No problem."

"Don't go—"

Kate stifled a laugh. "Don't worry. This is your play, I understand. I won't get in the middle."

"See you soon."

Present Day: Friday Morning

She'd snuck into the house from the back door in the wee hours. Duchess had given Lily keys months ago. Parked her truck where it couldn't be seen. Chose the attic of the old house instead of a bedroom. A cozy top floor abode she'd made her own.

It had been a long time since she'd had a full night's sleep. Lily had conked out and didn't rustle when Duchess awoke and started her day.

On the walk outside, she saw Lily's truck. Relieved. Duchess had controlled her maternal instincts. Lily couldn't be sculpted. The demands of her gift were dangerous. Inexperience bred bad risks. Duchess had first-hand experience with this passage herself.

Sleep will strengthen her.

She tended to the birdfeeders, cleaned and filled them. Past 8:00 a.m., there were light clouds. A gorgeous fall day ahead. But the forecast warned of a whopper storm on the way.

Two feral kitties hid under a nearby shrub. Waited for breakfast.

Duchess stopped, took in a deep breath. Sat down on a nearby chair in the backyard. Another breath, she closed her eyes. Listened to the outdoor sounds. Slipped into meditation, her mind relaxed. Receptive mode. Swept away chatter and the busy brain cycle that kept her intuitive tools tied up.

The channeled experience at Riverbend Road had left Duchess drained. Sleep had helped. The residual fatigue acted like the day after a hard gym workout.

Outside, in a place she controlled, there were no worries to distract. Important to leave the experience behind her. Otherwise, the intensity would clog receptors she used to sense new energy patterns.

Opened her consciousness to welcome another day's cycles.

Nothing more soothing than quiet.

It was in this space where her guides worked. A moment to let messages find her and drop in. Pure Law of Attraction energy.

She heard...

Tires on gravel. Nothing important. A neighbor's car in the distance.

Another breath.

The wind changed.

A malevolent whisper carried in the breeze. Inaudible. Duchess's spine stretched. She sat taller in her chair. Grabbed the armrests. She reached into the darkness that clouded her head.

Eyes shot open.

The psychic rose from her chair and headed toward her house. Walked into the kitchen to return the kettle of water to heat. Lid off, important not to wake Lily. Not long after, the water bubbled to a boil.

This is for me to handle.

Another whisper.

Time closed fast.

She stopped to listen. Took in a whiff of air. *What's that?* Shook her head. Walked over to the fridge and took out a small container of whipped cream.

Duchess reached deep into the back of a drawer. Retrieved a small key. Dragged a chair close to the sink, stepped onto it. Inside the cupboard, high above the sink, was a case. Opened the case, reached in and brought out a packet. It contained several small vials. She put one into her pocket. Closed the case.

Filled the pitcher with water. Continued the preparations.

A knock on the door.

When Duchess flipped the lock, and the door opened, it was no surprise.

"You must be Amanda."

"But we've never met."

Duchess cocked her head. "Educated guess. I'm Duchess. Lily's told me about you."

"She's here, right?"

"Come in."

"Lily's here?"

A pause. "I haven't seen her in several days."

The truth is always the best course. The literal meaning meant to evade an answer to a question posed by someone you don't know, so cannot trust.

Shit. What now? Amanda looked at the woman, unsure.

"Have a seat."

She ignored the offer. Walked over to the fireplace and looked up. "This is exotic."

"I painted it a long time ago."

Amanda turned, stared at Duchess. Eyes locked, the two women were quiet. Duchess hit an opaque denseness from her guest. No receptors. The woman was unreachable.

"What does it mean?"

"You tell me." Duchess waited.

Reared back, Amanda balked. "You painted it."

"Each person sees into it a different way. What is your perception? I'm curious." Duchess tried again to access the woman's energy. There was no entry. No connection.

Shrug. *I'm not playing this game.* "When do you think Lily might be back?"

"Any minute." Duchess waited. "You're welcome to wait."

A look at her hostess. *This old woman is harmless.*

"Your choice. I was about to have tea." She walked past Amanda, into the kitchen. *You're in the right place. Relax. You're safe here.* Said this mantra in her head over and over.

Amanda sat down on the couch. Looked to make certain she was alone. Opened her purse. In quick movements, she removed the syringe meant for Straker Kent, checked it and slipped it behind the cushion on the couch. There must be no witnesses. She'd wait until Lily came home to the surprise of her life.

Duchess entered and sat the large tray on the table between them. Three different herb tea blends from which to choose. There was one small teapot for Amanda. A carafe of water and several treats.

"You can pick what herb tea you'd prefer. Then fill up the little infuser and make sure the clasp is tight before you put it in your pot."

"Nah, I'll pass."

Amanda picked up a double chocolate chunk cookie. Smelled it. "Did you make these?"

"Yes. Chocolate, my favorite thing."

"They look good." She set the cookie on a napkin.

"My secret recipe." Sipped her tea. Broke off a piece of cookie. Duchess took a spoon and scooped whipped cream to put on her plate. "You sure you don't want any tea?"

"Is that whipped cream?"

"It is."

Amanda scooped up a large spoonful. Picked up the cookie, slathered whipped cream on it and took a big bite.

"How long have you lived here?"

"Forever. I'm from Santa Cruz, California."

"Always wanted to go there."

"So, Lily didn't tell you anything about me?"

"She mentioned this house. Said she stayed in Mechanicsville."

She's lying. But I don't think she has a clue who I am. Didn't do her homework. So arrogant.

Duchess watched her guest. Aware of Lily asleep upstairs, she wanted no confrontation inside her home. The outdoors was better for her purposes.

"It's a gorgeous morning. Let's take this outside. It's not cold today."

"Sure." She grabbed her purse. Held it close to her side.

Duchess walked behind Amanda. She had talked to Lily many times about privacy. This young woman wasn't here for a pleasant visit.

Summer long past, the vines across a giant pergola made for a magnificent feature. A spectacular wood table, with benches. A pond at the crest of a small hill.

Duchess sat the tray of refreshments on the table.

"Wow, this is amazing."

"My piece of tranquility."

Amanda stumbled. Her purse fell open when she hit the ground.

A split-second flash of a metal object.

At least it isn't a gun. "Be careful. The backyard isn't level. Lots of holes to catch you."

"Yeah, thanks." Cleared her throat. Looked down at the pond. "Is this natural?"

"With a little help from my gardener, we expanded it."

"Is that anise?" Amanda walked closer to an area where different herbs grew.

Duchess nodded, walked in the same direction.

Near the hill, the grass thinned. Muddy ground in the bald spots. Amanda took a step forward. Lost her footing. Her feet slid beneath her. Landed with a thud on her butt.

"Ouch, shit. Oh, that hurt."

"Let me help you."

"I'm fine." Struggled to stand. "This is slippery. You should be careful out here. It's dangerous for an old..." Stopped herself.

Duchess leaned down to help her up. "Dangerous for an old woman? Is that what you were about to say?"

A sheepish look. "Sorry. Mom hates it."

"What?"

"Being old. I didn't mean anything."

Oh, yes you did. Duchess waved her off. "Let's sit."

The two women walked back under the pergola, to the chairs around the table. Amanda rummaged in her bag. Found the zipper. Took out her inhaler.

"Asthma?"

Nodded. "Yeah, it's a pain. Had it since I was a kid." Breathed in deep, held it. She looked down. Grabbed the carafe of water to pour herself a glass. Took a drink.

Duchess saw a dull red blotch on her shirt. "What's that spot on your sleeve? It looks like blood."

Amanda pulled her jacket over her shirt. "Nothing." It came out in a husky growl. She took a breath, then coughed. More water.

"Thirsty?"

Amanda nodded. She took another drink. Grabbed the inhaler, breathed in again. Her coughing escalated. She tried to stand.

Duchess watched her.

Amanda sat back down.

"Anything I can do?"

She stared at Duchess. Gasped for air. Her breathing shallow.

"Maybe another sip of water." Duchess handed her the glass of water she had poured. Amanda batted it away.

"It would have been my first instinct." Duchess stared at her.

"Huh?" Amanda stopped. The realization hit like a punch to the face.

"No one ever suspects the water." A brief smile. Duchess glared at her guest.

Panic, first. Resignation turned to fury.

Amanda looked down. Shook her head. "I was thirsty. So stupid. An old woman." Hands on her thighs, she tried to will her body into submission.

Duchess leaned over, grabbed Amanda's purse. Inside she found Straker's knife. "Is this for me or Lily?"

A weak smile. "I hadn't decided yet."

"Well, I have." Duchess took ahold of it.

Amanda grabbed for the knife, but she couldn't control her body. Duchess slipped it into her waistband.

"Oh, I'm dizzy." She couldn't focus. Staggered.

Amanda had made a fatal mistake. She underestimated her adversary.

Duchess stepped closer, looked into her eyes. "I smelled you from a mile away."

Her eyes widened. Amanda dropped where she stood.

The mystic watched the life leave her body. Convulsions. *Evil piece of work. Only one end for you.*

No time now. Lily would be up and about soon, and Duchess wouldn't allow her to witness what had been done.

Off with her shawl, jacket, and a long scarf belt. The layers of clothes which were her signature fashion statement. Clothing meant to disguise the strength Duchess possessed.

Who quakes at an older woman's presence?

Dressed in all black, a bejeweled brace on her right knee, work gloves and leather work boots. Her persona shifted.

Sleeves pushed up, Duchess headed toward a large shed beyond the pond. Not too far from where Amanda lay.

An engine started.

Duchess drove a few yards out of the shed in an ATV, all-terrain vehicle. Backed up inside the shed. Her work continued until she drove the ATV out with a lawn and garden utility trailer attached.

Stopped near where Amanda had fallen. Got out and pushed the quick release, which tipped the trailer.

A check of her surroundings.

Duchess had the utility trailer close enough to the body. Got rope underneath and around Amanda's shoulders. With a winch, she tightened and pulled until Amanda's lifeless body was inside the trailer.

The five-acre property offered many options. She drove the ATV past the pond, down the small hill, and behind a large area with leaves and other debris, which hadn't been cleared since September.

Duchess dumped Amanda's dead body amid the pile of garden refuse. In quick movements, she labored to cover the corpse.

A temporary fix.

She drove the ATV and trailer back inside the shed. Gathered up Amanda's things. But instincts drove her back into the house and over to where Amanda had sat when she first entered the house. She reached behind the pillows. Deep underneath a cushion, she found the syringe. A silent meditation.

No time, Duchess visualized what waited for her if she didn't control what happened next. For that, she'd need help.

Present Day: Friday Morning

Kate arrived at Straker Kent's compound before Clay. When she buzzed, no one answered. Waited.

When they arrived, Clay pulled in behind her. Got out and walked up.

"Nobody answered."

Tack got out of the car and walked up to the large metal box next to the locked gate. Put in a code on a keypad inside it, then shut the metal box. The gate opened. Kate drove through and parked her car while Tack walked up to the front door and unlocked it. Clay walked back to his car and drove it inside the gate.

Kate followed Tack inside Straker Kent's compound.

"Straker." Tack waited. "Let me check in back." He walked through the French doors. A few minutes later he walked back out. "Straker must have split. Back door was still open."

There was no one downstairs.

"It's too quiet." Kate walked over to the stairs and took them up to the loft.

Clay walked in.

Straker Kent's dead body lay on the floor in the loft.

"Up here."

Clay took the stairs two at a time. Saw the arterial spray on the wall. Glanced over at Kate. She'd taken a pair of gloves out of her purse. A pair of white booties over her shoes.

"When sex isn't enough."

"Don't come any further without gloves and booties."

"Not me. I don't walk through crime scenes."

Kate surveyed the room. "Think we'll ever discover who did it?"

"There is no perfect crime."

Tack came up behind Clay. "Want me to get the camera?"

"Can you do it without disturbing anything?"

They watched Tack hoist himself up and onto the top of an oversized armoire. Swift movements from a muscular man. Reached high on the wall and ripped a camera from a ledge of a beam, part of the industrial ceiling.

"Got it." Lowered himself down and handed the equipment to Clay.

Kate shook her head. "I'd bet my next month's salary Amanda murdered Straker. It'll be on that camera."

Tack and Clay stared at her.

Present Day: Friday Morning

When she peeked out of the window in the attic, she saw Duchess. Her body obstructed the view of Amanda on the ground. No way to tell what she was doing, but nothing Lily saw alarmed her. Hopped out of bed to take a shower.

Dressed as fast as possible. Fled down the stairs, through the main room. Outside on the porch, she saw Duchess walking toward her.

"What happened?"

"Hush, now. Move Amanda's car into the barn. It's down the road." Pointed in the direction. "Through the grove of trees."

Lily didn't move.

"Go."

"What happened?"

Duchess grabbed both of her shoulders. "No time. Move."

Lily took the keys and ran through the house. She got into Amanda's car and drove past the house and followed the road.

Duchess took out her phone. Rifled through her contacts until she got to the entry with a number, no name. Pushed it.

"Clay Zach."

"It's Duchess. You said I—"

"What's wrong? I can hear it in your voice."

"I assume Kate is with you?"

"Want to speak to her?"

"No time. There's an issue. Kate can show you where I live."

"As soon as we're finished here."

"Be quick. There is no time."

Clay stared into space.

Kate walked up to him. "What now?"

"That was Duchess."

"Okay." *What's with the look on his face?* "What?"

"Sounded like a 911 call."

He tossed his keys to Tack. They had finished what they could do.

"As soon as you sweep the place for the rest of the cameras, get out of here. Tell no one you have footage from Straker's bedroom and compound. Make copies. Use the safe in my office."

"Yep. I'm on it." Tack took the stairs to retrieve the other equipment.

"Oh, and get the cleaners in here."

Tack stopped. "Do I confirm to investigators the compound has been swept for prints first?"

"No."

"Got it." Tack went back to work.

Clay looked at Kate. "You've been to Duchess's house, right?"

She tried to process what happened. Amanda murdering a man like Straker Kent. Kate didn't have the brain space. "Yes."

"You drive."

Present Day: Late Friday Morning

Lily flew through the front door, her mind at war with itself.

"Duchess. Where are you?" She walked through the house and out to the backyard.

"Is it done?"

She nodded. "Amanda was here? Where is she?"

"Not your concern. Come. Sit."

She sat down in front of her.

"Take this." In Duchess's palm was a piece of paper.

"What is it?"

"It's an address."

Lily read the note. "In California?"

"Santa Cruz. A special place."

No idea where she was going with this. Lily waited.

"I want you to get in your car and drive until dusk. It should take you three days, longer if you stop to sightsee, which I wouldn't recommend."

"I don't understand." Lily shook her head.

A stern look. Duchess edged off her chair to get closer to Lily. "I'll say this once. You need to go. Now. And you can never come back. Understand?"

"No."

"Okay, then don't understand. You've wanted to leave for years. Back when you were a child it was fun. Now it has become—"

"I don't want to leave you. You're all…"

"Listen to me." Duchess looked into Lily's eyes. "I'll never be further than a thought away."

Unconvinced.

"It's dangerous for you. There is no life for you here. Your instincts tell you the same thing, yes?"

Deep exhale. "True."

Duchess reached deep into one of her pockets. "This is a card to a bank account. The pin number is on this piece of paper. It will tide you over until you get a job. There is a phone number on the paper, too. When you get to Santa Cruz, call it. Tell her who you are. We've talked, and she's agreed. She will shelter you, guide you."

"I can't leave."

"Yes, you can."

Tears trickled down Lily's cheeks. She grabbed Duchess and hugged her tight. "When will I see you again?"

The look on Duchess's face made Lily cry harder.

"Stop it. Every tear you cry lessens your power. When you mourn, you attract what can harm you. There are other ways you will learn to release your emotions. Be patient."

A blank stare.

"Remember who you are. The gift of your powers. Do not tell others. My friend will teach you. And when you're ready. Share what you've learned *your* way. It is your purpose."

"This is ridiculous. I'm not a witch or a wizard."

"No, you're not. You're not a fantasy. You are one of the few humans I've met who've accessed power to the enlightened and accepted its strength. A warrior empath. You've braved your peer's laughter and derision to hone it, even when you didn't understand what you were doing. You are a presence so strong, entities from the unknowable world reach out to you through their pain. Those of us who have chosen a similar road have the duty to protect you and others who navigate the invisible world beyond. You are part of the next generation of light seekers. The future."

Lily looked down at the paper and the bank card. "I've got a savings account." A bleak smile.

Duchess shook her head no. "You must not access it. Before you leave, trust me with your pin number and everything I'll need to access the money. I'll get it to you when you're settled, after... When it's safe."

"I can transfer the bal—"

"No, you cannot. My dear, you must disappear. Understand?"

Lily shook her head no again.

Duchess leaned her head back and laughed. "Of course, you don't. No matter. You trust me?"

"With my life."

"Ah, now you understand. I've been doing it since we met. My purpose is your protection. You landed on my doorstep because of it."

"I've gotten comfortable with the channeled voices. But this is too much. You're talking about fate. We have choices and I'm not leaving you until you tell me what happened with Amanda."

"I'm not used to explaining myself. So, this once. Amanda wanted to harm you. I stopped her. You're safe. Nothing else is important."

Lily looked at Duchess. *She won't tell me a thing right now. I've wanted to leave for months and months. Why am I scared?* "Okay, I'll do as you say."

Their arms came around one another. Lily cried. Duchess held her.

"You're the only mother I've ever known. How will I..."

Heart torn apart, it took all of her will to keep it together. Duchess had never had a child, longed for one. Then one day, Lily walked into her life. She was grateful beyond words she could pray.

"And you are the child who came across my threshold. The best of my knowledge, you have. I love you, my darling daughter, more than I can express. But now you must fly."

Lily nodded. "Okay. I'll pack."

"No. You will go. The bank account is more than enough for you to start over. Grab what you must but go." Paused. "Think of all the new clothes you can buy."

"First thing, I'm buying a shawl."

Duchess beamed.

They hugged. Lily wouldn't let go.

"Okay. Come on. It's time." Duchess kissed her on the forehead. Closed her eyes. A silent meditation.

"I love you."

The last words from the mystic to her apprentice.

Lily fled into the house. Turned to wave goodbye before she entered.

Duchess stayed outdoors. Waited. The faint sounds of Lily upstairs packing. She'd memorized her steps through the house.

Time ticked by. The memories of their years together flooded into the mystic's mind. Her soul center full, her human side was inconsolable.

Sensed when Lily passed across her front door for the last time.

One honk. Another, and then a third. Tires crunched on dirt and gravel. She heard Lily turn on the road beyond her house.

A silent meditation for the young woman she'd cared for as her daughter.

Duchess had one last task to complete.

Present Day: Friday Afternoon

Duchess heard their car.

They hadn't stopped before Clay opened the passenger door and fled into the house. No one in the main room, the door to the backyard was open. He saw her outside through the screen.

"What happened?"

"Amanda came by. It didn't go as she planned."

"Where is she now?"

Duchess shook her head.

Kate came toward them. Stood across from Duchess. "What happened?"

Clay shrugged. "I'm trying to find out."

"Is Lily here?" Brows squinched, confusion across Kate's face.

"No, she isn't." Duchess was a portrait of calm.

Kate stared at Clay. He threw his hands up.

"Where is she?"

Duchess stared at Kate. "I'm not sure."

Kate smiled at her. "Okay, I get it."

"Fill me in, please."

Kate thought she had a thread. "Where should we—?"

"Amanda's car is in my barn, down the road." Duchess pointed in the direction.

Clay looked at Duchess. "But you can't tell us how it got there?"

"I can tell you what might have happened."

He smiled. "Please."

"Amanda split town. Lily, too. It's a guess."

Kate shook her head. Threw up her hands.

Duchess laughed. "Come on, you two. It's not like they had a lot going for them here."

"Too convenient." Clay turned around and walked toward the sound of the pond. Ran his hands through his hair.

"You're not telling us everything." Kate was sure Duchess was lying.

"So true. And yet, how will you prove it?"

"That's your play? You think we wouldn't figure it out if we brought teams in here?"

"I didn't say that."

Kate sat down. Mouth open, she stared at her new friend. "I won't say a word. But you need to be honest with me."

"What do you need?"

"Where Lily is?"

Duchess sat down across from her, leaned forward. Looked straight into Kate's eyes. "She's gone."

"Okay. Where's Amanda?"

Duchess winced. "Rephrase your question, please."

Roll of her eyes, Kate was on the threshold. *How to restate what I said?* "What happened to Amanda?"

"She underestimated an old woman." A wry smile on her face.

"Where is she?"

"Where she can't hurt people. You're welcome to search the house. As I told you earlier, Amanda's car is in my barn."

Clay walked up. "What did I miss?"

Kate shook her head. "Don't ask."

Present Day: Friday Night

"Are you going to tell her?" Tack waited for an answer from Clay.

"Few specifics. Kate and the Center can't be dragged into this. That's critical."

"What about the old woman?"

Clay shot a glance at him. "Duchess is her name." The message clear.

Hands up. "No disrespect. Clinical works for me. Names..." Shook his head. Tack didn't get personal. He never allowed himself to get close.

"Watch her movements. Call before you engage. Prepare for messy. Keep it quiet. Between you and me."

"Okay. I'll be in touch." Tack walked out of the nondescript building with a fenced-in perimeter near National Harbor, Maryland, which was temporary office space for Clay and his team. Drove his truck in the direction of Mechanicsville, Maryland.

Tack watched Duchess for three days. Home for dinner and to sleep. Back in Mechanicsville before dawn. Nothing to report.

Late Saturday night he blew through dinner. The sky was crystal clear and dark. No light from the moon.

After midnight, a faint squeak from the direction of the backyard.

Tack saw no one out front. Part of the backyard was visible, not the back door. A veteran of battles, he played a hunch. Got out of his truck. Walked toward the back of the house.

He focused on the large shed. Saw the woman, Duchess, walk inside and close the door. Tack moved closer.

Nothing.

Then...

A grunt. The grinding sound of an electric saw.

Silence.

Another grunt. The same sound, louder.

A pause.

Another grunt.

ZSHZSHZSH-CRACK.

Tack cursed under his breath. He recognized the sound.

"She's sawing through bone." It was hard to fathom. *If I walk up and knock on the door, she might shoot me.*

The sound pattern continued.

Tack was a patient man.

The sounds stopped.

The shed door opened.

The woman was bent over. Tack saw her heave. She held onto the back of an ATV. Puked again. What she had done had made her sick.

He walked toward the shed.

Duchess saw him. Tried to think where to find a weapon.

Hands up. Tack stopped.

Her eyes on the stranger. Nothing to do but trust.

"Hello, Duchess. Clay Zach sent me."

"Oh, goddess. You almost gave me a heart attack. Clay?"

"I'm Tack. I work with him."

Deep exhale. "I should have expected you."

"Clay sent me to watch you after Amanda disappeared. He had... Unanswered questions. Loose ends make him twitchy."

Duchess came around and leaned against the ATV. Tack walked close enough to see inside the shed.

Looked inside. Blood and body parts were splattered across the shed floor. The walls were covered in viscous matter.

"You did all this?"

Duchess looked at him, didn't respond.

Pointed to the shed. "Nasty business." Tack walked into the shed and picked up a heavy-duty trash bag. Looked around. Did the count in his head. Looked back at Duchess.

"It's none of Clay's business or yours."

Shook his head. "There is DNA all over this place. You're lucky her parents don't give a shit. But I wouldn't try this technique again."

"I'm counting on rain."

The left side of Tack's lip rose in a lopsided smile.

The mystic glared at him. "I didn't ask for help and expect none."

He chuckled. Leveled a gaze at her. "You don't get it. Clay doesn't care what you want. He sent me to finish things. Whatever it takes."

She stared at him.

Tack picked up the hatchet.

Duchess followed him inside the shed and closed the door behind them.

One Month Later: Morning

Evidence from cameras inside the Straker Kent compound revealed the grizzly death of a notorious criminal.

No one cried.

Videotape exposed Amanda Stone as the murderer. Police put out an APB for Jack Stone's daughter, but weeks later, there was still no sign of her. The illegality of the surveillance Clay had put in Straker Kent's compound gave them answers they couldn't use in court. Authorities needed to question her.

Clay Zach had his forensic team dispensed to Straker Kent's compound. What they found rocked the Ransom Center. A crude pill processing operation where capsules were filled with toxic opioid mixtures at a fraction of the cost which meant big profits. Money that had been laundered through the Ransom Center. Chemical manufacturing in China is unregulated, so the black-market counterfeit drugs Straker Kent imported through the dark web led nowhere.

Stoney was unmasked. He pled guilty to tax evasion, bank fraud, money laundering, and drug possession. The information he offered prosecutors was about Straker Kent, whose associates split once his operation was exposed. No deal to make, Jack Stone faced a long prison term.

One thing stayed the same. When they asked Stoney about his daughter, he had no answers. Told she'd disappeared, there was no emotional reaction from him. Stoney said they'd never had a good relationship. Amanda's mother said she was old enough to take care of herself.

Lily was gone.

No one questioned why.

Amanda was gone, too. For her father and mother, she'd never existed. Their own primal needs drove them. Collateral damage from a relationship between desperate people who didn't love themselves. So, they had no capacity to love one another. She was a child born to indifferent parents into a savage world.

Some thought Amanda had run after the murder of Straker Kent. Others wondered if she'd met a fate through his associates. Officials pronounced Amanda Stone dead months after her "disappearance."

Three people knew what happened. They stayed silent to protect Kate.

The legal gymnastics she'd hurdled to save and solidify her place at the top of the Ransom Center were over. Stoney had balked when Kate triggered the clause in their contract that ended his reign. Her lawyer explained the details he'd agreed to over ten years prior. Stoney's prison term turned the screw.

Clay made the turn into the Ransom Center parking lot. Kate in the passenger seat. It was her first day back since the catastrophe that had threatened her dreams, and the livelihood of a group of young geniuses. A generation who grew up in an era where information had become as important as privacy.

She turned to Clay. "I hope…"

"What?"

"Stoney was a force inside the Center. He was everyone's hero." She smiled. "Bigger-than-life personality." A look at Clay. "I'm no salesman. I'm a behavioral psychologist."

"Don't sell yourself short. Stoney was a businessman, but he was lousy at people. Your expertise opened financial doors. A female partner made him look good. Your star has risen."

Kate looked down. Deep exhale. "We've lost so many people."

Clay had a grin on his face. His attention focused on the front of the Center. "You haven't lost as much talent as you think."

"Are you kidding? What about—"

A nod in the direction of the Center.

"What?" Kate followed Clay's gaze. It took a minute to get it but when she did, her reaction was instantaneous.

It came out in a shriek.

"Oh, my god." She opened the car door, jumped out and walked toward the Center. Half-way there she jogged. Clay's laughter behind her.

Kate's smile spread across her face. "You're here. How?"

Trevor was tanned and looked relaxed. "So glad to be back."

"Your brother? What happened?"

"Hey, what about me?" Callie came out of the Center doors.

"Oh, this is too much." Kate walked forward. "I've never been happier to see you." She hugged Callie.

"Do I still have a job?"

Kate's answer came in the form of a guttural laugh that echoed across the parking lot. Clay came up behind them, his hand out.

Trevor took it. "Thanks for everything, man. Good to be back."

Clay looked at Trevor. "Don't forget our deal."

"What did I miss?" Kate stared at Clay.

"Nothing. I told Trevor our plan to link the Center with my outfit. He'll report to me now. He's on board and so is Callie. She'll be the liaison officer."

"I'm psyched." Trevor had a big smile across his face.

Clay put his arm around him. "Wait until you're a month in and you haven't had a day off."

Callie looked at Kate. "You ready? I've assembled the teams." Looked at her watch. "It's time."

"As ready as I'll ever be." Kate walked forward, with Clay behind her. Next to him was Trevor and Callie, who rushed to open the doors for their new boss.

Dr. Kate Winter walked into the new Ransom Center as president and CEO. Jack Stone's name wiped from the organization as a bad memory.

When she stepped through the doorway, Kate froze. Her throat tightened, and she had to choke back emotion.

Applause erupted.

Cheers exploded from the teams gathered in the front of the bullpen to welcome her. Whoops and hollers traveled above the noise.

Overwhelm hit Kate.

Clay came up behind her. "You've got this, Dr. Winter." A soft whisper in her ear.

She turned to look at him. Tears in her eyes. A mouthed, "Thank you." Kate walked further into the room.

The teams gathered around the new boss. Congratulations from all took time. Both Kate and Clay made certain to talk to every team member.

Trevor came up to hand Kate a memorandum. She took a quick look. "Okay, send it out."

The announcement was brief. There was a new boss inside Ransom Center. A woman had replaced an immoral, corrupt man with horrendous impulse control, and no brain for economics.

The excitement died down.

Clay walked over to Kate. "I'll head out now. Great start."

"Yes, it is. Thank you for everything. Let me walk you out."

The room hummed back into action. Sounds of a normal day at the Center.

Kate and Clay walked toward his car.

"We need to formalize the partnership between your outfit and mine."

Clay stopped. "Yeah, I want to talk to you about that."

She stopped. "What's up?"

"We don't have to do it now."

"Give me a hint."

"Okay. Why go through the liaison bullshit? The memos. The strategy sessions. It's a time suck."

Kate smiled. "Suggestions?"

"It's easy. We merge under Ransom Center."

No response. Kate walked a few feet away. She was deep in thought. Clay waited.

She turned. "How would it work?"

"However you want it to."

"I would shape the Center."

"Your call. I don't like the administrative bullshit I have to do. Hated it at the bureau. And trust comes hard with me. It's your company. I'm not into anything except the work."

Kate laughed.

"This is where I also inform you, I've taken on a couple of new Capitol Hill clients."

"You can't help yourself. You're addicted to their drama."

"Hey, there's a lot of money in Washington, D.C. We might as well get our share. What do you think?"

"Never liked the liaison setup either." Kate looked at him. "Do you think we can pull it off? Stoney and I…"

"I'm not a criminal dirtbag. And I've got no issues reporting to a woman."

"That would be the least complicated thing about it." Kate thought for a minute. "I could buy you out. Collapse your outfit."

"We can work it out."

"It's the smart move. I like it. You'll come in as a separate division. Your own boss. Lawyers can sort out the details."

"Great. I'll move my crew into the Center. My temporary lease is up."

"Callie will organize it."

Kate began to chart the company in her mind. Stopped. "We've been thrown together before."

Clay nodded.

"Too much has happened in the last months for me to ignore it. I'm not sure what we're supposed to do together but I'm certain it's real."

Clay had a big smile on his face.

Kate laughed.

"Get out of here. I've got work to do."

"I'm off to Montana." Clay looked at his watch. "I've got a plane to catch. It's a new case we haven't talked about."

"How long will you be gone?"

Clay shook his head. "Not sure. My contacts inside the bureau think it's the same guy who was in Idaho. I'll call you once I'm on the ground."

It would never be easy for them.

"Sounds good."

Kate walked over to him. "This will work, right?"

"We'll figure it out."

"It might be great." Kate felt giddy.

"Oh, yeah."

She watched him walk to his car. Smiled. "Hey, Clay."

He stopped, looked back at her.

"When you get back from Montana... You can tell me all about the blonde."

The look on Clay's face was priceless. His hands came up. "What blonde?"

Kate laughed. "That's your play?"

"Yep." He smiled. One-handed wave.

Kate stood staring out as Clay drove away.

Dr. Kate Winter was a changed woman. For the first time in her life she no longer doubted her instincts, and the fear she'd carried for so long about how she intuited events was gone.

A quick call.

"Hello."

"I'm about to walk into Ransom Center."

"Excited?"

"I've waited my whole life for a chance like this."

"First you had to embrace your gifts. To accept your purpose."

"One step at a time. This is the big one."

"Whenever a woman steps into her power it's a big moment." Duchess grinned. "You've done it before in your work. You've seen for yourself there's a wider force to tap."

"Your offer stands?"

"Yes, but I doubt you'll need a guide at this point."

Kate laughed.

Duchess waited. *She's nervous. That's good. She'll be on guard.*

"Easy for you to say."

"Remember, the more enlightened you become, the bigger target you are for malevolent forces. Expect challenges. Stay in your power no matter what you face."

"I'm so grateful to have met you. I'll never be able to return the favor."

"Oh, my dear, you already have. Enjoy your day. You've earned it."

Kate hung up. Walked into the Center like she owned the place which, at last, she did.

Duchess hung up the phone. Walked out to the backyard. The weather had turned grim.

"It's always best to tie up things at the end of a cycle."

For that, she'd have to wait.

Two Weeks Later: Cold Winter Night

The light of the full moon guided her.

Not for long.

Another wicked storm was predicted.

Duchess had been through a lifetime of battles, rebirth, and reinvention. Faced challenges, and the horror when her body betrayed her. Age was a powerful tool, a weapon, a dagger. But her strength today rivaled the younger girl she once was and who defied the odds to survive.

The brace on her right knee was gone.

Work gloves, leather work boots, and an all-black appearance included a headscarf. She had charcoal-colored smudge marks across her face. A ritualized presence revved her psyche.

No time. Tack had driven the point home after Duchess had demanded to finish what she had done alone.

Dead body broken down.

When she opened the shed door, the stench slapped her in the face.

Duchess gagged and kept working.

She had uncommon habits. She'd set firewood ablaze in the outdoor pit, in the wee hours on many nights. A night owl, no one who lived nearby would think it odd she chose to be out late at night on her property.

"I should have cleaned up better. Too much all at once." Looked around in the shed. Shook her head. A chainsaw lay nearby. Crusted blood on the jagged blade. Viscous fluids frozen to the ground. Several heavy-duty trash bags piled around her. Each light enough so she could move them without help.

A silent meditation of thanks. Tack had made the difference.

The last trash bag Duchess picked up had a hole in it. Three digits of a woman's hand had poked through. The stench overpowered her for a second. Pulled out an empty heavy-duty trash bag. Put the bag with a hole in it inside.

A tedious, gruesome job was almost done.

The grotesque task overwhelmed her senses more than once. But the last bags filled with body parts were ready to transport.

She drove the ATV out of the shed. A slow drive through her property. It was imperative to be as quiet as possible.

Duchess got out to survey the area. Night vision binoculars for a quick search. The ones she'd bought on a whim after she purchased the property. She walked the area, no movement, no curious creatures. There wasn't a neighbor close enough to see her. There were piles of broken branches nearby. The usual maintenance required for a property this size had piled up.

Retraced her steps.

Turned on the gas-powered wood chipper.

Pulled one of the bags off the trailer. Opened it.

Part of Amanda Stone's left leg went into the chipper.

ZZZZZZ-ttt.

The sound of bones and flesh pureed into pulp.

"Hmm... Not as loud as I feared."

A section of the right leg followed, along with her left foot.

ZZZZZZ-ttt. ZZZZZZ-ttt.

One by one, Amanda Stone's body parts were pulverized in the chipper.

"This isn't half as bad as sawing the body into pieces."

The memory made her shudder. Tack had quickened the end.

Grotesque images mingled with her current task.

Amanda's severed head was wrapped. A quick toss.

SHSHSH. SHSHSH. ZZZZZZ-ttt.

Clouds wafted over the bright winter moon.

The crisp air aided her mission. Kept Duchess moving.

If anyone had been out in the middle of the night, the sound of bones and cartilage being mutilated might have gotten their attention. But few people in rural America cared what their neighbors did at midnight on their own property.

It's why they lived where they did.

It was nobody else's business.

Duchess paused and looked up into the sky. She didn't speak. Closed her eyes, deep breaths, an incantation.

The bloody job was done.

There would be a mess to clean up at sunrise. It didn't worry her. She'd do it again.

"A demon came to my door. Nothing else to do." A fleeting thought of Amanda segued into her love for Lily. There had been no choice.

A blinding strike of lightning overhead.

Thunder cracked.

A downpour.

The sound of the ATV was quieter than the shriek of laughter from Duchess when the rain started to fall.

"Thank you, goddess."

It had begun forever ago.

One new moon, Duchess had opened the door to the unknown and walked through.

She had tutored many women since. Guiding people to reach beyond the traditional, the comfortable, the acceptable.

There was an infinite resource of energy from the force.

Duchess dared to confront the conventional through her powers. She helped people like Lily, Dr. Kate Winter, and even Clay Zach, who braved what they didn't understand to tap into the world beyond.

Some doors spring open through the divine act of discovery.

Some doors should stay shut.

It doesn't mean they will.

Notes from the Author

What if the universe sent you a message?

Would you recognize it?

At my core, I'm a thinker, a feminist, and a light seeker.

My mother, however, started me off with the journey of Christianity. Faith is central to my human existence. But when doubt rolled in it sparked my journey into the unknown.

Decades would pass before I tapped meditation to revolutionize my life, my thinking, and my writing.

Dark and light energies compete in my thrillers.

The women I write about are fighting for the life they want. It doesn't come easy. It has been an inhospitable world for women until recently. For the first time, #metoo inspired me to own the horrors I'd seen, experienced, and hidden.

I approach the mystic arts with respect. There are hundreds of seekers and spiritual guides exchanging ideas online through astrological videos, tarot interpretations, psychic predictions, and more. There are so many inspiring YouTubers who dispense mystic wisdom. Marie White's Mary-el Tarot was a wonder to explore.

Maryland is a magical state, our adopted home. My fictional Maryland utilizes known street names, cities, events, and monuments, but it can't be found on a map.

Instincts guide me.

Tapping mystical themes opened a wide canvas.

Meditation has turned into a divine creative portal.

If you enjoyed this book, I'd appreciate your continued support. A review on Amazon. Please consider being part of my ARC team of reviewers. Let's connect on social media. It all starts with signing up for my (news)Letter.

Thank you for reading... and listening.

I'm grateful.

About the Author

Taylor Marsh writes **thrillers**. Psychological thrillers found on the shelf with Barbara Copperthwaite, Megan Abbott, Rachel Hargrove... Taylor's badass women characters tread where safe space is hard to find.

Marsh is an accomplished speaker and communicator. A former Broadway performer and beauty queen who was the Relationship Consultant for *LA WEEKLY*, then the nation's top alternative newsweekly. She wrote and produced her one-woman show, "Weeping for J.F.K.," and dipped into talk radio. The author of two traditionally published non-fiction books, Taylor turned to fiction in 2016.

"The women characters in my novels have to fight for what they want, sometimes against forceful odds. It's a kinetic experience, an intense ride." –Taylor Marsh

On **Audible**, the **5-star audiobook** of *Olivia's Turn* is an auditory ride. Narrated by Taylor Marsh, engineered and produced by Audiobook Theater, a division of MM Press.

Check out Taylor's recent interview with **New in Books**.

Taylor has been interviewed by *The New York Times*, *The Los Angeles Times*, *New York Daily News*, **BBC**, **CNN**, **MSNBC**, **C-SPAN's Washington Journal**, and **Al Jazeera** Media Network, among other outlets. She was profiled in *The Washington Post* and *The New Republic* for her coverage of Hillary Clinton during the 2008 Democratic primary season. She was an early contributor to **The Huffington Post** (2006) and has written for **Zócalo Public Square** in Los Angeles, **U.S. News & World Report**, and Washington, D.C.'s **The Hill**, among others.

Made in the USA
Columbia, SC
23 January 2019